ALEXANDRA CON

◆

THE WITCH MARK

Complete and Unabridged

CHARNWOOD
Leicester

First published in Great Britain in 1986

First Charnwood Edition
published 2016

A catalogue record for this book is available
from the British Library.

ISBN 978–1–4448–2848–1

Published by
F. A. Thorpe (Publishing)
Anstey, Leicestershire

Set by Words & Graphics Ltd.
Anstey, Leicestershire
Printed and bound in Great Britain by
T. J. International Ltd., Padstow, Cornwall

This book is printed on acid-free paper

For my grandmother, Bessie Worthington

If someone had been able to lift off the front of our house that day, as one would the front portion of a doll's house, they would have been able to see the layout of our lives, each one of us. The ground floor would have appeared quiet to them, after the mourners had left, with that kind of ominous, insincere silence which continues long after it is truly felt. Only the lounge would be occupied, and then by just the two of us. The dining room, study, and kitchen would have been empty, as would the outbuildings, and the garden which surrounded the house and ran down to the wall beyond, would have been deserted also. Likewise the first floor, although the furniture would be arranged neatly, each item in its place, as it had always been. Nothing would have changed, except that the owner had gone away, and in going, had taken a little breath from each stone of the building.

Then, if the onlooker had peered in very closely he would have seen at the back of one of the attic rooms, a patch of dampness on a far wall, that in some lights looked like a witch . . . or had done, many years earlier, when we were young.

1

'It's a witch!' she repeated over and over again to me, so that I buried my head well down under the blankets, with my hands over my ears. After a minute I lifted them to see if she had stopped; but she was still chanting the same few words. 'It's a witch! A witch!' she continued, her perfect face then only half visible, her eyes bright in the hesitant darkness of a ten o'clock summer's evening. Alison, my sister, my beloved, beautiful, elder sister, was crooning into the half light like a barn owl into an empty field.

'Stop!' I said, my voice high with fright, my head reappearing over the covers. 'Stop it, Alison! It's not a witch, it's a mark on the wallpaper.' My insistence did no good, she merely laughed briefly and turned away from me.

Her face was now obscured, so that she appeared to be only a shape in the bed. We were separated by two feet of space in that high attic room where we were to sleep until the floor below had been made ready for us. Temporary and inadequate curtains had been rigged at the windows, so that the light still came through until darkness, and in the mornings it burst in on us strongly, just after dawn. The attics hadn't been used for years, they had been merely storerooms, their L-shaped area piled high with packing boxes and tea chests, the haphazard

3

order of belongings classed together indifferently, their purposes forgotten or no longer of importance.

I had seen the damp patch only two days after we had moved into that room, and at first it had provided a diversion for a child who found sleep difficult after the quick and horribly brutal death of her parents, or should I say, our parents. I had been only six then, coming to live with my grandparents in the walled house, with my sister, Alison, who was nine. I cried for several nights, and then found that I didn't miss them as much as I thought I should, because my new life was comfortable and secure. So I stopped crying even though Alison continued for months, especially when there was anyone about. People frequently gave her money and sweets to comfort her, and she managed to smile, but not too much. I seldom smiled — except when I was with Nancy.

Nancy was my grandmother, and if I had mentioned the stain on the wallpaper to her she would have laughed and told me that it wasn't a witch but a fairy or an elf bringing me pleasant dreams, or putting toffee under my pillow. I wouldn't have believed her, of course, but the explanation would have kicked the witch right into touch. As it was, I never told her, or asked for her opinion, and instead I believed Alison, and the witch came out every night and looked for me.

Because believing Alison was easy. Everyone believed her, as it was hard not to. If she had the face of an angel, she had the personality of one

4

also; that oddly sweet, docile nature which captivated everyone who came into contact with it. Alison would not have been cruel, not unnecessarily so; therefore, if she said it was a witch — it was. I was conditioned early on, even before the age of six, that my elder sister would take care of me, and that I must listen to her. Agreeably, I did so. This did not, however, prevent me from forming my own opinions, and when we both came to live with my grandparents, I clung hungrily onto Nancy instead.

My grandfather was quite another matter. He hardly seemed to take any notice of the two sisters who had come into his care after his daughter and son-in-law had been killed in an air crash, and we seldom discussed him. Pipe smoke, tobacco knocked out against the sides of a pot ashtray, a head imprint on a cushion — little images he left behind which I recall more strongly than the man himself. Fishing tackle on the floor of the back entrance, the rod leant up against the wall, the basket oozing moisture from its sides and making a damp patch on the red tiles underneath. But none of his words remained, no sayings which people treasured and remembered when they spoke of him — not that any of us did that much. Hot summer nights would pull him into the garden, digging ferociously under a choking sky, and tossing aside the weeds with his small, hard hands. It was not that he was incapable of strength, only that he had impaled himself early on, and had never struggled sufficiently to free himself. He was a bank manager by profession

— which was what he looked like, and if he had loved us, he had kept the fact a secret.

We had been with them for a year when it was decided that we should be taken away on holiday to the Lake District. We stayed at a small hotel which overlooked a large and chilly lake and, in the mornings, deep shafts of sunlight struck fiercely on the linings of the curtains, trying to break in. It was still very cold, although it was early June, and the air was full of that clear high light which you only get by water and mountains. My grandfather was mixing business with pleasure, and had left us in Nancy's capable hands whilst he had gone into the town.

I can still feel the sharp snap of the icy water on my toes and hear the birds over my head, wheeling and circling in the cold air. The sun squinted painfully down on the pristine surface of the lake, and far away, it struck the white sail of the boat, no bigger than a handkerchief from where we stood. I had been watching Alison for quite a while, seeing how easily she moved as she ran along the lakeside; it was cold, but there was no trace of redness in her face, she merely jogged effortlessly along. I was irritated by her, by her sureness; and in the way we behave when we are children, I acted without thinking and threw a stone at her. For a moment I waited to see if it had hit her, horribly fascinated, half hoping that it would, half hoping that it wouldn't; but she seemed not to react at all, and only when I thought it had missed her, only then, did she suddenly crumple from the waist, her fingers over her forehead, her back to the water's edge.

6

There were still birds in the high air, flying over the sharp sunlight. I could hear them but I didn't look up, I merely watched as Nancy turned to glance at me, the question apparent on her face. She told my grandfather later that it had been merely an accident, a game which had gone wrong, but she was being blindly kind — I had known what I was doing, and I had wanted to harm my sister, to disrupt the routinely beautiful stillness of Alison's world.

The incident made only a fleeting impression on her, although the blow itself left a mark which faded over the years to a faint oval of paler skin, like a jewel in the forehead of a maharajah's daughter. Even when Alison tanned in the summer, the scar remained, and as she never wore a fringe to cover it, everyone noticed. Oddly, because of her astonishing beauty it didn't detract one iota from the perfection of her face, it seemed instead to enhance it, to point out how exquisite she was. And for all this splendid physical appearance, for all her calm and peaceful nature, Alison could be wonderfully funny, and for that, if nothing else, I grudgingly loved her.

It must be apparent by now how hopelessly jealous I was of her. The difference between us was marked, to say the least, and even a stranger, who had not met either of us, would have come to the same conclusion looking at the selection of photographs arranged on the top of Nancy's piano lid. Picture after picture charted the course of the second infant, through a grizzling babyhood into a messy toddler, whilst alongside was the radiant, neat little figure of Alison, smiling peerlessly out of her frame. At four I discovered I could fight back, and after that momentous insight, the photographs altered to show a plain child pulling faces for the camera, the hair bristling out from the self-mocking face, the eyes short-sighted and sensitive behind glasses.

'We're going out,' Nancy would say, pulling down a hopelessly battered, wicker picnic basket.

'Where?' we would chorus, already getting ourselves ready to go.

'I don't know,' she'd say, reaching over and snatching things off the shelves; ' . . . but we're going.'

And we would set off gratefully, usually ending up in Richmond Park.

The bland, unemotional personality of my grandfather (whom Nancy picturesquely referred to as the 'junket') had exhausted her long before we appeared, and so when we did, she took it as a blessing and at every opportunity we were taken out on treats, mainly so that she could be out of the company of her spouse. He never came with us. I often think back and wonder what we looked like to the outside world. Nancy, nearly thirteen stone in girth, her weight deposited around her limbs like the padding on a cream settee, her face plumply pretty, holding on one hand the defiantly solid figure of a be-spectacled, awkward little girl, and on the other — Alice in Wonderland. Did we really sail down the park's paths like a battleship with a tug boat and a yacht in tow? And God, how I loved

8

her, how I loved her bigness and her laugh, and that bloody bad temper when we argued with her. How I wish she had stayed where she was, and let me grow up past her, instead of getting older and thinner and . . . like everyone else.

But then she was gloriously fat and we were children. Two sisters, three years apart in age, and a hundred years apart in appearance. Even at six, that had been made very obvious by the way that people flattered Alison and then dismissively patted the top of my head, although Nancy always tried to compensate for each thoughtless remark by a well-placed kindness. When we were alone she would read to me, one vast arm looped around my shoulders, the dog leaning against the settee and leaving patches of hair on the dark velvet. Sometimes, if it was summer, she would tell me to shell the peas, giving me a colander and depositing me on the back step with a warning not to eat any and to keep whistling. I would stop now and then — not to steal any, I didn't even like peas — to make her rush out of the kitchen in a mock fury and flick the tea towel round my ears.

Alison would be at ballet classes or piano lessons, and because my grandfather would be way down the garden, weeding, with his pipe clenched fiercely between his teeth, I could imagine that we were alone and that no one else existed in that small, safe world behind the walled garden.

Like summer, daydreams always come to an end, and before long the gate would be opened and Alison would walk in, waving to us, her feet

9

hardly making an imprint on the smooth grass. It isn't difficult to see how beautiful she is now, and it wasn't then, even for me, even for the child I was. She was slender and delicate, her face small, her eyes surrounded by long, curling eyelashes above which two perfectly arched brows interrupted the line of her forehead. She was picture-book pretty, the rosewood coloured hair held back with a band, the long neck slender and creamy against the fall of colour behind. A picture-book princess, the head girl at school, the heroine of romances. I knew that she would grow more handsome as the years passed, and that I would never have the satisfaction of seeing her turn from a pretty child into an indifferent teenager. She was only a little less beautiful than the angels, and they had chosen her.

Nancy compensated by trying to make me look more presentable, and toiled with me round numerous opticians in the attempt to make a seven-year-old look less like a stunted, middle-aged adult. She spent a good deal of money on pairs of glasses which would be broken playing netball, or fall rapidly out of favour; or she would spend evenings straightening my hair, only to find the following morning that it was as unruly as ever. I was not truly ugly, not really, it was just that in comparison with Alison, I was on a par with one of the dwarfs in a Velasquez painting — the little, grotesque figure which stands beside the Royal Princess and makes her appear even lovelier. But I know one thing for certain and it is this — that ugly children remain ugly, their plainness marking them out, and it alters them inside so that they are deficient from their beginnings. Within the space of eight child years, I understood that beauty is not important, it is vital, and because I did not possess that beloved necessity, I hated whoever did. By the same token, I had come to hate Alison.

She, to her credit, never set out to make me feel inferior, never lorded over me, and always defended me if someone was unkind. Certainly by doing so, she appeared in an even better light, as people thought she was kindness itself. I cannot say definitely if that was why she did it, only that it was certainly a part of the reason. She had no need to feel threatened by me, or by anything I did in the years which followed our childhood, because she had the whip hand, she was beautiful.

So from such beginnings develops the story of three women — even though some left, some changed, and some remained. We stayed, on and off, in the walled house, at different times for different reasons, and the attics reverted to their old use, although whenever it rained, a damp patch would appear across the wallpaper in a far corner.

'It's a witch!' Alison had said when we were children, and in a way she was right.

For another child it would have been a flower, or a kite, or even a seashore; to her it was a symbol of power, a life force — to me, it was fearful and threatening and it kept me awake as long as I could see it. The witch became our talisman, and long after she had forgotten it, I could see the stain spreading and growing, just as my jealousy did. Over the years, we battled and we competed; sometimes one lost and sometimes the other, and at night, the witch came out of the wallpaper to look for me.

2

Our parents were killed in an accident abroad, which gave the whole episode a detached and curiously unreal quality, once removed from grief. We had been staying with my grandparents at the time, and after they broke the news to us we stayed on with them, as if it had been carefully prearranged to ensure the minimum of inconvenience. Nancy parried her grief at the loss of her only daughter by becoming completely absorbed in us, and though she turned to her husband for comfort, I never saw him respond.

'It's good to have the children with us, isn't it?'

'It's fine.'

'Do you enjoy having them here?' she pressed him.

He looked away from her abruptly, and grunted, pulling down some sort of mental trapdoor between himself and his wife. After a while, Nancy, (as we always called her) gave up.

So he remained numbly inarticulate, hopelessly unloving and unloved; wandering aimlessly through the house like an Ancient Mariner, who had once had a tale to tell, but had forgotten it many years back. Nancy never referred to him by name, indeed, it was only after he died that someone spoke of 'Harold', and I wondered fleetingly who they meant.

13

Nancy, by contrast, heaped affection upon us like an amateur gardener ladling water and nourishment on some straggly houseplants. She made huge teas for us, piling up plates with fresh scones, their tops flour-smudged, their insides fat with cream and jam. When we finished, there remained only a light, and interrupted, coating of white flour on the plate, or the odd curl of sticky scarlet on the table cloth. The kettle was always on the boil, or being filled, or topping up the teapot's contents for friends, or the few business acquaintances of her husband's. She made us all those silly, forbidden dishes which children love — egg and chips, baked beans and mashed potatoes, and she filled up our plates almost as high as her own.

We came to her when she was still only middle aged, having married very young and borne her only child a year later. The sumptuous, voluptuous flesh which cushioned her body, belied her true nature, which was not soft, but resilient and durable, one which enabled her to come to terms with her husband's lack of love and her own indifference to him. Being bored, she turned to outsiders for diversion and became intensely involved in the unending round of charity works and garden fetes, of the type which abound in some profusion in London's suburbs. A pretty woman, run to fat, some said, not that outsiders' opinions mattered to Nancy, and when we arrived, she rejoiced.

Because having children in the house again meant that she could enjoy herself doing all

14

those irresponsible, indulgent things that children do, and adults reluctantly grow out of. With us she relaxed, and gradually over the years her contacts outside fell off as she spent more and more time with her granddaughters. We became a team; each completely different from the other; each totally opposed in appearance and manner; and because of that we became interdependent, and the pattern of our lives was set.

We lived in Richmond, outside London, not in one of the best areas, but not in one of the worst either. It was a large house, set back from the road a little, behind a high stone wall, which reached up to the second branch of the apple tree outside my bedroom window. My grandfather, who had always been a careful gardener, picked out flowers and shrubs which grew in shade, so that at any time of the year, something bloomed in the yard of cool shadow which lay along the base of the wall.

The downstairs rooms were darker than upstairs, due to the profusion of vegetation which clustered around the windows. Dark winter mornings threw navy shadows along the snow which coated the lawn, and thick wedges of white hung stoically onto the ledges around doors and window panes. Alison and I built a snowman, and borrowed one of our grandfather's pipes, pushing it firmly into the frozen mouth. But by morning it had gone, although he never mentioned it, and we replaced it with a dark twig in the shape of a bent thorn. When the daylight faded, the snowman's shadow reached up to the lounge window, the absurd stick

15

lurching out of its mouth like a miniature boomerang.

I soon forgot the few memories of my parents — children do — and I settled into my new environment happily, although Alison took longer to adjust, the seniority of her three years making her recall longer. But if Nancy tried to force her to do something she didn't like, she would respond skilfully, using what memory she had like a lethal weapon.

'I don't care what you say,' Nancy reasoned once, 'I want this house kept tidy when I've got people coming.'

'Mummy never used to mind if I played in her lounge,' my sister responded with perfect accuracy, knowing that our grandmother would give way.

'Do you still miss her?'

Alison looked down.

'Sometimes,' she said, and the battle was won. Nancy, by this time stricken with remorse and convinced that she had hurt the child, acquiesced. It was clear, even to my child's eyes, that such contests were uneven, and left Nancy more deeply affected than my sister. By the age of seven Alison had developed a perfect ability to manipulate people.

'Let me do the dusting for you, Nancy,' she might offer, spending the next hour carefully going over the furniture, returning obediently for praise.

'Thank you, love, you're such a help.'

'Can I have those piano lessons?' Alison asked, her head just a little to one side.

'I told you, maybe next year.'

'But — '

'No buts, next year we'll think about it, and that's final.'

But it never was. Alison fell quiet, or tears would appear in her eyes on cue, and because she was always so amenable, and so pleasant, she achieved her purpose. The following week, she was walking down the path with a new piano case.

She played the role of Orphan Annie to perfection, and only the occasional sidelong glance, or faint, upward curl of her mouth betrayed her to me. If anything affected her adversely, she reacted; if not, then the whole world, and all the world's children could go to hell in a handcart and she would probably have helped them on their way.

So I learnt quickly that beauty is a potent persuader, and that it can achieve holds on people. Looking at a pretty face, it becomes impossible to believe that the mind is not pretty also — so that the first impression is formed at a glance. I realised early on that Alison could effortlessly gain what I had to strive for, and that a well-placed smile from her could avoid the unpleasantness which is a normal part of growing up.

'What a beautiful child,' a friend of Nancy's said once, looking at Alison's little upturned face. 'I can imagine she'll break some hearts when she grows up.'

Then I was introduced and watched the reaction turn from interest to puzzlement. If

17

Alison was going to break hearts, it said, I would break mirrors.

But school was paradise to me, and in that place I was happy. High on a raised area of land it perched, like a squat brown bird with its wings spread out. On either side of the main complex were playing fields, and behind them a small car park for the staff. Short, brown painted railings surrounded short, brown painted outbuildings, and over the entrance door was a motto, written in Latin, which was repeated on the front of the prayer books in the assembly hall. I was caught talking shortly after I had begun there, and had to write out the quotation fifty times, with its English translation underneath, something about 'By Truth, to Victory.' When I handed the paper in I forgot the incident, although even now the sight of writing above a door reminds me of the smell of school gravy and the ringing of a high-pitched bell.

Winter terms smelled of paint on hot radiators, and dinners from the dining hall behind the art room. September terms led into Christmas, and the carol service after the turkey and plum pudding dinner, before the holidays began. Then New Year came and we moved on into the spring, with its mixture of blossom and cold games of netball on the hardcourt.

'Now, you'll watch your sister, won't you?' Nancy asked Alison as she fastened her satchel, cramming one of the chocolate biscuits she gave to both of us into the front pocket.

'I always do,' my sister responded calmly,

glancing over to me with an angelic smile. 'Don't I, Jill?'

I nodded, and jumped off the hall table, taking Alison's outstretched hand. As soon as we were out of sight, she would collar me.

'Are you going to eat all your biscuit?' she said, the smooth line of her hair glowing under the early April sun.

'It's my biscuit,' I said defensively, my hand automatically tightening around the object in my pocket, my eyes glued to the pavement.

She began again, after only a moment's silence.

'Miss Urquhart says that our class can have a rabbit this term.' She paused, knowing that my interest was roused. 'She says that we can let some other people — people we *liked* play with it sometimes.'

As ever with Alison, the implication was enough. I stopped and offered her the biscuit, my hand extended for the other half when she had broken it, only to see her snatch the lot and run off, laughing. She was waiting around the next corner, I knew that, but I would still walk past without looking up, and pretend to jump when she leapt out. We played set roles, both of us, rehearsing the parts we were best equipped to take.

It took me nearly two years to realise that it was always Alison who organised what we did, and because of that she had the lead role in everything. Time was the only leveller, and gradually I grew big enough to pose a serious threat to her should she overstep the mark.

19

Skilfully, she changed her tactics.

At school, she quickly won over most of the teachers and the girls. She was always voted monitor and games captain, even though she was no earthly good at any form of physical exercise. With a form of arrogance which usually accompanies early confidence, Alison tied up the school, its teachers, and its pupils, and I trailed behind at her hem, like an afterthought. She whistled, I ran.

So our positions at home and at school were marked out for us. By her beauty and charm, Alison won most people over; by my appearance and lack of charm, I alienated the people I came into contact with. Nancy loved Alison because she was her granddaughter, not because of what she was, and she loved me for the same reason, becoming closer to me as time passed, and therefore providing the life line I needed. I understood that I could never rival my sister in beauty, and so, through Nancy's encouragement, I outshone her academically. But even then I was jealous of Alison, and if my grandmother did not recognise it, I did.

Exactly at which moment the envy began, I can't tell, neither can I be sure if it was one particular incident or remark which triggered it off. Rather, it was an amalgamation of feelings and resentments which had been smouldering on a low light for all the years I had been able to reason. Alison the beautiful, I thought of her as, and recognised that the world was unjust, and there was nothing which could be done about that injustice.

Yet with this resentment, a curious bonding took place. There was one incident, when an older girl had picked on me, when I actively sought Alison's help.

'I'm going to get my sister!' I shouted to the girl, who was fat and spotty, and wore two thin plaits. 'You come out into the playground after school, and she'll fight you!'

We all waited with bated breath for the massacre, although Alison managed, through sheer diplomacy, to placate the oafish girl.

'You don't really want to fight with me now, do you?'

The girl eyed her suspiciously.

'Miss Urquhart might like to know how you've been bullying my sister,' Alison continued smoothly, watching her opponent deflate like a tyre with a hole in it. 'Why don't we forget what happened?'

And with that, she linked arms with me and we walked out of the playground together. Out of everyone's sight, her mature demeanour vanished. She loosened my arm and plinked the elastic on my school hat, so that it snapped back on the skin under my chin and made a red mark.

'Idiot,' she said thoughtfully, and we walked the remainder of the way home in silence.

During those childhood years, summers erupted and smouldered in the enclosed grounds behind the house walls and the garden swelled into a hot magnificence. Nancy and I used to sit at the back of the house, on the porch steps, talking for hours on summer evenings. Sometimes, my grandfather passed near to us, with a

21

brief nod of his head to acknowledge our presence, nothing more, but a few minutes later he built a fire which boiled up savagely from a pile of wood cuttings and weeds.

'Damn and blast, the man's built a fire again!' Nancy bellowed, knowing that he would hear her, and ignore what she said. 'All over the place, you'd think he'd have more sense.'

Fragments of ash blew across to us on breezy nights and stuck to our faces, like beauty spots in a Hogarth painting, and the smoke would get into our clothes and nuzzle our hair. Sometimes she would be working on a newspaper crossword, although I never knew her to finish one, and I watched as her arms moved heavily in the heat, their round fleshiness free of marks and wrinkles, the skin young. Under the soft line of her jaw, the bellied curve of her throat grew pink with the warmth, and although she never wore perfume, there was always a heady, flowery scent of powder which came from her as she moved.

'What's another word for alchemist? she asked me, and I snapped back impatiently because I didn't know the answer. She responded with a well-aimed slap with one of her plump, but surprisingly hard, hands, and returned to her crossword. At that time, arguments flared up quickly, and died down as fast, and conversations were rapid and free of rancour.

The year that I was ten, and Alison thirteen, Nancy brought us a dog, which we called Belinda, telling us some story about it being a stray and needing a home. Alison and I both knew that she had belonged to a woman whose husband had left her, but we never let on to Nancy. It was the only thing I recall that my grandfather cared about, although for days it hid under the beds and piddled on the carpets. When Belinda did finally settle down, she waited for him to come home every night, and after dinner he let her creep onto his lap and stay there until bedtime. Nancy was convinced that the animal was deranged, an opinion she voiced to several of her friends, but Belinda continued to be besotted by my grandfather, and when she was injured in an accident a while later, he was the one who nursed her back to health.

The age of ten presented another milestone for me, as I entered puberty and developed both mentally and physically at a rate which was bordering on supersonic. I found that my school friends had little in common with me, and forged ahead with my academic work with all the frustrated energy of someone who is not at all certain where they belong. It was that summer that we had the prize-giving day, to which all the parents were invited.

'You will come, won't you, Nancy?' I asked her.

'Of course, I'll come. Give me that spoon, will you?'

I passed her the object. 'You promise?'

'I promise, on my honour, God strike me dead and push me into this apple tart if I'm lying!'

She did come, naturally, dressed to the nines and looking like something out of the Henley regatta, sitting on a seat on the front row. Alison glided up for her medals and badges, her hair smooth against the back of her uniform, her skin translucent, and her smile so brilliant that the headmistress responded with a warmth unknown to the rest of us.

When I went up to collect my prize for History, Nancy applauded me vigorously, leaning forwards in her seat, and smiling encouragingly at me, her large navy hat tilted rakishly on her mass of hair. When we got home she praised both of us, arranging the cups in the glass-fronted cabinet. It was only afterwards that I noticed she had put my solitary trophy at the front. Such kindness, such little, careful gifts of thought.

That year the summer was hot; that year when I was ten. Uncomfortable, and hating the heat, I stayed indoors mostly, and tried to keep cool, watching Alison from my bedroom window as she turned from pale translucency to golden brown.

'It's not fair,' I wailed to Nancy, 'why does she get tanned and I burn. It's not fair!'

'Go out for a little at a time, and get your skin used to the sun,' she encouraged me. 'Do it bit by bit. Alison's skin is darker than yours, that's all.'

I wouldn't listen, of course, and when Nancy was out the next day I sat out and burned. When she came back later all hell broke loose.

'It's your own blasted fault!' she began, dabbing Calamine on my arms and legs, and along the bridge of my nose. 'I told you not to go out so long, I can't think why you're so pig headed.'

For days afterwards, I scratched and snivelled, walking around the house and leaving trails of pink powder like the Easter Bunny.

It was typical of me. I was the one who jumped into the swimming pool at school with my glasses on, or who came last in the Booby race, and although I made light of it, just a glimpse of Alison's pretty, poised figure could turn my stomach to stone.

So one day, in the dinner hour, when the school was empty of children, I crept into Alison's classroom and took a pen out of the desk of the girl who sat next to her. It was a navy blue pen, with the owner's name scratched into it — Sarah Owens — and when I held it in my hand, it felt light, as if it was empty. I thought for a moment and then made my way down to the cloakrooms, finding Alison's locker immediately. Inside it was tidy, her school hat placed on the top shelf, her cloak flat against the back wall. I looked around quickly and then put the pen in the furthest corner of the top shelf, shutting the door and running out into the playground without looking back.

One o'clock passed, as did two o'clock, and the doubts set in. What if they found the pen in Alison's locker? What if they expelled her? Suddenly, my hatred for her was displaced by a stronger feeling, a dread of losing her. At the end of the period I went out into the corridor with the other girls, just in time to hear various comments about the missing pen. Who could have stolen it? Someone volunteered the information that Sarah Owen's father had

25

bought it for her. Everyone knew.

When the bell rang to mark the next lesson, I jumped, and whilst all the girls made their way to the next classroom, I stayed in the corridor, my head banging, and my face scarlet.

It took me longer to get back to the cloakrooms, because this time there were pupils milling about, and I was terrified that someone from one of the senior forms would ask me what I was doing. Finally, they all left, and I had just opened Alison's locker and lifted the pen, when I heard a voice behind me.

'What are you doing?'

I spun round, a reflex action making me drop the pen back onto the locker shelf. It was a prefect. 'Nothing.'

'This isn't your locker.'

'No.'

'Then why are you here?'

'It's my sister's, Alison's.'

Her attitude changed immediately, and her expression altered; she even apologised to me before walking off. When her footsteps had faded, I grabbed the pen and made my way back to Alison's classroom. The rest was easy. I merely dropped the pen by the foot of Sarah Owen's desk, half-hidden, and left, only to be told off for being late.

That night, Alison told Nancy about the incident.

'There was such a commotion . . . you should have seen it. Sarah was going mad, saying that her father would kill her, and the teachers were muttering about a thief being about.'

I played with Belinda and kept my head turned away from both of them as she continued.

'They were so cross with her when they found it under her desk that she was kept in for an hour after school for being careless.'

Silently, I swore that I would never do anything so stupid again. That I would never hurt my sister like that . . . not ever. And, for a time, I didn't.

3

My grandfather had never been ill before, Nancy told the doctor on the phone, and then she hesitated, listening to his response.

'Of course I wouldn't be calling you if I wasn't worried,' she snapped, her face particularly white under the hall light.

Alison was sitting on the second step of the stairs, her face turned towards my grandmother, her arms clasped around her knees. We waited in silence, hearing only the staccato response on the other end.

'Yes . . . , I'll do that. You'll see to it? Well, when will they come? Not before that? Very well.'

She replaced the receiver with the look of someone who is not well pleased, and told me to get off the hall table as she walked past. Neither Alison nor I spoke, we waited for her to say something.

Our grandfather had come in from work that evening, grunting a greeting to us, and stroking the dog, before retiring to the lounge to read his paper: exactly the sequence of events he always followed. Then, suddenly, he had called out for his wife, and in the time it took Nancy to reach him, he had slumped over the side of the chair, his hand just brushing the carpet, his mouth open and a small trickle of saliva oozing from one corner.

As Nancy rushed in she banged the door shut

behind her, leaving us in the hall. Neither of us dared to reopen it and so we waited, seeing her re-emerge only instants later, and ring for the doctor. When we glanced into the lounge again, he was upright, his mouth wiped clean, his hands together on his lap.

The doctor came quickly and told us that he had had a stroke, and that he would have to be taken to hospital, where they were best able to look after him.

'What are his chances?' Nancy asked, her voice steady, although she was too pale.

'I can't tell you with any degree of certainty what his prognosis is. He might recover easily and get back to his usual self, or he might have another stroke, which may, or may not, kill him.'

She took the news with complete calm, although her hands shook when she touched her hair, and her eyes were harder than was normal. The doctor left soon afterwards.

Half an hour later, we were still waiting for the ambulance to arrive. Nancy paced in and out of the lounge, her hands fluttering above her husband's head like a pigeon looking for a place to land, and her breaths coming in quick, uneven gulps. Alison and I kept very quiet. We waited.

When the ambulance finally came, the men were cheerful, telling my grandmother that they would be at the hospital in a jiffy.

'Don't you worry now, we'll take care of the old fellow,' one of the men said, and I saw her jaw set.

She went with them in the ambulance, calling in the woman from next door to sit with us until

29

she got back. When she did return, she told us that she had given the hospital her number, and instructed them to call her if he asked for her, or if he deteriorated. She didn't say 'died'.

That was Thursday: it took him four days to die. Four days in which we visited him and sat by his bedside, watching him. He was almost totally paralysed, and what movements he had were restricted to the left side of his face, so that his expression, which had always been minimal, altered hardly at all. Oddly though, he seemed to sense when we were there, even though they said the stroke had left him deaf. He would open his eyes and glance around, the inevitable thin trickle of moisture escaping from his lips, a slow recall settling in his glance. Nancy sat very close to his bedside, and when he slept, she worked on her interminable crossword puzzles with a fixed, almost manic concentration.

Alison and I would walk to the hospital from school every evening, and stay there until Nancy was ready to leave, sitting in the corridor and eating the sandwiches she had made for us. To our eternal discredit, our grandfather's condition hardly affected our appetites, or our spirits, and we would chat and discuss the passing traffic of ill patients, and weary visitors, with two pairs of merciless eyes.

'Will you look at that hat?' Alison said, nudging me with her elbow, a sandwich clasped daintily in one hand. 'Can you imagine going to see anyone *sick* in that hat?'

It wasn't really funny, it just seemed so, in that over-heated, over-emotional atmosphere, and we

30

started to laugh, choking our food down in lumps, the tears rolling uncontrollably down our cheeks.

A sister came over to us.

'This is hardly the place for giggling, I would have thought,' she said sternly, eyeing us both. 'I think you should be ashamed of your behaviour.'

Alison sobered up immediately and looked up at her, shyly, putting on her Botticelli face, her eyes brimming with sincerity; whilst I kept my head down and scratched a nettle rash on my knee.

When we had finished eating, we took our turn to sit with our grandfather and talk to him, because Nancy was convinced that he could partially hear, and she wanted him to know that we were there, and that we cared. For a woman who had long ago fallen out of love with her husband, she took to his dying with a concern which was remarkable, as much as it was genuine. Looking back now I realise that she was trying to obliterate those years of indifference by a few last days of complete devotion. She almost succeeded.

Over those four long days he shrank, probably not literally, but to me at least he seemed to grow smaller. His frame became less obvious, the shape under the bedclothes as unreal as a marble effigy in a country church. I could not touch him, although Nancy kept asking me to hold his hand — it was too much like a betrayal, as if I was lying to him. So I remained at the foot of the bed, and watched the man I had never really known, never really loved, and never really

31

thought I would miss — slip away.

But life can have cruel twists in store, and so it proved the day my grandfather died. Nancy had been with him all through that last Sunday, reading her newspaper and dozing under the hypnotic peal of bells from a neighbouring church, so that when we arrived she was pleased to see us and took great pains arranging the few insignificant flowers we had stolen from someone's garden on the way. She had watched him constantly those long days, and knew that he was fading, and that he would never leave the hospital, although she denied the fact, and it was only when Alison asked her an innocent question that she flared up.

'Will he get better?'

'I don't know, Alison, no one's sure yet, but I think he will.'

'Does he really know you're here all the time?'

She looked across to her husband.

'I think so, some of the time.'

'But not all of the time?' Alison persisted.

'No. Why?'

'Because,' continued my sister calmly, 'I was thinking that maybe you didn't need to keep sitting with him, not if he doesn't really understand.'

Nancy moved faster than anything I have ever seen, leaping out of her seat and slapping Alison across the face in one movement, making Alison yelp with pain and step back.

'I only meant . . . ' she started, and began to cry.

'I'm sorry,' Nancy said, grabbing hold of her

32

and comforting her. 'I didn't mean it, I'm sorry.'

Alison, however, was not about to be placated so easily. She sobbed violently for a few seconds and when she pulled away from Nancy there was a mark on her cheek. Having grown up with Nancy we had become accustomed to a certain amount of physical persuasion, and I must admit that I was getting considerable pleasure from watching Alison being clobbered instead of me, but in my moment of triumph I glanced over to my grandfather and then, transfixed, watched him.

He wasn't moving — which wasn't remarkable in itself, but suddenly it appeared to me that he was even less mobile than usual; that there was a different type of stillness about him. I walked over to Nancy and tugged her sleeve.

'Nancy?'

'Just a minute,' she said, turning her attention back to Alison, whose face was already recovering.

'But — '

'Not now — '

Risking a swift back hander, I tugged her sleeve again and this time she reacted, looking at me and then, as if instinctively, towards where her husband lay.

I still see that expression, even now, when I think of her, that stilted, suspended glance of total disbelief, like a person having got off a train to buy a sandwich, and returned to find the platform empty. She looked — cheated, and surprised, almost as if he had defeated her, or worse, that she had been caught out, that in the end, her neglect would prove the final impression he took with him. She walked away from us and sat down on her seat, taking first one hand and then the other, her plump fingers curling protectively around his, her head laying on the pillow besides his. We watched, stunned, until Alison went out and came back almost immediately with a nurse.

We buried him three days later in a nearby churchyard, and erected a large, white marble headstone, with his name, and 'beloved husband, father and grandfather' written underneath in Gothic script. The funeral was not well attended and it seemed that he had achieved some form of recognition by being forgotten almost immediately. The bank sent a nice card and wreath, from which Nancy cut a piece of fern to place in the back of his photograph, on the top of the piano. But other than that, he was missed little, and even Belinda stopped waiting behind the door for him after a couple of weeks had passed. We sorted out his belongings with little pain, and when we moved his smoking things, I saw Alison take the same old pipe we had borrowed for the snowman, without uttering a word. His fishing tackle was moved up into the attic, and his dressing gown was taken off the back of the bathroom door, his slippers tucked into a pocket. After that — there was nothing of him left.

But if the death of my grandfather passed Nancy and I with hardly a ripple, its effect on Alison was immense. It appeared that whilst he had made little impression on her whilst he lived, his demise altered her, and made her embrace

34

religion with a fervour which was truly remarkable. I was then thirteen and Alison sixteen, a pretty girl free of acne, weight problems and short sight — all of which beleaguered me. I always think that it was the potency of the church's rituals which drew her; the moment when she went up for Communion, with all eyes upon her. That was her instant of glory.

Because she was glorious: dressed neatly, her face now showing something of what she would become, her hands clasped together under her slightly inclined head. We had all attended church, but intermittently, like most people, going at Christmas before we gorged ourselves, or when life had taken a sticky turn, and we wanted to convince ourselves that someone was looking out for us. But her absorption was unnatural, and although it bemused Nancy, it amused me, because I understood what she was trying to do.

She was assuring that even more attention would be drawn to her, so that people seeing her would say, 'Look how she misses her grandfather, not like the other two.' I knew it, and so did Nancy really, although she wouldn't admit it, and because we were both more honest, we overreacted in a different way, and instead of making ourselves hypocrites, we carried on as normal. Every Sunday she set off for church, greeting everyone she saw with her usual charm, and we would stay at home, feeling alternately angry and then guilty, as if maybe she was right, after all. Because she was such a fervent believer,

I became an atheist, although I hardly knew what the term meant, and long, violent arguments would break out between us, after which I apologised and Alison responded by giving me a withering look, and tossing in a reference to 'turning the other cheek'. In short, she became a bore.

Nancy intervened in time though, and although Alison was momentarily lost for means by which she could promote herself, she soon found one.

The alternative turned out to be the drama society at school, which was something we should have seen coming. I was studying for the first set of exams which I hoped would finally take me to university, and Alison, never one to waste time on academic pursuits, was cast as the lead in the school's forgettable production of *The King and I*. She attended all the rehearsals, and soon won over the drama teacher, and the other members of cast, by helping everyone, whether they liked it or not. Her costumes were splendid, as was her make-up, and the only fly in the otherwise balmy ointment was the fact that Alison couldn't sing, something which should have proved a drawback in a musical.

But it didn't stop her, and it was a matter of some astonishment to me how the admiration of a person's beauty could render a whole audience tone deaf. On the opening night, I was with her in the wings.

'Are you nervous?' I asked.

'No,' she said honestly, twitching at a piece of her wig, and smiling regally to one of the teachers who passed.

'But there's loads of people out there, watching.'

'Lucky them,' she answered and swept on.

I remember when I first heard her sing, a sort of ghastly pleasure took hold of me, as if I had at least found something she couldn't do. I even encouraged her, certain she would be laughed off stage . . . It served me right, though, I should have realised that all she had to do was to remain upright and blink now and then for the whole theatre to be captivated.

She finished the play and walked off, taking three curtain calls, and I waited for her in the wings, chewing the edge of my thumb nail. On my estimation, she had hit four or five notes.

So as she shone, I went into the shadows, inflicting my own Elba on myself, and settling into my studies which began to occupy more and more of my time. Nancy was as determined as I was that I should do well, and sat for hours asking me questions, the pages of my text books curling at the edges with repeated use.

'What instigated the Seige of Paris?' she asked me, her eyes obscured by the glasses she wore to correct her long sight. The same ones she left on the top of the cooker, or in the airing cupboard — the ones we could never find.

'It . . . ' I hesitated, seeing her lay down the book with a sigh.

'Think Jill, it's not difficult,' she began, and then seeing the expression on my face, said patiently: 'You were doing so well, now, think back and remember. We only did this last night.'

37

And because I wanted to please her, I remembered, pulling the facts out of the back of my mind, so that she smiled and hugged me with pleasure. Not that she couldn't be ruthlessly harsh on occasions, and even in our teenage years, we earned a slap to any part of available anatomy if we cheeked her. But if she was strict, she was just, and willing to hear my side of the story, so that as time progressed, she became a little less susceptible to Alison's manipulations, and a little more amenable to my version of events.

My appearance had not improved, although I tried hard to make myself more presentable, watching what I ate to avoid the ominous deposits of flesh which already threatened to engulf my hips and the tops of my thighs; or trying in vain to master the wearing of contact lenses. The same mirror which told Alison every day how beautiful she was, showed me a stocky, heavily built young girl, with poor skin and glasses. Tirelessly, Nancy assured me that I would improve as I got older; in vain we struggled with hair styles and clothes and lotions for spots; in vain she tried to prise out of me that slim creature who lived inside. What Alison did, I emulated; what she wore, I copied, but it seemed different on me, and lacked charm. I sat on my sister's bed and watched her apply make-up with the skill of a professional, altering herself from her usual perfection, to some form of hybrid, surreal being, who was unlike ordinary mortals. Her beauty accelerated, from prettiness, to extreme attraction, which could not avoid turning heads and inviting comment.

Alison coped with her appearance as if she had been given something very precious to hold and feared dropping it. She grew into her beauty, whilst I became imprisoned by my lack. Yet there was something I treasured, and grew inordinately vain about — my hands. They were delicate and slender, with long fingers and fine, oval nails. I cared for them from an early age, filing the nails religiously and applying coats of clear polish with a precision I would have found hard to master in other fields. I became conceited about them, and as soon as Nancy realised how I felt, she bought me pieces of jewellery to draw attention to them. Alison had unremarkable hands.

Nancy bought me a ring one day, a large amethyst in an elaborate Victorian setting.

'Now, only wear it for special occasions. It's worth a bomb, so I don't want you to lose it. Promise?'

I nodded, but at night I slipped it onto my finger and peered into it, seeing the bedroom reflected in the face of the jewel, and imagining myself inside the violet stone.

That year Alison was seventeen, and she left school to be signed up only days later by a modelling agency in London. They told her that she would never be short of work, and that she would have endless opportunities to travel. Being placid by nature, she reacted as if it was merely her due, and showed no other emotion, although Nancy was delighted, and spent a whole evening on the phone, calling up people she hadn't spoken to for years, just to tell them the news.

At school I told no one. It was too much for me to handle that Alison should enter so easily into a profession which epitomised all that was glamorous and exciting; but the news got out some how and girls kept coming up to me and asking for photographs of her. Even the teachers seemed to catch the fever — forgetting her unremarkable scholastic record and asking questions, just like any other star-struck teenager.

And with the modelling came the boyfriends — men of certain and uncertain ages. Like Alastair, who was forty and deeply in love . . . although he could hardly string together three words when Alison was there, struck by a form of catalepsy when she was around. After Alastair, came Tony, who was younger and faster, and overdressed, his hair looking as if it had been fixed to his head with staples.

They came and went, and only occasionally did one make a more lasting impression, although Michael was the best value. He would come with the obvious belief that to win Alison he had first to win Nancy and myself, and would therefore embark on a splendid series of 'softening up' techniques, flowers for Nancy and books for me. He could also do tricks, like 'find the lady' and if pressed, would pull a coin from out of his ear. We pretended to be very impressed, but the odd, badly placed giggle could reduce him to a gibbering wreck in seconds, and Alison would be left to spend the evening with a very nervous young man. We got rid of the slick ones quickly, combining our formidable talents, and kicking them into touch hardly before they had chance to get a grip; and the soft, unambitious ones soon met the same fate. In short, we became a graveyard for lost lovers, and Alison took our sorting out of her love life as par for the course.

But if Nancy and I remained unimpressed, a shift in our relationship began at that point. Alison took to discussing her men with my grandmother, and after I had gone up to bed I could hear their voices, and the occasional bellow of laughter from Nancy, and I began to feel an outsider. I started to cut myself off, divorcing myself from the woman I loved best; and the one I admired and feared.

Letters pattered on the doormat in the mornings; and the phone rang on and off into the evening with offers of work, or dinner, all of which were chewed over later with Nancy, when some were dismissed and others accepted graciously. Alison could have done better in her profession, had she chosen to, but she was too indolent, too determined for her own comfort to reach the sunny summits, and instead of clawing to the top, she climbed three quarters of the way, and rested, watching all the others trying to get that far. Flowers arrived from the nearby florists, with tiny notes in tiny envelopes, some lyrical and some cryptic, and all of which were destined for the rubbish bin. I salvaged a few and rubbed out my sister's name, carefully substituting my own, and when I was alone I pretended they had come for me. Silly, childish things which still turn the heart.

41

So we three grew apart in different ways. Alison, because she no longer really needed Nancy or her sister; Nancy, because she loved her eldest granddaughter enough to let her go; and myself, because I had driven a wedge in between us and I no longer knew how to remove the obstruction. I listened to their closeness and was jealous, hating the world for its unfairness in excluding me, whilst I longed to be a part of that same place. Only whilst I worked was I content.

In this way a year passed and two others followed, bringing me to the edge of eighteen, when I was due to sit my final exams in order to obtain a place at university. I imagined, as I suppose we all do, that it would be a seat of wisdom, resplendent with libraries, piled high with leather-bound books, and ivy tapping at the windows beside fires which burned into the early hours as we discussed philosophy. I thought it would be the place depicted in old black and white films, with earnest, studious types rising to assume positions of power, or the occasional lost soul who died young and was spoken about in whispers.

Then only three weeks before the examinations were to begin, the school invited Alison to give a talk. Being something of a celebrity now, they said, perhaps she could tell them something about her exciting life and the places she had visited. Back she walked, through the same gates she had put behind her four years earlier, her tall, upright figure composed, her attitude regal.

42

. . . Bali is captivating, the sun shines constantly and the tropical birds are spellbinding. I did some work for a cosmetic house out there, and they made me up with exotic paints and gave me a monkey to hold — the photograph will be on next month's Queen magazine.

She rattled on, and captivated them — each one of them, speaking easily and confidently about places they would never visit, or if they did, they would probably be fifty-odd and too old and too fat to see it with her eyes. I watched her, mesmerised.

. . . the photographer I worked with was Sicillian, and you know how excitable they can be.

There was a rush of laughter, even from the teachers, although if anyone else had said it, they would have been reaching for the soap to wash out their mouth. She walked skilfully down that sticky line which separates the prim from the risqué, and she didn't fluff her chance. They saw her on the beaches, with the beautiful people, and they went with her to hotels and opera houses, as my sister dragged those unlovely, spotty, idealistic girls into her Martini world. They loved her for it.

. . . Russia is fascinating, and the Hermitage Gallery there is out of this world. Catherine the Great built onto the Winter Palace, and there she met her various . . . pause, a discreet smile, men friends.

She paused again to let the implication sink in, and they were all smothered by the romance

43

of her images. Alison herself looked the part; wearing the palest of peach silk, she appeared even more tanned than she actually was, so that her long slim legs, in their short skirt, tapered elegantly down to a pair of strappy sandals. When she wanted to make a point, she would toss her hair, just enough to make the sides flip back and expose the perfect smooth line of her cheek and throat. It was obvious to me that she realised her power, and equally obvious that she was relishing it; when she finally finished, the girls pressed forwards for her autograph and asked her questions, and she responded as if she really believed the world was as she had described it, or worse, that it was possible for anyone to achieve. I watched her from the back of the hall, watched her as she talked, her rosewood coloured hair resting on her shoulders, the teeth small and almost artificially white. I watched her re-enter my existence and disturb it, so that for ever more I would have to live up to her. I saw her, and I hated her, and when I left she did not look up.

I returned to the walled house alone, Alison having gone on somewhere, and although I had left the school as quickly as possible, I still had not managed to avoid several girls who told me how beautiful Alison was, and how she would be certain to steal any boyfriends I ever had. When they asked me if I was jealous of her I shook my head and walked off, back to Nancy. She was baking in the kitchen, a cookery book propped up against a packet of flour, her plump hands free of rings. She looked up and smiled a

44

welcome, but I couldn't settle with her and soon went upstairs.

The results of the examinations I had taken came through in August, telling me I had failed two of the three I had sat. Nancy was outraged. 'It isn't good enough, Jill, and I can't understand it. You knew all those facts . . . it doesn't make sense.' She grabbed me by the arm and pulled me to face her. 'What happened?'

'Nothing.'

'For God's sake!' she bellowed. 'Don't tell me that, tell me something; make something up if you have to, but don't say 'nothing'.'

But I didn't respond, remaining tongue-tied.

'Answer me, young lady. I didn't invest all that money in you just to have you humiliate me by lack of common courtesy.' She increased the pressure on my arm. 'Now — why did you fail your exams?'

'I — ' I still couldn't find words.

'Yes?' she prompted me, her face dangerously pink, her eyes hard. 'Yes? Answer me! What the hell are you going to do with your life, if you can't pass a few infantile exams? What's the point..?'

I cut her short.

'Yes, you tell me, what is the point? What is the point of exams anyway?' I shook free of her grip. 'Oh yes, I thought I could do something, that I could be someone. Stupid, isn't it?'

'What are you talking about?' she asked, incredulous.

'Alison! Alison! Alison! That's what I'm talking about. Alison, winning at everything; Alison the beautiful who captivates everyone. Alison the great.'

Nancy raised her hand to slap me but I stepped back out of her reach, unable to stop myself talking.

'I actually believed that if I got a place at university, then I would finally feel as if I was real — part of this bloody world, instead of somewhere on a doorstep, waiting to be let in. I can't be beautiful, because I'm ugly, and I'm ugly inside because of it. I don't want to be classed as second-rate because no one would turn around on the street to look at me.' I choked, tears welling up behind my eyes and in my throat. 'Oh God, it's so unfair, and it shouldn't matter what a person looks like but it does. I see men look at me and then over my head to see who's coming up behind. And I can't compete with that — I should know, after all these years living with Alison. I really thought that someone would *listen* to me if I had something witty or intelligent to say, but it's not like that. All the world loves a pretty face. Frankly that's why I failed the exams, because I couldn't see the point in keep trying when she will always beat me . . . and the worst of it is, I can see why.'

She stood transfixed, not moving or speaking, and then she took me in her arms and held me, rocking me against her so tightly I could hear the quick stamp of her heart.

4

The autumn was not slow to start, leaves fell from trees in a kind of hurry, and made a stained glass window effect on the lawn. We built fires every weekend, just myself and Nancy, since Alison travelled more and more, and chopped wood to take in and put on the open fire in the lounge. We learned to talk again, or rather I should say, I did, and Nancy listened, although I found it impossible to determine which direction to go, or how to plan my future. So for a time, I became tied to the house and my grandmother.

Alison came and went, bringing us presents and tales of other countries, and although Nancy's attitude did not alter towards her, she seemed less willing to enthuse about her career. If Alison noticed, which is doubtful, the slight reserve on her grandmother's part did not trouble her.

We called the decorators in and they repainted the house, in all the same colours, so that nothing changed, it just seemed brighter and refreshed, like a plant which had been given some much needed water. Because there were now only the two of us, we used the morning room more and more, keeping to that room and the kitchen, and hardly using the lounge unless people came. Then we would unblock the chimney and lay out a tray with the best china, slipping small damask napkins under the tiny plates. Always on the piano lid, alongside the photographs, was a vase of flowers, the type dependent on the season. At Christmas we bought some blooms for a ridiculous price, and filled them out with artificial foliage, but after a while the water rusted the stems of the fakes, and made a brown smudge on the bottom of the glass.

Daylight hours began with housework, the steady repetition of duties which seldom altered, although Mrs Edwards, the cleaner, came in three mornings to help out. She was a small woman, with a peevish tongue and a pair of quick, pale eyes which scanned you like a metal detector, but she could work faster than anyone I know, or have yet met. Nancy detested her, and was always careful not to let anything slip in her conversation, whilst Mrs Edwards hung on her every word like a monkey waiting for ripe bananas to fall off a tree.

When we were on our own, we listened to the radio a good deal, both liking plays, and we talked for hours about my mother and father, or about Nancy's childhood in Scotland.

'Tell me about your home.'

'I've told you, hundreds of time, there's nothing left.'

'Please, Nancy.'

If I said it in the right tone, and if she was feeling amenable, she would begin, 'You know about the farm, where my brother and I lived?'

I nodded.

'And the stream which ran down from the mountain and made the back walls damp?'

I nodded again.

'There was a well too . . . '

Then off she would go, grabbing hold of me and taking me back with her, through her upbringing and her school days, until the momentous afternoon she met my grandfather, the then glamorous figure from far away London. She fell in love, and believed his promises of Eden, marrying him and returning with him to England. Her wedding fascinated me, as did the story of her preparations.

'Most people lose weight before they get married, but no, not me, I gained it. I went back for my last fitting and split a seam in the back, so that the dressmaker went around telling everyone I was pregnant and had to be married.'

After marriage, maternity did follow, but not as quickly as gossip would have it. She gave birth in London to her only child, bringing the baby home to a small flat in Whitechapel.

'At night I had to wash and dry the nappies in front of the fire, so that the windows were always running with condensation.' She stopped and jerked her head towards the lounge, where her husband's photograph was. 'We thought he'd do better, and quicker, than he did, but there were too many other bright boys about. He got there in the end, but I had, well, fallen out of love with him by then, and I missed home badly.'

'What did he think?'

She bellowed with laughter.

'God knows, I don't, and *he* never said a word, just clammed up. I got involved in committees and outside friends, but I didn't invite him to join in. He wouldn't have wanted to anyway.'

She could rattle on happily unless I stopped her, and I seldom did that. Nancy talking about her past separated me further from my uncertain present, and I clung to that security. How long this would have gone on I can't say, only that fate intervened and offered me a way out of the wood. It was a Saturday, and Nancy and I had been shopping, arriving back exhausted in time to hear the phone ring.

'Yes!' Nancy snapped, and then listened. 'Oh yes, I do remember you, how are you?' She looked over to me and motioned for a chair, sitting down heavily and kicking off her shoes. 'Jill? Well, she's not doing anything at the moment, having a bit of a rest after the exams.' There was a long pause as she listened. 'No, not as well as we thought, but not through her own fault and certainly not through any lack of effort.'

I tried to get her attention but she ignored me and carried on talking;

'No, I don't think she has . . . she wasn't well at the time,' she continued, lying with consider-able ease. 'I don't tell everyone, they'd think it was an excuse, you know how people are, but I think it was a good deal of the reason why she did so badly.'

In exasperation I gave up and went off to make some tea, eavesdropping as I did so.

' . . . she got her History with flying colours.' I blushed — I had only just scraped through.

' . . . oh yes, well, she always had the ability to learn, not unlike her mother for that. Just a

50

minute — I'll get a pen.' She scrambled to her feet and over to the sideboard, knocking over the toast rack before finding a pad with a pen attached. 'Right, got it — go on. Edward Worthington, yes, I've got that, and the number?' She repeated the name and the address once more and settled back with a satisfied expression on her face. 'It's been so nice to talk to you, I'll let you know how she gets on. You must come over for bridge one night. Who? Eileen Phillips?' She frowned. 'Yes, I do remember her . . . absolutely . . . anytime . . . lovely, I look forward to it. Bye.'

She replaced the receiver and spun round to face me, waving the paper in her hand.

'This is your future, my dear. What did I tell you? Like Mr Micawber always said — something will turn up.'

The 'something' was the name, address and phone number of a gentleman who lived in London, in Kensington, and who had recently returned from Egypt where he had been working for several years as an archaeologist. He had returned to England because of ill-health, and was now concentrating on the conservation of old, historic buildings and was looking for an assistant, cum general dogsbody.

Nancy's friend had thought of me. Possibly, I mused because I would be cheap and also because I was hardly likely to be distracted by outside influences. I was curious but not overly interested, although Nancy seemed to think that the job was already mine.

'You'll love it! You know how interested you

51

are in history, and besides, you never know who you might meet.'

'I'm not sure . . . ' I began lamely.

'Oh, don't be such a flaming pessimist! Go and talk to the man.' She looked back at the piece of paper. 'Did I remember Eileen Phillips? How could I forget her! I lent her a hat once, for a wedding, and I never got it back.'

For Nancy that was it — I had a job. I rang the number that evening and spoke to Edward Worthington, whose voice was high and insubstantial, like talking to a child. We agreed a time for the following afternoon.

He looked for all the world as if he would crumble if touched; his limbs were lost under the material of his suit, and were so fragile that they hardly seemed to lift the cloth. Many years before he would have been tall, but the decades had bowed him until he had become a splendid bracket of a man, his head driven down between his shoulders like a vulture's, his eyes huge and pink-rimmed behind thick glasses; his skin like a crumpled paper bag. But when he shook my hand it was with a firm grip, and his voice seemed stronger in person.

'Are you interested in this type of work?' he asked, inviting me to launch into my prepared piece. He watched with interest, and not a little amusement, and then with an alarming cough, clapped his hands together. It was a mannerism I was to see many times, when he was particularly pleased with something.

'Now — what do you really think?' he asked, and from then on, we were colleagues.

I began to work there the following week, arriving at eight thirty in the morning and working until four, because after that he would be tired and needed to rest before setting out on one of the many functions he attended. Almost daily some invitation would arrive, asking him to talk at a dinner, or at a school, and he seldom refused.

It can't have been the money, because most institutions paid badly; he simply liked to work. His family had returned to England before him, his wife dying soon after, and approximately once a month one of his three children would visit him, sometimes one of his two daughters, sometimes his only son. The women were similar, their voices monotonous and their attitude riddled with bigotry, and they sat at the back of his beautifully faded town house, with an expression of abject martyrdom on their faces. Although they never came together, they became interchangeable in my mind, and although they had children, no grandsons or granddaughters set foot in the house.

His son was another matter. He was reckless and superficial, and parked outside the house blowing his horn as if he was picking up a girl for a drive in the country. He seemed oddly stuck in the past time, taking on the appearance of an ageing juvenile lead in an Ealing comedy. Geoffrey was his name, and when he rang on the phone, he always said, 'Hello, this is Geoffrey, darling, how's the old man?' From then on, I referred to him as 'Geoffrey darling', and when Mr Worthington overheard me one day, he

53

clapped his hands together with a childish delight and repeated it to the next person who came in.

I learnt to type and file because I had to, and because I could do it my own way, it didn't seem so bad. My office was small and wood panelled, and smelt of wax polish, and in front of my desk was a large sporting print in a dark oak frame.

We had a housekeeper called Anna, who was of indeterminate blood, with a mass of thick, black hair, held down with a brightly coloured scarf, worn gypsy-style around her head. She answered the door in her slippers, which infuriated Mr Worthington, and he told her about it repeatedly, after which she would wear shoes for a couple of weeks and then revert to her old ways. It was a contest between them.

I was happy there, and because I worked with old, ruined and mostly forgotten objects, the work became yet another retreat from reality. I dealt with the dead, and their possessions, weaving fantasies around the articles; inventing life histories for people who had been dead for centuries. If that makes it sound macabre, it wasn't — it was merely safe.

Meanwhile, Alison continued to travel on her modelling jobs, and when she came back there would be the ususal flurry of activity from Nancy and Mrs Edwards, to welcome her. When she left again, folders from airline tickets lay at the bottom of her wastepaper basket, or little swabs of make-up covered cotton wool lined the inside of the bathroom bin. Sometimes she left an article behind, or a piece of clothing. They say

54

that everyone has their own smell, and my sister's clothes always smelled faintly of warmth, as if they had just been ironed.

Her bedroom was the same one she had had since she was a child, when we had come down from the attic. It looked out over the back garden and caught the late afternoon sun. When she was fourteen, she had chosen the colours and fabrics she had wanted, and the walls were transformed with soft shades like the inside of a scallop shell. The furniture was pale ivory, interset with gold, and her dressing table was besides the window, so that the light was good but did not fall directly onto the mirror. At four o'clock on a summer's afternoon, deep shafts of sunlight fell onto the rounded sides of her perfume bottles, casting liquid shadows on the glass beneath, or slid under the oval of the mirror and made patterns on pieces of jewellery she left lying there.

Inside her drawers she laid out her various sets of delicate underwear, in every colour to match her outfits, and in the next she placed her jumpers and scarves, putting scented drawer liners underneath so that if you moved anything, a heady draught of perfume idled up to greet you. Likewise her wardrobes were meticulously laid out; every dress next to the jacket it matched, and her silver fox fur and mink jacket placed carefully under old shirts, a luxurious inch or so peeking out at the bottom. I ran my hands along the fur and watched the effect such movement had, seeing how the hairs bent to my touch and then settled, the deep bands of colour almost warm. In another cupboard she kept her rows of shoes, again in colours to match the outfits, but all with high heels, and behind them, she arranged her boots, the staggering slim heels polished and upright, the toes turned towards the door.

The room was full of her, of each exquisite object she possessed, or had touched, or would touch, and when she was away the atmosphere in there became almost oppressive, as if the walls were holding their breath and waiting for her.

By contrast, Nancy's room was a mess of cushions and newspapers, her books piled high on a bedside table, so that after a few weeks of stacking they descended with a resounding thud onto the rug underneath. She ran up huge bills at the local library, and they threatened to take her to court once unless she returned a book she swore she didn't have. The argument raged for nearly three months, and they finally gave in, although only a week later we found the offending article at the back of the drier in the laundry, where it must have fallen weeks earlier. I burned it in the brazier at the bottom of the garden, convinced that at any moment a policeman would tap me on the shoulder, although Nancy told me she couldn't see what all the fuss was about, and that it had been a lousy book anyway.

We developed a wonderful life style between us, needing each other's company, which is a measure of our closeness; and because I was totally relaxed with her, I never minded what I looked like. She was large and solid and in the summer her plump arms, dimpled at the elbows, would beat the hell out of the garden as she weeded. The contrast between her thrashing, good-natured attack, and my dead grandfather's precise, careful approach, was comical and oddly touching. I followed her around, from flower bed to flower bed, sitting down next to her and getting covered now and then with earth, as she wrenched at anything which faintly resembled a weed. Those evenings were elastic, stretching on and on, and yet even then, we never had enough time to say everything. She had a pair of gardening shoes, which were baggy and ringed around the toes with dirt . . . I have them still, although she stopped wearing them years ago.

At night, when I got in from work I sat in the lounge and read, although I spent most of the time looking out of the window. There I forgot Alison and I was safe, hearing Nancy's movements in the room next door, or the dull, erratic tick of a grandfather clock she had bought in a sale, and which never kept going for more than two days at a time. The envy I felt for Alison was hardly apparent at that time, and I believed that as long as she led her life and I could remain in the walled house with Nancy, it would not recur.

Without her I could believe I was beautiful, and witty, and successful; that men would come into my life and love me; that cigarettes would be lit for me; doors would be opened for me; poems would be written for me; and that some day I would marry and have children — who would naturally love me. Yes, it does sound childish and immature, but I thought that was how the world was, if you were one of the lucky ones, and having never ventured far myself, I relied on books and cinema and all the other distorting media to tell me what I could expect. Had I had close girlfriends, some common sense might have prevailed, but I kept my relationships superficial, never wanting to confide in anyone outside the walled house, and no one pressed me for my thoughts.

5

Edward Worthington could talk about his subject for hours on end, and seldom repeat himself, which was probably why he was so sought after as a speaker. It was a rare gift and made him a natural, if unwilling, teacher. Eight thirty found him in my office, wiping the remainder of one of Anna's breakfasts off his chin, a periodical clutched in one hand.

'It's outrageous,' he began one morning, 'I knew Bernard Millings long ago and he never once came up with an original thought, or found anything that someone hadn't found first and thrown back.'

Ten minutes usually passed before he calmed down and began to dictate letters, or make plans for the day.

'Listen, let's go and have a look at it for ourselves, what do you say?' he asked and I nodded. 'You get here early tomorrow and we'll make a day of it.'

It was the beginning of many such jaunts, and because I liked him and was eager to learn, I went along willingly. He made the ideal travelling companion, falling asleep almost immediately and waking only minutes before we were due to arrive. Before such outings, he left long reams of paper on my desk in the mornings, the handwriting firm and forward-slanting, although he wrote after the pen needed filling sometimes, and then all I could make out were the halves of letters, like Egyptian hieroglyphics. He had tremendous cleaning up bouts too, emptying all his drawers and piling up notes on the scratched top of his desk. After a few days they would be rearranged and put back in perfect order, but it took only weeks for things to return to normal, or as long as it took him to haul a briefcase across London to give a lecture. Afterwards, the files re-emerged out of the case with their edges torn, or stippled with ash, and occasionally the mark of a good brandy found its way onto the title pages. I offered to re-do them, but he declined politely, saying that he preferred to do them his way, and after the first time I never pressed him.

Relics of bone were flung unceremoniously onto my desk, or a packing case might remain in the hallway, its cargo removed, although the box and its acreage of sawdust chippings lingered until one of the daughters bullied Anna into moving it. He was all precision and carelessness, but his memory was fiercely accurate and he taught me to think. Many times he asked me my opinion, knowing that I had only a rudimentary knowledge, and because I was flattered I spent time looking up facts and asking serious questions, so that my information grew. Standing besides him on sites we visited, taking from his hands pieces of pot or weapon found in unexpected places behind supermarkets in old towns, I was in my element, and nodded gravely when he dictated notes to me, following up his every word like a private running behind the general. Each day he taught me something, and once, standing by a windy bog in the middle of Dartmoor, I refused to get back into the hired car and instead hung on grimly as we watched the workers gradually uncover part of a wall.

'You see!' he shouted. 'You see! Just as I said all those years ago.'

The light faded and the damp set in, sinking through my coat and making a ring of vapour around my collar. The wind started up quickly, stabbing at my hair and lashing it across my face, streaking the lens of my glasses. It took nearly three hours to remove all the earth, and when they had finished, working by the light of hastily erected arc-lamps, all we could see before us was a small, grubby wall, but my throat constricted and my heart bellied with pride.

'Well done,' he said, patting me on the back lightly, 'you were a good help.'

If my life had ended at that point, I would have sworn to St Peter that it had been worthwhile, and I would have meant it.

So at work I was accepted readily, and became absorbed by the subject and by the people involved. I could work for weeks at 78 Chestnut Walk, without even mentioning Alison's name, and I hugged my working life to myself greedily. When Mr Worthington invited me to attend a dinner as his assistant, my world seemed finally golden.

They had invited a guest speaker who unfortunately drank too much and hung onto the lectern in front of him like a man about to fall down a volcano crater. But he was marvellously funny, and within minutes we were all willing him to remain upright and keep talking, so that when he did finish, a rush of applause broke out spontaneously and Mr Worthington leaned over and shook his hand.

The hall where the dinner was held was quite large, its ceiling high and its walls decorated with that formal type of robust mural so beloved of the early Victorians. On my left, some small, black natives were being converted to religion by a robed figure; whilst on my right Queen Victoria was honouring Wellington, who appeared to be kneeling on an orange box, but when I studied it for a while I realised it was meant to be a marble step. Glasses clattered and smoke rose up to a smog about ten feet above us, and all the men's wives in their beaded dresses exchanged gossip, or inclined their heads towards me in brief acknowledgement. Some of the dinner jackets looked tight across the back, and at the end of the farthest table, a middle-aged man dozed happily, his head down on his chest, his thin white hair floating around his skull like seaweed in the breeze which came from an open window above.

I chose a simple velvet dress for the occasion, in deep navy because I thought it made me look slimmer, and I borrowed a heavy gold chain from Nancy to hang around my neck; but when I looked in the mirror there was only the usual stocky figure looking back at me, and although I had spent hours arranging my hair, I knew that by ten o'clock it would revert to its usual state. Nerves kept me from getting into the taxi and nerves nearly made me late, but I arrived in time to greet my boss and his associates in the entrance hall.

'You're Edward's assistant?' someone said, stating the obvious.

'Yes, that's right,' I replied brilliantly.

'Would you like a sherry?' the man asked, and I nodded gratefully.

He was small and already sweating on his forehead, although he said he was a professor and an old friend of Edward's. I drank the first glassful, and felt the effect almost immediately, so that within minutes I was chatting happily to anyone who even looked in my direction.

'He's a wonderful man,' a rather plump middle-aged woman said.

'Wonderful,' I echoed.

'His wife was a wonderful woman.'

'Yes, wonderful.'

'Did you know her?' she said, her eyebrows raised. I moved away quickly.

I returned home to Nancy full of sights and experiences, telling her about the woman in the Powder Room who had taken off her rings to wash her hands and walked out without them. Consternation broke out when she got back to the table, and the head waiter and two of his staff rushed around questioning and cross-questioning, until the woman, with a screech of relief, found the jewellery in her bag where she had put it for safe keeping. The head waiter insisted to her and her husband that it had been no trouble, but when he moved away his eyes were as hard as a cat's.

When I slept I dreamt of a man who was locked in a crypt, and found a whole tea service under one of the marble floor slabs; and when I awoke I laughed because it made no sense. We spent a magical time, Nancy and I, invigorated by the first warm days of the year — those few warm days that promise summer, forcing you to open windows and plant cuttings in the dark earth still full of April rains. Mrs Edwards cleaned the windows indoors, leaving a damp ring on the carpet with her bucket, and the gardener began his yearly litany of complaints, standing barefoot in the kitchen drinking his tea, the earth-encrusted wellingtons propped up in the back porch.

Nancy seemed somehow altered; and although I was busy at work and away from home more, the slight difference was noticeable and worried me. After Alison mentioned it on one of her visits, I became anxious. I was also infuriated that she appeared more concerned about Nancy than I was — that she had again managed, simply by chance, to make me feel inadequate.

'I don't think it's anything serious,' she said, packing a suitcase, her hair hanging over one side of her face as she bent down, 'it's just that she seems to have less energy. Maybe she needs a tonic.'

I was wrapping one of Alison's belts around my first finger at the time, a very soft leather belt which was deep scarlet — a strange colour, which looked black in the creases. I heard her talk and longed for her to go, watching as she turned around to assure herself that she had left nothing behind.

I sat on her bed and waited, seeing every movement she made in slow motion: the putting on of her rings; the placing of her passport in the zip compartment of her bag; and the final correction of her make-up in the mirror before she left. When she walked out, calling for Nancy, I could still imagine her face reflected in the glass and, dropping the belt on her bedside chair, I followed her.

For the next two days after she had gone, I watched Nancy, looking for any clear sign which would indicate that she was unwell. I knew better than to ask her outright, because she wouldn't have told me anyway, so I waited for her to give herself away. I had just begun to relax, thinking that we had imagined something which did not exist, when I saw her in the garden weeding one of the smaller beds, and suddenly, without warning, she slumped like a drunk onto the grass, her limbs relaxed, her face turned away from the house.

6

She proved to be about the worst patient anyone could have had the misfortune to look after. Nothing suited her, nothing tempted her, the food was too hot or too cold, the bed too hard, the books I got from the library too dull. How I kept hold of my temper was nothing short of miraculous, but after nearly three days, I exploded into a diatribe which rendered her mercifully silent. She looked at me with her mouth open, and then, thank God, she began to laugh.

'You don't care,' she said finally, tears rolling down her cheeks, her large chest heaving. 'I've got a bad heart.'

'At this rate, you won't be the only one,' I replied, bending down and picking up another pile of scattered books, their covers dangling rakishly off their hard backs. 'Come on now, eat what I've brought for you.'

The doctor had informed me that it was indeed a heart condition, and that she had had an angina attack and not the heart attack I had feared. He told me in all earnestness that she would have to lose some weight; that carrying around three stone of unnecessary flesh was no good to her condition, and could shorten her chances. I asked him for a prognosis and he told me that she could go on for years, or . . . After he left, I went into my bathroom and cried, making dull sobs into a towel, and screwing up my face like a child does when it's confused and bewildered. Nancy awoke soon after and called me, making an impressive amount of noise, and when I rushed in, she looked at me blankly.

'Whatever is the matter with you? I'm not going to die, Jill,' she said, her eyes peering at my face. 'Have you been crying?'

I shook my head and, like a fool, broke into tears again, so that she did as she had always done, and comforted me.

But it was one thing to talk and another to live up to the words, and within days it became apparent that she was no longer as mobile and as vigorous as she had been. When I was with her, she pretended to be in high spirits, and pain free, but if I stopped outside the door and watched her, I could see how she would lean back heavily against the pillows, her weight a strain then, her eyes dull and devoid of expression. I believe now that she was afraid, that the first feelings of anxiety crept in with her illness, making her timorous and uncertain — although never whilst I was there.

When we were together, she was all energy and strength, her voice clear and animated, her laugh as raucous as ever. If the phone rang with an enquiry about her health, she bellowed at me until I transferred it to her bedroom extension, and then she convinced the caller that she was well and that we all fussed over her too much. I thought it was bravery, and it was in a way, but it was also the only means she had by which she could hold onto her position — as a matriarch, grandmother and head of the household. If she believed she had lost that, she would have lost her will to live, and although it was blindingly clear to me what the position was, I was careful that she never felt her role had been usurped. I continued to ask her what I should buy, and where from, and how I should cook it, even though I could have done all those things automatically; and she played her part by scolding me for paying too high a price, or for letting Mrs Edwards get away with arriving fifteen minutes late, and leaving ten minutes early. She ran that walled house from her bed, ordering and controlling us, but she tired easily and by five in the afternoon she was exhausted and soon after fell deeply to sleep. She began to grow old from the outside, inwards. When I spoke to some of her friends about it, they told me that it was just an effect of the illness, but I knew differently, and I also knew that she would never be quite what she was again.

'Did you get the beef from Whittakers?' she asked me, coming back to life after a brief sleep. 'You did remember what I said, didn't you?'

'It's done, and we'll have it on Friday, with some new potatoes,' I responded, detailing all the little trivia of our lives as if it were of paramount importance.

The weather changed only a few days after she had been taken ill, becoming windy, the air running down the chimney and making faint cries in the corridor. I had to go up into the attics to find an old tray, the type with legs, upon which we used to bring Nancy breakfast in bed when we were children. It was in one of the tea chests under the rafters, she told me, but when I went up to look, the first thing I came across was a small, almost mummified wren, which had got in somehow and died. When I picked it up it was weightless, its feathers dull, but not rotted, its eyes closed. The gardener buried it for me, not without a brief complaint, and lumped an unspectacular bush on top of the little grave as I asked him, insisting that it wouldn't grow. The breakfast tray was where Nancy had said it would be, and I pulled it out hurriedly in order to leave the attic as quickly as I could. Over my head, a small skylight tapped with the onslaught of a slight shower, and intermittent rushes of wind sighed around the crossbeams and along the bare boards. The wallpaper had deteriorated a little more, its pattern faded and indecipherable in parts, and when I moved to leave, I couldn't stop myself from glancing back. There was no mark on the wallpaper then, but I knew that if it rained until evening, the witch would be back, and I shuddered briefly and moved downstairs.

I grew up then, in those two weeks when Nancy was confined to bed, and it was about time. I let her harrass me as much as she wanted, because her real power had diminished, and even if she didn't recognise it, it was obvious to me. The order in the house was changing, and gradually, the various roles we had assumed would change also.

When she slept Nancy looked young again, her face relaxed, the full line of her cheek and

69

chin making her oddly childlike. Sometimes she would be restless and turn over with a heavy clumsiness which was untypical of her; other times she awakened suddenly and I hadn't noticed, so that when I did glance across, she unnerved me when I saw that her eyes were open. It took only a fraction of a second for her to smile, but before she had, there was another expression in her eyes that I did not fully understand; an expression of loneliness, and possibly even regret. After the first few days of illness she began to lose weight, not generally, but from specific areas, such as her hands, so that the skin wrinkled slightly and made the blue tinge of her veins apparent underneath.

'You have lovely hands,' she said, knowing that the compliment gave me pleasure. 'Mine look so . . . unlike me now.'

'It won't last,' I insisted, as much for her benefit as mine. 'When you get back on your feet, you'll see.'

Mrs Edwards and I carried the small television upstairs and placed it close to Nancy's bed, so that she could see it easily, but the programmes hardly ever kept her interest for long. She had been active all her life and enforced inactivity was making her irritable.

'Are you sure that doctor told you that I had to stay in bed?' she asked me repeatedly, and repeatedly I assured her that that was exactly what he had advised. When he did visit, he told her that she was much better, and complimented her on her loss of weight.

'A whole stone, Mrs Longman! Well done!

70

You'll be quite a beauty queen when you've finished.'

I saw her wince as I did, and when I closed the door after he had gone, I wondered if he really did prefer the older, tireder, thinner version of my grandmother, or whether he could even remember what she had previously looked like.

For my part, I detested the rapid change in her. I loathed the shrinking of her size, because it seemed her personality shrank also. Wanting to encourage her, and because I knew it was better for her health, I complimented her, but she saw through it.

'Don't tell me tales, Jill, I know what I look like, and I look my age.'

It wasn't true — she looked older than her years.

By the end of ten days she had lost eleven pounds and when I came in to move her lunch tray one afternoon, she was standing by her wardrobe door, rifling through its contents.

'You can ring up Mr Worthington, Jill, and tell him that you will be back in the office on Monday. I'm well able to cope now.' I moved over to her, noticing how her nightdress hung on her, and how her feet seemed longer and bonier than before.

'You're not — ' I began.

'Don't boss me, my girl, I'm not a child. You may think you run this house, but — '

She stopped then and turned around to face me, her expression apologetic and somehow more like she used to be. Opening her arms, I walked over to her and she held me.

71

'I didn't mean that,' she began, rocking me slightly as she always did. 'You've been so good to me, and look what a cow I've turned out. It's just that this is my house, and it's all I've got. You have your career, and your life to live, and you'll find your own man, some day. But for me . . . this is everything.'

She stepped back, looking at me from an arm's length.

'Did I ever tell you that I loved you?' she asked, her voice serious.

I nodded. 'Many times.'

She smiled broadly. 'In that case, I won't bother repeating it.'

She dressed then and we talked about getting a woman from the town to alter her clothes, which were all too baggy and looked pathetic when she tried them on, just as her rings swivelled on her fingers, until she grew impatient with them and flung them to the back of her dressing table drawer. I had never thought of her as a vain woman, but when she looked in the mirror she frowned, and her eyes blazed with frustration, as if she had lost something and was horrified to learn that it could never be regained.

But although she wanted to return to her usual ways, she could not. An hour's pottering around the house exhausted her, and in the garden, the smallest attempt at pruning, even without bending down, would leave her white-faced in irritable defeat. Still I continued to ask her what to do and she tried with all her will to make my meals, but her progress was halting and

72

when Alison rang to say that she was coming home for the weekend, she looked impatient for once, as if even the idea of her granddaughter's coming was too much for her.

'You see,' she explained to me when she put the telephone down, 'you and I, well we're used to each other, but Alison's grown apart from us and I feel as if I should put on a show to welcome her, you know what I mean — make an effort.'

I nodded, and secretly rejoiced that my sister was now thought of as some form of beloved interloper, and with a different attitude I set about preparing for her arrival.

A wet evening saw her getting out of the taxi cab, her hair swinging across her face as she leant forwards to pay the driver. When she turned, she was already smiling, her hands gripping the handles of two suitcases, her face almost free of make-up, her belted coat making her waist look even smaller than it was.

'Hello Jill, give me a hand with these, will you?' she asked, and I walked out to her, kissing her lightly on the cheek. She smelled of rain and wet wool, and her skin was cool, like alabaster. Inside, she hardly had a chance to remove her coat when Nancy walked into the hallway and kissed her. Alison's face registered surprise, but she hugged Nancy in response, and looked over her shoulder towards me — and the question blatant in her face, the smile gone.

'You look . . . tired,' she began tactfully, studying her grandmother's face and figure. 'What's been happening whilst I was away?'

73

I opened my mouth to speak, but Nancy got there first.

'I had a little trouble with my heart — '

'What!' Alison exploded, throwing an accusing look over to me. I had neither written, nor telephoned her about Nancy's condition.

'Now don't go on about it,' the other woman continued.

'I'm perfectly all right now. It wasn't a heart attack, just a little warning that I have to take things a bit easier. Pace myself.'

Neither of us believed her, of course, and Alison remained rooted to the hall carpet as if she had been nailed there. I could see the tell-tale signs of Nancy's impatience beginning — the slow drain of colour from her face, and the little, rapid movements of her hands when she was trying to keep her temper. With a diplomacy that was not usual in my nature, I intervened, 'We didn't want to worry you,' I began smoothly, feeling the full force of two perfectly shaped eyes boring into me. 'It seemed pointless to worry you.'

The position of the three of us shifted as obviously as if there had been an avalanche on a mountainside. Where we had once been, we were no longer; each woman's status was threatened, and other, more precarious footings had to be found. I watched Alison falter, uncertain what to say, and for an instant I felt sympathy for her, and wondered how I would have taken the exclusion had I been in her place.

'Now,' she began, recovering well, 'the important thing is that we are all together again.

We must take more care of you, Nancy, perhaps I could spend a little more time at home and travel less.'

She said it with a note of triumph in her voice, and my heart felt suddenly as if someone had packed it in ice. I looked across to Nancy, hoping to read a similar dread in her face, but she took the suggestion with obvious pleasure, and the hold I thought I had over her slipped out of my grasp.

Alison was back.

7

I need not have worried really. Alison stayed with us for nearly ten days, and then, when she could no longer refuse the work offers, she left for a weekend in Brussels. She had stayed long enough for us to grow used to including her again, but not long enough for us to find it impossible to revert to our old ways. Nancy, naturally, never mentioned any of this directly to me, she would never have obviously favoured one girl over the other, but her actions spoke for her. Alison left at eight thirty that Saturday morning, and when I saw the car turn out of the gate I felt relieved, and set about the house whistling and making beds with a pleasure such actions would not normally have aroused.

Coffee bubbled and hissed on the gas ring, and rounds of toast turned from ivory to gold under the red heat of the grill. I laid out marmalade and honey, taking care to put spoons on the plates for each of them, and I called for Nancy when it was ready, laying down the morning paper next to her plate. We were safe again, my actions said, our world was secure. I walked around the walled garden later, pinching the dead leaves off various bushes, and paused by the rose bed and turned, seeing the house standing four square and solid in front of me.

With a heady confidence I saw my future marked out before me with a clarity I could never before have imagined. Work was a pleasure to me, my employer needed me, and so did my grandmother. She would grow older from that moment on, I reasoned, and would need my help and support, which I would naturally give to her. It was only a returned compliment after all, to repay her for what she had done for me as a child. I conned myself into believing that I was invaluable to Nancy, whereas I needed her to make sense out of the life I had chosen.

I was then twenty years of age and had managed with a supreme effort of will, to rid myself of my weight and if I was not svelte, I was not heavy either. Because of my shape, I always appeared a stocky, box-like figure, but I studied magazines and found out various ways to disguise my faults, and became a little less plain. Smiling transformed me, someone said, and for months at the merest hint of something amusing I would grin like a startled racehorse, until Nancy tactfully suggested that I should dampen it down a little.

Work brought me in touch with a great many people, most of whom were deeply involved with their various projects, and none of whom asked me out. I comforted myself with the knowledge that I too could become serious-minded and develop my career until it consumed my whole life, but there was always a nagging doubt which never let up on me. These men had wives and children, and if they hardly ever saw them it didn't seem to matter, they were there anyway, waiting for them. I looked at the few women who were involved in the conservation work, and my

77

eyes developed a habit it took me years to get out of — when I saw a woman for the first time I looked instinctively at her left hand, and if she wore a ring I felt animosity, and if she did not, sympathy. I gravitated towards the plain ones, feeling that married women were already one step ahead of the rest of us, and when a girl confided to me once that she had just turned down an offer of marriage because she was not sure she really loved the man, I looked at her with amazement — what had true love got to do with it? I wondered, doubting that she would get another chance.

The decision was reached slowly, but irrevocably. I developed my career and looked after Nancy and the house, so that my life consisted of these few people and belongings, and as soon as I had made up my mind, a calmness settled on me. Alison came and went, but she never caused so much as a ripple, I never allowed her to, and she kept her private life well apart from the walled house and the two women who occupied it, preferring to continue her own separate existence outside. Possibly she was taking some form of revenge for my actions during Nancy's illness, possibly she had decided that she merely wished to live that way, and I never knew for sure, because I never asked her. But I was grateful that I no longer had to listen to her stories of the many admirers, or overhear her and Nancy gossiping into the small hours.

My grandmother was undergoing a sea change too, and became too preoccupied with her own

78

worries to notice the shift in our relationship, being too anxious to pretend that she had never been ill, and that she was as she had always been. But when friends rang to make arrangements for her to meet them for lunch, she arranged the dates for several weeks ahead, believing that by then she would be stronger. She didn't want them to see how she had altered, how she had aged, and one of the few times I ever saw her cry, was when she washed her hair and found that the previous slight patches of grey had almost tripled. We tinted it with a colour I got from the chemist, and when it was dry her hair glistened under the light as if it had been polished.

'What do you think?' she asked me, her eyes brilliant with achievement.

'It's wonderful,' I said simply, and meant it.

It was such a small thing, but it turned her luck, and from that day onwards she seemed to make progress. Time and time again I returned early from work to find empty pots of jam in the rubbish bins, or the crusts of innumerable rounds of toast hurriedly thrown out for the birds. She swore blind she was sticking to her diet, but the weight began to creep back, and by late June her rings fitted perfectly and her clothes were snug on her hips. The doctor took great pains to explain the situation to me.

'It's bad for her to carry so much weight,' he repeated, looking out of the lounge window and watching Nancy in the garden, gliding around the flower beds, a trug over her arm, the familiar white gardening gloves protecting her hands. 'She has a weak heart, and although she hasn't had another angina attack, it doesn't mean to say she won't.'

I followed his gaze, but all I could see was the woman I remembered from my childhood, and I knew for certain that she would live longer in her own way than she ever would if he insisted on restricting and shrinking her. As with her, though, I went through the motions.

'She's always enjoyed her food,' I began stiltedly, 'and although I try and stop her when I'm here, I can't tell you what she eats when I'm at work.'

He was suddenly bored and moved away from the window, picking up his case and walking to the door.

'Well, just keep reminding her, that's all I can suggest. It's her life, in the end.'

I walked out behind him, noticing that his hair was thinning on the back of his head, and that there was a faint dusting of dandruff on his collar. I was just wondering why his wife hadn't brushed it off before he left on his calls, when he turned back to me. 'I'll come in a fortnight, unless you need me before then,' he said and left.

I knew that his patience was exhausted with us — that he merely saw a stupid, middle-aged woman who hadn't the sense to keep to her diet, and a granddaughter who didn't try to force the matter. Possibly in his shoes I would have felt the same; he didn't understand us, or the manner in which Nancy's mind worked, and he would never have condoned her unconscious decision to live as she was happy, even if it did shorten her years.

Life came back into her — which is the only way I can truly describe the change she underwent. Certainly, she had aged, that was to be expected, she was now a member of that club, who have to 'pace' themselves; whose actions are curtailed by the ever present realisation that life suddenly has a cut-off point. Nancy knew all this, and came to her own peace by alternately accepting and rebelling against the knowledge. She spent days in the house, cleaning, and altering the layout of the furniture, heaving at chairs and tables, as if she was willing them to force her heart into submission, or acceptance. She tempted fate. I came in one day from work and saw what she had done, the anger burning in my throat.

'Why don't you get some bullets?'

'What the hell does that mean?' she asked me, putting down another crossword puzzle.

'It means — that if you were to put one bullet in the gun barrel, spin it, and then spend all afternoon firing it until you blew your head off, you couldn't be acting in a less responsible manner than you are now.'

She gave me a withering look.

'I can't live like an invalid, you know. I can't live to give you peace of mind.'

My anger lashed out unexpectedly. I had had a hard day, some objects had been lost and a letter that Mr Worthington had wanted sending off I had overlooked, and although he had not lost his temper, his disappointment was harder to bear. I took all my spleen out on Nancy.

'You can't live to give *me* peace of mind? How

81

selfish! God, how selfish could anyone get! I never thought of you like that, not once in all these years. I would never have believed that you were mean and unfeeling and selfish.'

She stood up, crossed her arms and watched me, her face showing nothing.

'What if you died?' I said, stopping immediately, having said the one thing I had sworn never to say.

'What if I had died?' she repeated softly. 'Well if I had, you would have buried me, and talked about me for years, saying all those lovely things that everyone says about their nearest and dearest. You would have dusted my photograph, and watered my plants,' she unfolded her arms and walked to the window, pausing for an instant before she continued; 'and every year, when it was my birthday, you would have thought about me. Sometimes, you'd have missed me, or wondered how to make pastry, or where something was, but otherwise you would do what everyone else does — you would carry on.'

'Oh God, I didn't mean — '

She continued as if she had not heard me. 'Yes, you would have regretted some things, and treasured others, and when you came to clearing out my bedroom you would have been rather more affected than we were when we sorted out your grandfather's things.'

She stopped, but I couldn't see her face as she was still facing the window. Because she sounded so unlike herself, I did not approach her, and I waited for her to go on, thinking that she might begin to laugh and the tension would be broken.

But for a long moment she said nothing, and then with a great effort she murmured, 'You would, wouldn't you?'

In all my years with her she had never been the weaker one mentally. I walked over to her and saw that she was frightened, that in my one reference to her death, she had seen it plainly for the first time herself.

'Nancy, I would do all that, and more. There would be nothing of you which didn't influence me, or remain with me. You're not going to die, not yet, but when you do, I shall go on loving you, just as I do now.'

She nodded her head and moved back to the chair, and without another word, continued with her crossword. I wondered if she was really concentrating, but after dinner I looked at the paper and saw that nearly all the spaces were filled. She had made the first of her stations to her own death, and although she did not die for many years, now and then she asked for a reaffirmation of her value, and as we grew to understand each other better, I understood how and when to provide what she wanted of me.

It was such a small price to pay for the rest of our time that I did not dwell upon it, and later that year, for my birthday, she bought me a jewellery box, which was red leather outside and lined in the deepest crimson. I laid out all my rings in the spaces provided, their brilliant faces turned up to me, their flashes of colour reflected in the mirrored lid. Along the left hand corner of the case were my inititals in deep gold script, and many times I ran my hand over their imprint, tracing a finger along the slanting, copperplate lines. It was an elegant gift, to an inelegant girl, but I loved it, and over the years I filled it with the various pieces I collected, charting the passage of my life with their accumulation.

Alison was abroad and arranged to have my gift sent from a nearby department store. It turned out to be a silk caftan, which was beautiful and exotic, and utterly splendid, on anyone else. I wrote and thanked her, and pushed it to the back of my wardrobe with a few other things she had sent in previous years — gifts that she never questioned me about, or wondered why I never wore them.

Even my boss remembered and bought me a card with a Siamese cat on it, and an inscription about me being a 'careful and loyal helper', and in its stilted way it pleased me, as did the bottle of sherry he left on the corner of my desk after he had gone out that evening. It was all so safe and uncomplicated, as if I was now accepted and would remain there all my working life. Anna had left me a bunch of flowers, and when I went upstairs to thank her, she blushed and wrapped her hair up in a towel, whilst apologising for her appearance, saying that she had just had a bath. She invited me in, and I accepted, walking around her two small rooms and asking about the few photographs she had hung in prominent places.

'It's my brother, Theo,' she explained, looking younger now that her hair was wrapped turban-like around her head. 'He did very well, very well, and got a business in Valletta.'

'You come from Malta?' I asked, wondering why she had confided to me a fact that she kept so assiduously hidden from everyone else. She looked at me for a long instant, her dark eyes slightly puffy, the deep tone of her skin making her appear unfairly sallow in the English daylight.

'I tell no one — they all want to know my business. But I tell you.' A slight look of cunning slid across her eyes. 'You tell no one?'

'No. Why should I?'

She seemed satisfied that I had passed her test, and from then on, she invited me once a month to take tea with her. It was a curiously British habit and yet I looked forward to our talks, as bit by bit she drew me a picture of her family and her children, telling me that she was fifty-three and that her daughter and son were back in Malta running the restaurant with her husband. I digested the information carefully.

'You mean that you're separated. Are you going to get a divorce?'

'I'm Roman Catholic,' she replied, crossing herself dramatically. 'No divorce, we live apart only.'

'Do you miss him?'

She shrugged and fingered the gold chain round her neck.

'I love him a great deal when we were young — but he like women . . . you know?' I nodded. No, I didn't know, but I wanted her to go on. 'Always women, women, women. I thought — he's married to me — he comes home always — why worry?' She looked over to me as if she

85

wanted some confirmation that she had behaved correctly. I nodded again sagely. 'Then suddenly he finds this woman, and he loves her . . . ' Another roll of the eyes, another pantomime gesture. 'So I came here. I earn good money and I save.'

I couldn't help wondering what she was saving for. It was unlikely that she would marry again, her religion made that an impossibility, so why was she working and scrimping to hoard money under a cloudy London sky, when she could have been living under perpetual sunshine in Malta, turning a blind eye to her husband's wanderings?

'I buy my own café,' she said simply, as if she had read my thoughts.

'To compete with him?' I asked, but she didn't seem to understand. 'To do better, make more money, than him?'

'Yes. Everyone will come to my place just to look at me and say that I was wrong to leave my family, and that I get old.' She laughed to herself, as if the prospect delighted her. 'They come to talk about me, but they come, hundreds of them . . . you see? People come — I make lots of money. If I tell them grand stories about London, and my men,' she winked ludicrously, 'they talk all the more, and they come to the café more and more, and my husband he thinks, maybe she's not so bad after all.'

I watched her in amazement, seeing her waiting and saving alone in two dull rooms in England, plotting like a female Machiavelli, towards her ultimate goal — the winning back of

86

a worthless husband. I marvelled that any woman would go to such lengths, and when I asked to see a photograph of him she got up and pulled out an album from the back of a cupboard drawer. There, on the front page, in pride of place, was her husband, small and dark, with a thick nose and the start of a paunch, planted squarely on the ground on two large feet, his arms akimbo. He looked like a thousand other men, with no presence and no charisma, at least, not that I could see from the shiny face of the photograph. But when she took it from my fingers and gazed at it herself she actually did appear younger for a second, and it did seem suddenly possible that she would one day get off an aeroplane and make her way back to her home town to wow them with fantasies, winking at the florid, dark men sitting by fly-blown mirrors in a small, hot café. Maybe some of them would wink back, and believe her tales, drooling over the visions of her life in famous and infamous London; maybe they would press her for details, and maybe she would roll her eyes and wiggle her finger at them. And maybe, just maybe, one day her husband would come in and ask her to walk with him when she closed . . . and maybe it would all be worthwhile.

Meanwhile, she saved and she dreamt, and once a month we drank tea together before I made my way home.

So the three marriages I had as examples were assorted, and spoke ill of the arrangement. My parents, who had lived and died together, and with whom I had never had the opportunity to

87

discuss the matter; Nancy's marriage to a curiously diffident and unloving husband; and Anna's love and absorption in a man who was selfish and thoughtless, and who probably seldom dwelt on the wife who had left him and his children or possibly he was even grateful to her, in that she provided him with a free hand to act as the deserted husband and to pursue comfort wherever he could find it. They all seemed unfulfilled and mismatched; as if none of them had been committed to the right partner, as if the god who was in charge of matching humans had muddled them, and drawn out the names at random, so that one woman may have got another's man, or vice versa. How many married for love? Or the hope of love? How many would have found happiness elsewhere? It was impossible for me to judge then, I only saw the results of their matching, not the reasons which drew them into their pairs.

July saw Alison on the front of one of the most prestigious magazine covers, her small face perfectly lovely, her eyes large and luminous, the expression sensuous. It was the face which belonged to another type of personality, not my sister's: it was the countenance of a woman who was all-knowing, pleasure loving, hedonistic, the look of the lotus eater, the predatory mate. It was not Alison who looked out from the glossy cover, but Alison's face, and for the first time it became apparent to me that the two were separate. I knew how her mind worked, that she was uncomplicated and shallow, that her sweetness was more to ensure an easy life, than to entice

88

people; that she reacted in the same way with men — they were amusing, or witty, or good company, but not to be taken seriously, nothing over which one lost sleep, or confidence. She painted on attitudes and emotions which she did not possess. Had Alison been more ambitious, or more demanding, she could have made a consummate actress; as it was, she preferred to continue in the limited, but lucrative channel she had dug for herself, and she seemed to need no more.

Nancy cut the photograph out and pasted it with the others, in the rapidly growing scrap books we kept. Oddly, when I saw her picture I did not feel the same trauma of jealousy she personally invoked, I did not resent her from a distance, and I would trim the photos and write the captions besides them with great care, discussing her progress with Nancy, although outside the walled house I never mentioned her — I even denied her existence.

At work, Anna had once asked me if I was an only child, and I had said yes before I had time to think, crossing Alison off with an alarming finality. Had I owned up to her, questions would have followed, and the whole history and triumph of my sister would have followed also, and much as I would like to say otherwise, I could not have endured that. So for a while, Alison faded into my background, and life revolved around Nancy and my work.

Reading the local paper at the weekends, Nancy called out if she came across the wedding of one of my previous school friends scrutinising the photographs mercilessly.

'Do you remember that girl you knew in your fourth year? The one with the foreign mother?'

'Which one?'

'You know — she was small and red-headed, and she spoke with a lisp — you couldn't stand her.'

'Marina Turner! Yes, I do remember her — why?'

'She got married last Saturday, and had the reception at the Hartlington Club. God, that must have cost a fortune.' She carried on reading the small print. 'Best man, John Fielding . . . that name's familiar . . . that's right, I've got it, his mother married Celia Brook's son.'

She rambled on, although I wasn't really listening. She could remember who married whom, and where and even what they wore, probably long after most of the people involved could. It was a hobby with her, watching how people progressed, and the friends who rang her were almost as bad, holding endless conversations on the phone about marriages and births, although the people who died were seldom mentioned, as if dying was the ultimate in a social faux pas. Otherwise, anything else was fair game, which is not to say that Nancy was malicious, only curious and fond of talking, and she never kicked anyone when they were down.

'I doubt if I'll marry,' I said, as I signed off a letter to Alison.

'Why ever not?' Nancy asked.

'Well, I'm hardly what you might call

good-looking, and besides, I'm not sure I want to get married.'

I meant it too. Really I did.

'Listen, the best wives aren't necessarily the best looking. You're not ugly, Jill, you know that, and although men like a pretty face, they don't always marry one. You wait and see, the right man will come along, and then you'll want to get married. It's the way of things.'

But inside I knew otherwise. I didn't want to join in the matrimonial stakes, I didn't want to invite rejection and humiliation. If I was not to get married, then I wanted it to be because I chose not to, not because no man had asked me. I was too frightened of rejection to risk loving, and too careful of my pride to invite a rebuttal.

July rained on into August, and a small pool filled the dip in the lawn. One morning, two ducks stopped off on their flight, swimming around for a time as we watched them through the lounge window.

Then, shortly afterwards, there was a fire at Chestnut Walk. It had started in the basement, from where the flames had curled up into the first floor, making brown blisters on the panelling in my office. When I walked in the morning after the fire, one wall looked as if it had been transformed into a weird sepia jungle scene, or like a mural which had gone horribly wrong, the long licks of scorch marks crawling upwards like some disturbed fossils, climbing towards the light.

Mr Worthington had been out that evening, and had come back at about one o'clock in the

91

morning, just in time to smell smoke. Wisely, he had rung for the fire service without stopping to investigate, and then he and Anna had waited in the street outside. The firemen put out the blaze almost immediately, so that the damage was restricted to the basement and to the one wall of my office, and the nearby floorboards. The smell continued to linger for days, long after the mess had been cleaned up, and Mr Worthington contracted some workmen to replace the panelling which had perished. When they did so, however, it looked too light and out of place, and even after they stained the wood, it appeared not to belong to the rest of the room, looking insubstantial and fragile. I bought some plants and arranged them on a table pushed against the wall, training them upwards on hastily built caning, and by the end of that September, nearly half of the area was disguised.

It had taken the fire to make me realise just how much I valued my job and career. The sudden and deforming alteration of my room had also disturbed me, as if, without warning, what was taken for granted could be changed or even destroyed. After things returned to normal, I worked avidly, giving much of my spare time and contributing a great deal of effort and interest to my work, and my employer began to rely on me more and more. He knew that I was to be trusted and so I was given a great deal of responsibility, and although my knowledge was moderate, it increased daily.

People began to ring and ask for me

92

personally, thinking of me as Mr Worthington's right hand.

'Could you get him to see us? I mean, you could convince him, we know that.' or 'If I ask you to do that for me, I know it will get done, which is more than I can say for most people.'

I treasured the compliments, and began to think of my work as another woman might have regarded a lover. It consumed me. When I woke, it was the first thought in my head, and when I went to sleep, the last which came to me; I felt genuine sadness when I closed the office door on Friday evenings, though I knew I would be back on the Monday and the room would be waiting for me.

And on the other hand, was Nancy, who became my child, the positions between us reversing neatly. She was growing older and I realised that she would, by stages, become dependent upon me, not that the realisation gave me a single uneasy thought, on the contrary, I welcomed the commitment. Life provided me with a substitute lover and a substitute child, and I was sensible enough to know that if I couldn't have the real thing, then second best could be made to do.

And what of Alison in all of this?

Alison continued to flourish apart from us. She never expressed an interest in Chestnut Walk, and I did not volunteer information about the place, and when we talked about Nancy, her interest was fleeting and superficial, as if she was fond of her, but relieved to see me taking on the daily responsibility. Perhaps she thought she had

93

carefully sidestepped the issue, pushing it on to the sister who was stuck at home, but her opinion was not forthcoming and I did not let on that the situation suited me too well, otherwise she might have sought to alter it.

In and out she came, taking calls in the late evenings, leaving after nine for dinners in the West End, and coming in almost silently. I knew she took off her shoes in the hall so that she would not disturb us; and I also knew that she took a telephone extension into her bedroom and made calls in the early hours. No, I did not wonder who she spoke to, or what she said, and when the morning came we greeted each other happily and started different days.

Then Nancy began to get tired earlier in the evenings, going up to bed about ten o'clock. She laughed about it the first few nights, saying that she had to have her beauty sleep, but after that she said nothing else, and her early retiring became routine. She would still read, but her light did not burn long after eleven, not as it had done before, remaining lit sometimes until dawn, when, with a triumphant bang as the finished book hit the floor, she would finally sleep.

Her humour, however, had not changed: she was as bawdy and as raucous as ever, and her temper was as sharp. She saw me off in the mornings and greeted me at night with snippets of news or conversation, and I valued her company as most people value a close friend. What she did during the day I never asked, unless it was made obvious by one of her furniture moving bouts of activity, and I supposed that the odious Mrs Edwards did most of the heavy work.

But one day I came home early and found Nancy asleep in a chair by the lounge window. I knew that if she woke and saw me she would be mortified, so I crept out and went back into town, returning at my usual time to find her ready and welcoming, a meal freshly cooked, and an article in the paper ringed with red ink.

They were the gentle, untroubled days, the long nights and tranquillity which soothed us all. It was good that we recognised and treasured them, because on the horizon was a ship whose coming would affect us all, and one which would rock us and wreck us in turn.

8

I remember the morning vividly because the car wouldn't start, and my boss was waiting for me to deliver some papers to him before he could leave on his trip. Repeatedly, I turned on the engine, only to hear a choking sound as it failed to catch, and in exasperation I called out to Nancy to get me a taxi. I snatched the keys up and went back into the house to wait.

' . . . fine, as soon as you can. Thank you.' She turned to me. 'Five minutes, they said.'

I nodded and rang the office, explaining to Mr Worthington what had happened. He assured me that it wasn't my fault, but his tone was controlled and lacked conviction. I stood cursing by the window, until the taxi drove up.

If I had believed in omens I would have been worried, but as I arrived just in time to thrust the file into Mr Worthington's hands as he walked down the steps, I felt that although the day had begun badly, it could only get better. I was wrong.

Half an hour later I received a phone call which informed me that I was wanted on site at a place just outside Oxford, where they had come across something 'interesting', and because my boss was away I had to go.

The place turned out to be a little sleepy hamlet which was falling down. The houses were all slanted, lurching drunkenly against one

96

another like men at a bar rail, and the only inhabitants appeared to be a woman pushing a large pram, and the landlord of a pub which was understandably deserted at ten in the morning. I walked in and asked for directions, and he told me, slowly, and with a great deal of lip movement, as if I was a deaf foreigner. I thanked him and walked out into the dull sunshine.

Because I had hired a car, I couldn't find the right gear at first, and drove past the turning by accident. Swearing under my breath, I reversed down what appeared to be a dirt track, and I had only gone thirty feet when a figure jumped out of the hedgerow.

'Bloody hell!' I exploded, slamming both feet down on the pedals. 'What in God's name — ?'

He turned to face me and I stopped in mid sentence, the words making dusty patches on my tongue. Holding a piece of what appeared to be dried clay, the man stood motionless, a thin smile of amusement on his features. He was tall and badly dressed, in the clothes of a person working in rough conditions, his trousers tucked into his wellingtons, the collar of his shirt turned back with the first buttons undone. His face was tanned, the eyes screwed up against the sunlight, the mouth wide and tilted at the corners. He appeared to be a workman, from the dusty, short hair to the ungainly feet, but his demeanour was too confident, too polished, for that. He made no movement towards me, neither did he apologise, and instead I walked over to him.

'I was reversing . . . ' I started, seeing his eyebrows raise.

97

'Have you killed many people that way?' he responded coolly, with the trace of an American accent.

As I walked the few feet towards him, I felt more ungainly than I had ever previously done. I felt ugly and overweight, knowing my legs were heavy, and my face, devoid of make-up, plain behind glasses. He saw my shortcomings also, and as I reached him, his smile set into a formal, rather than a genuine welcome.

'I was looking for the dig,' I continued. 'I'm here on behalf of Edward Worthington.'

He extended his hand and I took it, noticing that it was smoother than I had anticipated, and that he held mine longer than was necessary. He was all teeth, tan and talk, with a kind of unctuous charm mothers warn their daughters about. I should have known better, but the instant I saw him I felt as if I had been hit with a pickaxe. He released my hand and waved his arm expansively towards the next field.

'Here it is,' he announced, and I moved towards the direction he indicated, turning my ankle as I did so. The pain shot up my right leg and made me catch my breath, although I continued to look across the landscape with an interested expression on my face. I had no desire to appear even more of a fool.

He didn't stay long with me, seeming to lose interest rapidly, and he moved away as soon as he could without being rude. I watched him walk off, and then leant down and rubbed my ankle which was already swelling.

He was there all day, on and off, giving orders

because apparently he was a big wheel from New York, out here doing some research, and by sheer luck he had happened upon a find.

'Typical,' I heard one spindly young man mutter to another. 'We work here all flaming year, and that bright spark comes over here, trips over the first thing he steps on, and uncovers half of the Holy Roman Empire. That's justice for you.'

'Who is he?' I asked innocently, noticing the exchange of glances between the two men.

'Mark Ward. Comes from America and thinks he's a bit of a lad.' He laughed forcedly, his face shiny in the sunlight. I began to feel hot.

'How long is he here for?'

I knew the question was an obvious one, and that they would laugh about my asking it, later, in the village pub. But I asked anyway.

'Not sure. Maybe a week, maybe longer. It's difficult to say with these superstars.'

I thanked him and moved away and for the remainder of the day I made my usual notes and spent as much time as possible watching the tall man who was working only feet away from me. He was easy in his movements, and comfortable; if he slipped or dropped something he laughed, and everyone laughed with him, especially the women. He had glamour — that longed for, inexplicable style which dazzles. When we finished for lunch, he glanced over in my direction and without thinking I waved. Surprised, he paused, squinted his eyes against the sunlight and then looked around him.

I knew what he was doing. I knew that he was

99

looking for someone else with whom he could have lunch, for some other, better looking woman. But they had already left, and so he turned back to me, raising his hand in greeting as he walked over. Better to be with a plain woman, than no woman at all.

'So we meet again. Would you like to have lunch with me?' he asked, flinging his jacket over his shoulder and helping me to my feet.

'Lovely,' I replied inanely, as though I was invited to lunch every day of the week.

We walked down to the pub together and the two men with whom I had been talking glanced up, surprised to find me with the American. I felt inordinately proud and for the first time in my life, I had a pride in myself and my worth. It was heady stuff, and that combined with a lager made me reckless and light-headed. I talked too much; laughed too loud; made fatuous comments which I would have winced at, had I heard anyone else say them, but I couldn't stop myself. His expression veered from amusement to irritation, as he drummed his fingers on his trouser legs, and downed one drink, calling for another. I believe that I even saw him raise his eyes to someone — perhaps suggesting that I was being a bore, a fool, and a plain one at that. But for me it was simply the most exciting and humiliating thing that had ever happened to me, and when the lunch was finished he escorted me back to my place in the field, smiled, and walked off — no doubt greatly relieved.

The afternoon ground on, becoming hotter and dustier than before, the heat dancing along the horizon and under a line of oaks. I sat beneath a tree and jotted down what everyone said, making careful notes for Mr Worthington to read later, as I watched them all, especially the tall American. At four he left, nodding briefly to me as he passed. I heard his car start up, and dug my nails into the palms of my hands, annoyed at my own stupidity and consoling myself with the thought that he would be there the following day. That night I slept little, as I was prodded and nagged by whisperers who wouldn't let me rest. They hissed in my ears and made the night air hang on the bed clothes, so that by morning I was tired and drained of sleep. The long nights had begun.

I arrived early at the dig the next morning, nodding briefly to the thin young man and his companion, and settling myself in the same position as before, so that anyone wanting to find me would know where to look. At ten, he had not come, nor at eleven or twelve, and it was only by hearing a remark made by one of the other girls, that I knew he would not be coming back.

'Gone home yesterday night, although he didn't mention it to me. Gone back to the wife and the Stars and Stripes.' She sounded bitter, her voice pitched high. 'Well, he can go, I don't care.'

The other girl laughed.

'Listen, you know what he is — we all do. He'll sleep with anything in a skirt, and then it's 'wham, bam, thank you ma'am,' and off to the next. It's the way he is.'

There was a soft muffle, as if the first girl was crying, and then they both moved off.

It was easy for me to be practical and reason that I had been lucky not to make a fool of myself, that I hadn't fallen for his line — even if he hadn't thrown it in my direction. He was married, they said, and he lived abroad. He was ruthless, and a user, and definitely not to be trusted. I knew all of that, and yet, when I got home that night I snapped at Nancy, and ran upstairs, crying myself to sleep. He had shaken me, and after that day I was altered.

When I did sleep, he appeared, silhouetted against sunshine, the tall figure relaxed, the neat shape of his head making him appear younger than he in fact was. Sometimes my vision would move into close up, so that little details I could not have remembered awake, came back to me with a startling clarity whilst I slept. I saw lines around his eyes and down the sides of his mouth, and where his hair fell over his forehead there was a small mole, just above the right eyebrow. I woke heavy and filled with discomfort, rubbing the back of my neck as I sat up in bed, or throwing back the covers and going downstairs to make myself a cup of tea.

I did what I had never done before: I began to smoke upstairs, sitting by the bedroom window and looking out into the night garden, a cigarette clenched firmly between my fingers, my heart sick with disappointment, my mind exhausted with the constant unending, rewinding and replaying of a few minutes' conversation which nagged at me.

If I closed my eyes, he was there. If I thought of a man, he was there. If I considered anything, I would think how he would see it. I had met him for one day and shared a disastrous lunch with him, and yet he moved in and consumed my life like a serpent swallowing a brood of hen's eggs. Mark Ward, Mark Ward — came over the litany, chorusing into my thoughts and sleep like a tune which sticks in the mind, with the same insistent, wearying repetition.

Nancy noticed a change in me. It would have been hard not to, but she put it down to my being overworked, and suggested that I ask for a few days' holiday. I smiled to myself, and then, in the small hours, my imagination ran away with me and I thought of going over to America and looking him up, or bumping into him on the street, and saying that I was there on business. Yet, when I woke, I blushed at my own absurdity and tried to look on my job with the same enthusiasm and commitment I had before. I could not admit to myself that I wanted him, only that he intrigued me, and although I knew I would not see him again. I felt his loss as poignantly as if he had shared half a life with me.

It took me nearly three weeks to learn how to disguise how I felt; three weeks in which the walled house altered, and Nancy became a burden to me. Three weeks in which everything I had ever previously valued turned to ashes in my mouth.

'Jill, I don't want to nag, but you do seem a little, well, preoccupied. Is the job getting too much for you?'

It was Edward Worthington, stopping by the side of my desk and looking at me through his thick glasses. I reacted badly. 'Of course not. I can do this job perfectly. You wouldn't find anyone else — '

'I didn't mean that. You know I couldn't manage without you.'

I had the grace to blush.

'Mr Worthington — '

'Call me Edward. After all, we've known each other two years now, and it's about time we got rid of the formalities.'

He sat down opposite my desk.

'You do a splendid job here. I merely thought that you might be a little overworked. How about getting someone from the agency to come in and do the typing for you? It might be a good idea.'

I had been behaving badly and instead of a reprimand he offered me help.

'Mr . . . sorry, Edward,' I started awkwardly, 'that would be a great help for me, and thank you for the suggestion. I have been a bit tired lately.' I lied expertly, watching him clap his hands together with relief.

'Good, good. Now remember, if you want to take a little break, have a holiday, you do. I must look after the best assistant I've ever had.'

I glowed at the compliment, and after he had dictated several letters to me and left the room, I rang the secretarial agency.

'What kind of person are you looking for?' the woman's voice asked me, the tone authoritative, as if she hardly needed to ask the question.

'A middle-aged lady, with quiet habits and one

104

who doesn't smoke,' I responded, not expecting to be taken seriously.

The voice came back untroubled.

'I have Mrs Osborne here and I think she might do perfectly for you.'

'How old is she?'

'Just a moment.' There was a pause on the line and a soft shuffling of papers before she replied. 'Forty-three. She's a widow.'

I digested the information quickly. If she was a widow she would have a great deal of time on her hands, time which she might spend undermining my position.

'Hello?'

'Sorry, I was just thinking . . . Is there anyone else?'

I heard a quick intake of breath. 'You have a bias against widows of forty-three?' the voice asked coolly.

'Does she have children?' I pressed her, anxious to know if Mrs Osborne had any outside involvements.

'You have a bias against children also?' the voice continued acidly.

'Yes, and against Turks and goat's milk! I'm sorry I troubled you,' I snapped and put the phone down.

The next agency I tried was more helpful and more obliging. They offered me the choice of three women, all middle-aged, and none of them widows. They recommended strongly a Mrs Wren, who could only manage three mornings a week, as she was heavily involved in local politics and had a husband and two children to look after. I asked them to send her round.

Mrs Wren lived up to her name, being tiny and dressed in various russet shades. She had a small, secretive face, like a diary which was kept locked, but when she spoke, it opened up and she came to life in front of you.

She began the following Monday, typing vigorously and filing everything I gave her, showering compliments upon me like blossoms as she did so.

'It's so easy to follow your system. You should see some of the places I've worked in.'

She was, however, curiously ill at ease with Edward, and would avoid going into his room with papers, unless it was absolutely necessary. I asked her about it, and she looked troubled. 'He's so . . . formidable,' she said finally.

Funny, I never found him so.

We took to having lunch together on the days she was working there, and she unwrapped her sandwiches very carefully, as if she was going to use the greaseproof paper again, pushing it into her bag with quick, exact movements. Her husband disliked politics, and so she never discussed them with him, and gradually a picture began to emerge of a woman who was curiously excluded from her family's lives.

'David's going into the Navy,' she confided to me not long after she had begun, 'and Claire's going on to university to study German.'

I made all the right noises, and looked at her photographs, but I still could not imagine her having given birth to either of the children, and after the first initial scraps of information about

106

them, she offered nothing further. Once, her son came to pick her up — a diffident, shy young man, with his mother's face, and a slow mannered way of speaking which soon became irritating. He was eloquent, however, about the profession he had chosen, but when his mother began to tell him about what she had been doing that morning, he closed off from her as obviously as if he was listening to a stranger.

But in Chestnut Walk, Mrs Wren provided exactly the right balance, her role slipping nicely into the running of the office. She presented no threat, neither did she wish to undermine anyone's position, and within days she mastered her duties and the making of her own brand of paralysingly strong coffee with a determined assurance.

I staggered back into normality, making determined efforts to renew my previous equilibrium. I told myself that it was wrong of me to take out my frustrations on Nancy, and I tried to compensate by talking to her about taking a holiday.

'We could go to Scotland, you'd like that, wouldn't you?'

She pulled a face. 'Not really, if you want the truth. Scotland's the past for me, and I always think it's a waste of time going back anywhere. It's never the same.'

I persevered. 'Well, what about Wales?'

'Too many hills, and besides, the Welsh don't like the Scots.'

'Nancy, you don't sound Scottish, they won't know.'

She tapped the side of her nose with one finger. 'They would. It's instinct.'

I sighed and got up from where I was sitting, walking over to the window in the morning room and looking out. The gardener had kept all the flower beds in neat order, their contents growing in straight rows, the bushes scraped into shape, and looking as if they hardly dared to drop a leaf. Autumn had begun again, and instead of longing as I usually did for the run to Christmas, I shuddered at the thought of long nights and cold draughts and the rains bringing intermittent fogs.

She had turned back to her reading, the full arc of her cheek slanted downwards, her eyes following the lines of the words. On the right arm of her chair she had laid down her pale blue cardigan, and across her lap there was a plaid shawl, of the type referred to as a 'travelling rug'; the type you see in family magazines in the back of the car, or laid under a picnic spread. I watched her and realised with guilt that she irritated me; or rather, she irritated the altered me — all her movements I had taken as comfortable reassurance now grated on me, her action taking on a monotonous repetition which made me clench my teeth and turn away hurriedly.

She had almost fully regained her strength then, so that her life was the same as it had been previously, but condensed into fewer hours. She had shrunk from an eighteen-hour day to a twelve-hour one, and had adapted to the change. Her tinted hair gave her back the years her

108

illness had taken from her, and the weight she had ladled back on with such delight, padded her from old age. She was constant, and returned to the grandmother of my childhood, whilst I moved somewhere and somehow away from her and didn't even know if I wanted to get back.

The house, which I had so subtly contrived to gain full control over, was suddenly worthless, as if I had achieved a hollow victory. The rooms were exactly as they had always been, their contents as familiar to me as my own face, the little stories and anecdotes regarding them recorded faithfully by Nancy, and retold to me over the years. I knew how much the table in the lounge had cost, and if I concentrated for a moment, I could still feel the smarting on my legs where Nancy had hit me after I had scratched its top with my music case. The piano had been an anniversary present from her husband, although he hadn't played it much, and Nancy had spent long, tedious hours mastering a few pieces, until she could play Beethoven's 'Moonlight Sonata' perfectly. The display cabinet had been inherited from her parents up in Scotland, coming down to England after the funeral, the bottom drawer lined with a piece of yellow newspaper over eleven years old, the inside scrubbed from years of applied vinegar and water. Nancy told me she couldn't touch it for weeks after her mother's death; that she had merely left it in the corner where it still stood, unable to put her own things behind the protective glass doors.

109

'It was the nicest thing she had ever had, after all those years,' she told me. 'When we were little, my brother and I, we were forbidden to touch it, and the key was kept somewhere in my parents' bedroom, although when I was ten my mother and I took all the ornaments out and cleaned the shelves, putting each piece back carefully.' She looked across to the cabinet. 'I watched her look at that thing with such pride, and I knew that if I hung around long enough she would give me something for helping her, so I could go down to the village shop and brag to my friends.'

There were stories about each item: carpets saved up for; curtains lined and relined; and her real triumph — my grandfather's desk. Nancy had seen it in a sale in Barnes, and after some haggling she had managed to get it for a reasonable sum, insisting that it be delivered the next day. I was ten at the time and thought it was hideous, although by the time she had scrubbed and polished it, and replaced the handles, it looked quite splendid. We pushed it into the bay window, and Nancy put a clock, a desk set and a photograph of her daughter, my mother, on the leather top; then she invited my grandfather in to see it.

'Well — what do you think?'

He walked over to it.

'Well?' she repeated.

'What did it cost?'

'What's that got to do with it?' Nancy snapped. 'Do you like it?'

'Grand,' he said finally, and then without

110

warning, pecked her on the cheek.

Alison's face was a study; she paused for an instant and then looking across to me, rolled her eyes heavenwards.

'Are you going to be a tycoon?' she asked him cheekily, but he didn't reply, and after muttering a rough thank you to Nancy, left the room.

The desk was seldom used, but when I began to work at Edward's, I used it sometimes and, after Nancy's illness, I sorted out all our bills on its worn top, looking up sometimes to catch sight of the photograph of my mother in the tortoiseshell frame. And I had nearly lost all this for the sake of something ephemeral and worthless, and I now wanted it back. I walked around the house and by the time I had reached Nancy's room I could feel a change inside me, like one of those odd feelings you get as a child, that lodging somewhere in the chest, below the breast bone, that bubble of optimism. With a faint giddiness, I laid the memory of a man I had never even known, and set about reclaiming what was mine.

When Nancy had finished her crossword that night we ate our dinner and chatted, so that I listened and loved her again. We decided that we would go down to Cornwall for a few days' break, staying in a small pub we had once visited many years before, with Alison.

'We ought to ask her,' I said, with my new magnaninity. 'I know she'll be busy, but we should ask.'

And we did, but she was already booked that week for a job in France, and she declined

111

prettily, her relief almost as obvious as my own.

The holiday was a turning point. Away from the house and from the reminders of my dissatisfaction, some form of perspective returned. It had taken nearly two months for me to obliterate his image; two long months, during which time I had felt the first overwhelming strong pull of physical attraction, and I had not understood it. Dreams of being held by him would wake me: sweaty, my throat dry, and a peculiar, uncomfortable guilty feeling which lasted throughout the day. I had never believed that people became obsessed by another person, but suddenly, the hasty contempt I had had for Anna and her infatuation with her careless husband, turned to sympathetic understanding.

It is always difficult to be catapulted into feelings and emotions which you are not ready for — or maybe that's the whole point; perhaps no one is ever ready for them, that's why we all botch our chances, or cling too long to unsuitable people, or build gods out of tiny, tacky, sticks of men. Maybe we're supposed to. Either way, the sea air and the salt seemed to scrub him out of my pores and when I heard the fog horns at night, or smelled the sea wrack from the water, I could even laugh at my own stupidity.

I longed to confide in Nancy, but I was frightened that she would see me as foolish, and because I had come to terms with the situation and absolved it, I thought it wiser to let it rest.

We were walking along the beach, when I spotted them.

'Nancy, I've found some seagull feathers,' I shouted, calling across the autumn empty beach.

'They'll be full of disease,' she responded, winking as she said it, the sun making her skin pink.

We were an odd couple, a fat lady on a sea shore with a young woman in glasses, our shoes in our hands and the pebbles making imprints on the soles of our feet.

'I've always wanted to come back here,' Nancy said, sitting down on a large boulder, her jacket slapping against her sides as the wind caught it.

'You always said you never wanted to go back anywhere.'

'Anywhere's not here,' she responded, as if there was a difference. 'I'm glad we came, it's been a good break, and I think we'll be better for it.'

I turned to her, shielding my eyes with one hand. 'I've loved every minute of it.'

'They'll be glad to see you back at work, I suppose.'

'I suppose.'

'And tomorrow,' she continued idly, 'Mrs Edwards will be coming in to do the ironing and the gardener will be back in the place, moaning about whatever it is that he's going to moan about this week.' She paused and I looked at her, knowing she wanted to say something, and surprised she was finding it difficult.

'Everything goes on, it always does. All the best things, that is.'

'Like us?' I asked, hoping I had prompted her in the right direction.

'In a way,' she said, but the meaning had gone. She had let it pass, and I had not recognised it.

We sat for a while longer, watching the water turn from blue to green, and then black in the shadows where it met the walls of the quay. Moss hung along the stonework, and occasional dashes of bladderwrack clung grimly in the crevices, or under the breast of a fishing boat. The deep sun fell on the sea and laughed back at us, winking towards the salt sky and the sepia beach, and under the turn of the tide, the slow sigh of the water echoed and sang to itself.

Neither of us moved, though we both turned to the water and watched the evening come in on us, and at seven o'clock, we went back to the hotel.

I packed for the return next day and longed to see the walled house, and turn the key in my office door. I wanted to see Edward, Mrs Wren and Anna, anxious to count them and check that they had not changed. I slept hearing the sound of the waves on the shingle only yards from my window, and when the gulls came back with the daylight, I dressed with a singular lightness of heart.

Nancy was already waiting for me in her room, her stout figure bending over a full suitcase, slamming down the lid on a batch of clothes underneath with ill-disguised impatience.

'I'll do it,' I said, walking to the case and sitting on the lid. 'Now fasten it.'

She clicked the locks and rubbed her hands

114

together triumphantly.

'We'll have breakfast and get off, don't you think? No point hanging around.'

I could have laughed at her enthusiasm, but it was so close to my own that I linked arms with her and walked down to the dining room.

How slowly miles pass when you are anxious to be somewhere else. Every yard seems to yawn out before you into infinity, every minute that should bring you closer to your goal seems unfairly postponed. Perhaps there is a spirit of the railway tracks, some mischievous Puck, who alternately rushes and delays us, making our dreaded appointments too soon, and our longed for arrivals too slow.

Sheep slipped past in fields, crows flew up from the high trees, and in our compartment a man fell asleep with his mouth open, and his glasses up over one ear. He slept deeply and when he awoke he jumped up, snatching down the window and looking out for an instant before returning to his seat, his face flushed.

'I thought I'd missed my station,' he explained, drowsy with sleep still, his tiredness apparent.

'Which is your stop?' I asked him.

'Baddesley Marton.'

'Go back to sleep,' I said, smiling, 'I'll wake you when we get there.'

He looked at me for an instant, uncertain and then thanking me, settled back and dozed off almost immediately.

Nancy also slept, and as the passengers left the train no others came on to replace them, so that

115

we continued our journey alone. I read a little of a magazine I had bought, but the lines blurred and I turned to the window instead. We went through dusty tunnels, and across fields which had been doused with rain; we lapped ourselves under old poplars, and slipped past the windows of terraces in busy towns. When I woke our fellow passenger he smiled warmly and gathered his belongings, and when he got out of the train he turned and waved to me, the light from the station lamp catching the top of his head.

At ten o'clock we arrived in London, creeping in and parking under the archway of steel and glass. We got off slowly, because Nancy was tired then, her face looking less youthful than it had even that morning, her figure crumpled in her best suit, the marks of the traveller apparent. I hailed a taxi and we went home that way, avoiding the tubes and the buses because we were too tired to care how much it cost. When I opened the front door of the house and turned on the light, the hall was ready for us, and when Nancy had gone up to bed, and I had washed off the grime from the journey I could hardly stop myself singing.

9

Six months passed, taking us through the blackest of the winter and into the start of another spring. It had been almost a year since Nancy had been taken ill, and in that year she had recovered, dragging herself back into normality, although I continued to assume the premier role in the house. I sought her advice on every occasion, and although I asked her opinion, I would come to my own decisions, and she seemed no longer to resent the shift in our roles. I thought more of her as a 'grandmother', as if I had now to look after her and provide for her as she had done for me during my childhood; and although she had been left well-off by my grandfather, I prided myself for bringing in a good wage, and being able to buy things for us, and the home, with money I had earned myself.

Edward had asked me to go with him on a trip to Yorkshire, to follow up the discovery of some remains, but when we got there the find turned out to be bogus, and he gave a scorching interview to one of the daily papers about 'cowboys' infiltrating his beloved profession. I wondered privately if there was a big international market for old bones and bits of Roman baths, but I never voiced my opinion, and instead tut-tutted as he expected me to, and supported whatever he said.

Then one afternoon Anna came into my

office, and asked me to call up and see her after work.

'You come?'

'Yes, of course, as soon as I'm free.'

She nodded and walked out.

I worked until after five and then went upstairs and knocked on her door. She answered on the third rap. Her face was scarlet with crying.

'Good God, Anna, what's the matter?'

There was a sob from behind the handkerchief she had pushed into her face.

'It's my husband.'

'He's dead?' I said, my throat tightening with sympathy.

'Why you ask if he's dead?' she snapped.

'You're crying, it seemed the natural thing to assume,' I said, walking into the room behind her. 'Why? What *has* happened?'

She wiped her nose firmly and continued into the kitchen, and within a couple of seconds I could hear the familiar noises of tea being made. I sat down baffled and gazed out of the window, watching two sparrows fighting for position on the window ledge opposite.

'We have tea?' she asked, holding a loaded tray. I nodded, and she laid it down. 'My husband . . . he wants me to go back.'

I thought I had misheard, and waited for her to repeat it, but she didn't.

'He wants you to go back to him?'

She nodded twice, the gold chain around her neck catching the light.

'And you're *crying* about it?' I said, incredulous. 'Isn't that what you wanted?'

118

Her expression hardened from the eyes down, like putty setting.

'No,' she replied. 'I wanted to go back and buy myself a restaurant.'

'But he already has a restaurant, what would you want with another one?'

She looked at me with horror, thinking I should have understood what she meant without her having to spell it out. Then she looked away from me and down at her feet, as if the answer had been embroidered on her bedroom slippers.

'I wanted to go back with money, to show him I was . . . important,' she finished, clicking her tongue impatiently. 'This is not good, not good for me.'

'But he will think you're important having been over here all this time.'

'So I should go back now because he's old, and fat and lost his hair?'

The allusion she had previously built up about her husband was rapidly fading; now he was gaining weight and faults like maggots in a bruised apple.

'But if he loves you — ' I began pathetically.

'He *loves* me?' she repeated with a stage laugh. 'He loves me *now*, when no one else love him, when he needs help in the café — this is when he loves me.'

'Don't you love him?'

'I don't know . . . ' she replied honestly, pouring herself some more tea, the cup shaking a little as she held it.

She asked me what I would do, and I told her that it was her decision, which was a big help.

119

After a while she got out his photographs and looked at them, telling me about their courtship and showing me for the first time a picture of herself when she was young. The print had faded a little, but the fixed, sullenly bold face of the young woman was powerfully attractive, and bore little resemblance to Anna. She saw my amazement, and took it from me.

'I come over here, fourteen,' she thought for an instant, 'no, fifteen years ago. Then I was like this.' She tapped the photograph. 'Now, I go back an old lady, with no figure. You understand?'

I didn't. If she had aged, then he had also. Finally it occurred to me that they would both be looking for the person who had left, or who had left them — that fantasy figure who had come in and out of their lives, and around whom possibly a great many stories and dreams had been woven. She was frightened to see the look on his face when he saw her now, the disappointment — even separation was better than that, and I realised that all her plans for her restaurant in Malta were worthless, merely the pipedreams of a woman who would grow older and older plotting her victorious return, whilst she crept to her dying in London.

We talked for a little while longer, and she came to no decision, because she had made up her mind already, although she didn't know it. When I saw her three days later, she had written to her husband saying that she would not go back . . . not for a while anyway. She left the door open just a little. From then on, he wrote every month, asking her to return, and every month she refused. In time though, the correspondence took on a warmer tone, with Anna signing — 'your loving wife, Anna.'

It was a lousy, windy, rainy morning when the letter came from Alison, the address smudged on the envelope, the writing obviously hurried. I picked it off the mat and took it into the kitchen where Nancy was making breakfast, a pile of hot toast and marmalade smiling up from the plate.

'It's from Alison,' I said, putting it down on the kitchen table.

'Take it off there, Jill, it'll get sticky.'

Obediently I did so, looking around for somewhere else, and finding nowhere, I dropped it into my bag.

'I'll let you know what she says when I get home.'

Nancy nodded and read a piece out of the paper about rates, her voice rising with indignation. I was only half listening, concentrating instead on some papers Edward had asked me to type the previous evening. We sat there, both intent on our own interests for nearly twenty minutes, before I realised the time and left hurriedly, driving through the pouring rain and parking in the mews behind Chestnut Walk.

It was nearly three o'clock before I had time to open the letter. I made myself a cup of tea and sat down, propping my feet up on the bottom drawer of my desk, and splitting the envelope with a piece of bone.

121

Dear Jill,
*How are things with you at home? I know I
haven't written for a while, but things have
been hectic here.*

I paused and looked at the postmark, having
forgotten where she was writing from — it said,
'New York'. New York, USA. I turned back to the
letter.

*So many people and some good laughs, you
will be intrigued by the photographs when you
see them, some of the best I've done, or so
they say, but you know photographers, they
ooze insincerity. I've lost some weight
recently, must be the terrible food here —
all beefburgers and chips, no wonder all
American women have bad skins — they need
the healthy stuff of steamed puddings and
British beef to put some colour back into their
cheeks!*
*What's news with you? Still busy at work?
Or is the pressure off a little? I'm having to
stay on here a while to sort out some things,
but I'll write again when I have the time and
tell you when I'm coming home. Give all my
best love to Nancy, and take some for
yourself! Looking forward to seeing you — lots
of love,*
Yours — sister
Alison

The tone was the same as it always was, jolly
and light-hearted, the tone of someone at ease;

122

but underneath was something altogether different, and although I couldn't fathom out what it was, it bothered me, and I put the letter back in my bag, frowning. Not once had Alison ever said she was looking forward to coming home before — it was out of character. I put the words out of my mind and set to work, grateful for the constant phone calls and demands for my attention. When I drove back to the walled house, the lights were on in the lounge and Nancy was talking to someone.

'Come in, Jill, it's only Angela.'

I walked in, silently cursing myself for not removing my shoes and creeping upstairs. Angela was a bore, a woman with a great deal of time on her hands, and nothing in her head. She looked up at me when I came in, her ivory coloured face topped with a frothy pile of pale blonde hair, like whipped cream on a vanilla ice. I made small talk for nearly ten minutes, and excused myself, saying I had some work to do, and as I closed the door behind me, I heard her saying, 'She's always been the clever one, hasn't she?'

When Nancy read the letter later that night she saw nothing remarkable or worrying about it.

'Well, it's nice that she's looking forward to coming home, she travels so much it must be a relief to put her feet up now and again.'

'But it doesn't sound like her,' I persisted.

'Yes, it does. It sounds exactly like her.'

That was all we said about it, but when a second letter arrived soon after, I took it to work without telling Nancy, and read it with deepening curiosity;

123

Dear Jill,

Well, here I am again. I bet you can't believe it — two letters in as many weeks, quite something from your nearly illiterate sister, wouldn't you say? I'm coming back on the 15th, and I should be with you at the house about 10.30pm, so don't go to bed, and then we can have a talk. Seems ages since we had a real chinwag, doesn't it?

Do you remember when you were at school and you got your knuckles rapped for answering back? I thought that teacher was a bitch — I would have given her a mouthful myself if I'd known about it at the time. Why didn't you tell me 'til nearly a week later? Odd, wasn't it? You were always so secretive at school, not like you are now, not at all. I sometimes think of those days, don't you, and wonder how everyone turned out. I suppose a lot of them are married — not so much your set, but mine will, my being so old now! It would be nice to get married sometime and have children, but until I meet the right person it seems pointless, don't you think? It would be awful to get married and divorced, with all that heartache. They must feel such failures, people who can't make it work, I mean, although I don't suppose it's always their fault, sometimes it's just circumstances. Look at this! — me, babbling on and on, and I've got work to do.

Remember — the 15th at 10.30pm — so don't go out to avoid me!
Yours — sister,
Alison

124

Now this was not like Alison to talk of marriage and school, but her patronising attitude towards all the poor sods who couldn't make a marriage work, that was like her. How utterly, unthinkingly, selfishly typical of my sister.

With disgust I threw the letter to the bottom of my bag and forgot it, dreading the fifteenth when she was coming back. I was suspicious of this new, revised version of Alison; it seemed sickeningly reminiscent of her old ploys, when she was trying to get my backing in some wild scheme, or in order to curry favour with someone. She was talking to me as an equal, which was a novelty in itself, but also as if she wanted, and needed, my help, and that was unique.

The five days which passed before she arrived seemed to slip effortlessly through my fingers. At home, we did all the usual ritual dusting of her room, buying some flowers and arranging them in two vases, one for her dressing table, and the other for her bedside, winding up her clock, and opening the windows to freshen the place. Ten minutes later, I closed them, the air still too damp to be comfortable, the curtains already cool to the touch. I came home early that day, to find Nancy making Yorkshire pudding, her apron pulled tightly over her body like the cover on an overstuffed cushion. She smiled as I walked in. 'I'm nearly done. You wouldn't be a love and get me a gin and tonic, would you?'

'Bad for your heart,' I answered, and went into the lounge to pour one for her and one for myself. The room was prepared, the fire lighted, and the frames on the photographs blinked in the soft light. I snatched a handful of crisps off a side table as I passed and went back into the kitchen.

'Looks nice in there,' I said, passing her the glass.

She drained an inch before replying, 'That's delicious, just the ticket.'

'What are we having?'

'Yorkshire pudding, beef, vegetables and apple pie.' She glanced around her as she spoke, reaching for the dish cloth and wiping the top of the table.

'What if she's late?' I asked peevishly, regretting the words immediately I spoke them and saw their reaction on Nancy's face.

'Oh, you don't — '

'No, of course she won't be late! She can probably catch a whiff of your cooking already, somewhere over the Atlantic, and told the pilot — follow that smell!'

She laughed, and I hugged her, and when we finished tidying up, we sat down in the lounge and waited for Alison.

I had been right, she was late. At eleven o'clock, Nancy was asleep in her chair, at eleven thirty, I was turning down everything in the cooker, and at twelve, I had taken the food out, and prepared a sandwich instead. The joint of meat dried on the sideboard, and the vegetables looked as if they had seen better days. Still she didn't phone, and she didn't come. At twelve thirty, I was eating a large slice of the apple pie, my heart banging with annoyance, when the phone rang. I ran out into the hall, snatching it up quickly to avoid waking Nancy. It was Alison.

'Sorry, I didn't make it. I'm coming tomorrow.'

'Couldn't you have let us know sooner?' I asked, my voice high with irritation; hers controlled and bland.

'Why? It's only the difference of one day. Does it matter? I mean did you go to a lot of trouble on my behalf?'

'Oh — go to hell!' I shouted and slammed down the receiver.

I woke Nancy as carefully as I could, and explained to her what had happened, although she seemed very confused and too tired to take in anything properly. I helped her up to bed and she fell asleep quickly, like a child being brought in from a late car journey. When I turned out the light in her room and heard her steady breathing I cursed Alison, and walked off down the corridor to my own room.

She did arrive the following day, during the afternoon whilst I was at work, so that she was waiting for me when I got in, and ran out into the hall throwing her arms round me.

'Sorry! Sorry! Sorry! Will that do? I know I should have rung, but things were so hectic. Do say that it doesn't matter — Nancy's been fine about it.'

If someone had told me that she could have become more beautiful than ever, I would have doubted it, although it appeared that she had found, and tapped, some secret source of prettiness. Her face, almost free of make-up, glistened with colour, the deep tan of her skin turning to pink along the line of her cheek bones, the whites of her eyes appearing bluish against the brown of her pupils. She had swept back her hair, away from the sides of her face, so that she appeared to be little over twenty, and in the centre of her forehead was the pale disc of skin where the stone had hit her, years before.

'Hello, Alison.'

'Hello Alison,' she mimicked, drawing down the sides of her mouth in a mock grimace, before relaxing again and smiling so brilliantly that I relented and smiled back.

'You were such a cow, not coming like that, after all that time and effort Nancy had gone to, making your homecoming special.'

'Oh, don't go on! It's done with,' she said, squeezing my arm and leading me towards the lounge, whispering, 'she's thoroughly for-given me, so don't you go in there and stir it up again.'

I didn't, of course. Who would have made life unpleasant for Alison? I merely did what I had always done, and let her take centre stage for a while. I slipped off my shoes and sat down by the fire, watching the interplay between Nancy and my sister with a detached, if curious, gaze. She told us where she had been, and of the shops in Fifth Avenue, running upstairs and coming down again with three parcels — two for Nancy and one for me. For my grandmother, there was a chain and matching earrings, for myself, a watch with a dark blue face, and a gold surround. It was understated and for once perfectly in keeping with the recipient.

'It's wonderful, Alison, it really is. Thank you.'

'Well, we took a lot of time picking it out — ' she stopped suddenly.

'We?' I asked her, breaking my rule for once and showing some interest in her men friends. She blushed and looked away.

'Just a friend,' she said quickly, and changed the subject.

' . . . so this photographer came in and asked for more lights, saying that he couldn't work in such bad conditions, and when they had set them up, it must have been over 120° in that place.' She chatted on, her face animated with something other than tales of her travels; she was too lively, too bubbly for the sister I knew; and like her letters, there was something altered about her, a quality of gaiety, but also of slight edginess which was unlike her.

I dipped in and out of her conversation like a child ducking for apples. I heard snippets of her voice and noticed that Nancy was leaning forwards, watching her.

' . . . it was a good idea, I'll give them that, the *Ancient and Modern* they called it, and brought in a very nice American who knows all about pottery and things. He's in archaeology. I thought of you, Jill . . . Jill?'

I snapped back to attention. 'Sorry. What did you say?'

'I said that they brought in an American bloke who was an expert on ancient pots and things, and I thought about you, and wondered if you knew him. Honestly, Jill, weren't you

129

listening to anything I said?'

'Yes, I was just a bit tired. Go on, Alison.'

'Well, they set up this shot for the morning but it rained, and being out of doors we couldn't go on with it. It cost the advertising company thousands of dollars, and some big wig from Manhattan called them up and said they had to get some results — or else.' She started to laugh. 'Just like the Cosa Nostra! You should have been there!'

I was mentally thanking God that I hadn't, when Nancy tapped me on the knee.

'You're half dead, Jill. Go on up and you can catch up on all the news tomorrow.'

I accepted, grateful to get to bed, and knowing that Nancy wanted some time with Alison. I undressed and turned back the covers on my bed, hearing the murmur of voices below, like an echo of a time years before. Within minutes, I fell asleep.

There was a terrible storm in my dream, or at least I thought there was, but when I awoke, my bedroom window was banging against the outside wall in the wind, its handle jerking erratically. I got up, pulling the window closed and looking out to see the branches of the apple tree shaken in a tremendous gale. The squall was ripping the leaves off its branches and pulling at the creeper on the house walls, tearing strips off the body of the plant, so that they danced and juddered in the wind like horrible puppets. The clouds blew across the white moon; and over the long stretch of the lawn, pale ivory shapes danced between shadows, and ran for the dark of the wall.

I thought that the weather had woken me, but as I stood there I could hear someone moving around. Walking to the door, I paused, before continuing out into the corridor.

Nancy's room was in darkness, not a slice of light showed under her closed door, but further along, a thin strip of yellow poured out from Alison's. I heard another movement, and then she walked out into the corridor, seeing me and putting a finger to her mouth, before beckoning me to follow her back to her room.

Inside, the place was in total disorder. Cases lay on top of the bed and on an easy chair, and the wind blew against the windows fiercely, making macabre shapes behind the curtains. I looked to her bed, yawning.

'Haven't you slept yet?'

'I couldn't,' she said simply, pulling the window closed, and beginning to rub her wet hair with a towel. 'I had a bath and washed my hair — I wasn't sleepy.'

Now that her hair was undone she was her proper age again, and under the marvellous eyes, two blurs of shadow spoke of several sleepness nights.

'You look tired, you should sleep. We'll go out tomorrow.'

She continued to rub her hair and didn't look at me. Her arms moved idly, her hands obscured under the towel, her back almost stiff with tension.

'Alison?'

'Yes?'

131

'Is something wrong? Did you have a bad time in New York?'

'No,' she said quietly, turning back to me. 'No, nothing like that. I just don't sleep so well these days.'

I was tired and I couldn't think clearly, so I slumped back into a small velvet chair and waited for her to speak.

'Your hands look lovely. You always had pretty hands,' she said suddenly, and I thanked her, wondering if I would ever find the energy to get up again. The wind continued outside, making dull noises in the house, and battering on the doors like children's fists.

She still continued to dry her hair, and then she combed it so that it lay flat against her head, framing the little face. My eyes came in and out of focus as I fought to stay awake, but she said nothing and sat staring at the carpet in front of her, her arms folded across her middle, like a Buddha.

'I must go,' I said finally, leaning forwards, 'I really must.'

Immediately she burst into tears, so that I snapped awake as if someone had hit me on the back of the head with a mallet. She cried loudly, which was out of character, and it was all I could do to try and prevent her from waking Nancy.

'Alison, what is it? Whatever is it?'

'I can't — '

'What? Oh, do stop crying, and tell me, you'll wake Nancy. What is it?'

I didn't get the answer for nearly two minutes, during which time she sobbed as if her heart would break. Bit by bit she came back to reason, and then she sighed deeply and smiled one bright, quick smile, patting me on the hand.

'It's so daft. But I miss him so much.'

'Who?'

'This man I met in New York,' she said and looked away, embarrassed, her colour rising slightly. 'I miss him, I can't tell you how much, it even hurts — there.' She prodded my chest with one finger. 'I won't be able to see him until he comes over here to work — and that's nearly a week.'

'A week!' I said, laughing despite myself. 'Oh, my God, one whole week! How can you stand it?'

She began to laugh too, and for the first time in years we were comfortable together, rocking backwards and forwards on her bed. Minutes later, she sobered up.

'Jill, he's so . . . special.'

'And what's his name?' I asked, the smile still on my face.

'Mark,' she said simply. 'Mark Ward, and . . . '

I didn't hear anything else, not for several minutes, I just sat with my hands in my lap, unmoving. Someone had taken out my heart, I was sure of that, and put a huge lump of pastry there instead, because I couldn't feel anything, although I knew I should have been hurting badly. I remembered that someone once told me that you don't feel pain when you're first injured, it's only later, when you can think again. She was talking, I could see her lips move, but none of the words came through.

133

After a while she got into bed, and I tucked the covers around her. I pecked her on her forehead, just above the scar, and I believe she thanked me as I walked out. I had been a big help, she said, a comfort, yes, that was it.

The wind blew for the remainder of the night and when I got up the following morning my eyes were dry and itchy with tiredness, and my clothes felt heavy on my limbs.

All day I concentrated and kept myself under control; no one would have guessed how it was with me.

When I got home that night Alison was there, she had even made me dinner, and the three of us ate together, just like old times. Afterwards, she talked to me about her lover and I listened, and as I listened, I formed a plan.

She did not know that he was married, and I was not going to tell her; neither did she know that he was worthless. Alison had no idea that he had slept with many women, of all shapes and sizes, and of all types, or that he had left them all, at some time, and had taken the big silver bird across the Atlantic, home to his ever-loving wife. She didn't know it.

So I encouraged her to love him. I listened to her description of him, all the little details I had noticed long before she had even met him. It was difficult for her, because she had never before felt deeply for any man, and the territory was strange to her. He had been a considerate lover, she said, and the words bit into me as deeply as acid into a copper plate.

I knew I would have to be clever, and I knew I

134

would have to stop my heart banging when she mentioned his name, or the palms of my hands from becoming sticky when she told me stories of their days together.

He was coming to London in a week's time, and in that time I had to win her confidence completely. She had to rely on me, and need me, and accept my opinion, so that she would follow whatever I said. Whatever I said.

Alison, pretty, foolish Alison, took my interest as I knew she would. Suspecting nothing, she was grateful for my help and a shoulder to cry on. I told her that he sounded a fine man, and that he couldn't help but love her. I told her that she had nothing to worry about, and that he was a reliable sort. I poured the honeyed words into her ears with all the dexterity of Claudius pouring poison into the ear of Hamlet's father, and I felt nothing.

Something died inside me. Which is what everyone says when they are ashamed of their actions, but something did fold up and shrivel and get blown to dust. I grew inwards again, seeing the old envy and jealousy claw its way out of the dark, and swell as I fed it. I watched my beautiful sister, and I drew her further and further into a cage which I knew would slam down and crush her. I couldn't stop myself.

And just like the old days, the witch in the wallpaper came out to look for me.

10

'Alison, come in here a minute, will you?' I called out through the open door of my bedroom, pausing for a moment until I heard her feet approaching. She walked in and sat down by the window, her figure a shape against the apple tree outside.

'What is it?' she asked, her manner relaxed, the smooth oval of her face interested, but not troubled.

'I was thinking ... about what we talked about last night.'

A slight flutter of uncertainty moved across her eyes.

'Alison, I think that we should keep this a secret from Nancy, not for any devious reason, you understand, but so she won't worry ... not until something's certain.'

She nodded eagerly, swallowing the suggestion like a hungry pike.

'I really think it would be for the best. After a while, when you two have sorted yourselves out, then we'll tell her. But otherwise, it would be a mistake. Can you imagine how she would worry? 'No one's good enough for my girls' — I can just hear it.'

I kept up the casual chatter, embroidering it as I went along, confident that I had covered myself against Nancy's intervention. Alison smiled again and leaned forwards towards me.

'He'll be here in another day, just think — only one more day.' She looked away. 'I feel such an idiot, longing for him like this, but . . . '

'It's natural,' I responded smoothly.

'He does love me, doesn't he?' she asked, and for an instant all I could think of was the dig near that tiny hamlet, the houses looking stubby and sun-hot under the heavy sky. I remembered the girls' voices, and the quick sob from one of them when they discussed this same man my sister was now talking about. He had left that girl, that sad girl in the hot field, just as he would leave Alison, one day.

'Did he say that he loved you?'

'Time and time again. He said that I was the most beautiful girl he had ever met.' She threw back her head with a sharp gesture. 'But then, that's what they all say, isn't it?'

Was it?

'What time is he here? I mean, what time is he arriving in London?'

'Seven-thirty at Heathrow, and I'm going to be there, waiting at the barrier, just like they do in all those daft black and white movies.' She stopped talking again, as if her attention had been catapulted off into another direction. 'What shall I wear? You will help me, won't you?'

She asked me for reassurance constantly, like a small dog begging for biscuits. I told her that I would help all I could, and when we went into her room we began to sort out her clothes methodically. It was like dressing a pretty child for her first party.

Nancy called up to us soon after, asking what we were doing and without consulting Alison, I told her that my sister was going out the following night with a business colleague, and that we were trying to sort out what she should wear to impress him. Nancy lost interest quickly, and after telling us dinner would be ready in half an hour, moved back into the kitchen.

Alison tried on almost a dozen outfits, winding her hair under hats, or shaking it loose again and glancing in the mirror with a critical eye.

'What do you think?' she asked, dressed entirely from head to foot in black.

'He'll think someone's died,' I said and she agreed with me.

'This then?' she asked a minute later, wearing a multicoloured dress and jacket.

'You look like you've just fallen off a float,' I volunteered ungenerously. She looked away from the mirror, and turned slowly in front of me.

'You may be right, but it suits my hair colour, and he'll be bound to see me easily.'

'In that outfit, he could see you from a thousand feet up,' I responded and she laughed, taking the clothes off again and choosing a quiet, well-cut dress, which belted around her waist.

'It's perfect,' I said, and meant it. 'You look beautiful.'

She smiled that secret smile that she used to employ when we were children, a smile of utter contentment, or total composure. I had seen her use it when she got her own way, or when she had been spoilt, or petted, or when she was deeply pleased. She had that same smile now and I turned away suddenly, unable to look at her.

'I'd like you to meet him — ' she began, but I cut her off short.

'No, not yet. Not until you're more settled, until things are more certain between you. If you bring in the family now, he'll think you're after him and run a mile.'

'But I am!' she cried out, delighted. 'Isn't it appalling, running after a man?'

For a fleeting instant I wanted to tell her that he wasn't worth it, but I stopped myself. Even if Alison did get hurt later on, I reasoned, she would get over it. She was my sister, after all, and nothing went too deep with her.

So the following evening when I got home, she was waiting, dressed to the nines, ready long before she needed to leave. She clutched my arm and I walked into the lounge with her.

'I've just had a thought — could you drive me in, to Heathrow, I mean? He has a flat in town and I know he'll drive me home later, but if you would take me in it would save me having to get the car out.' She put her head slightly on one side, 'Would you mind?'

We set off thirty-five minutes later, driving through the evening traffic without a hitch. The radio was playing Vivaldi, I remember that, and after a few minutes a slight drizzle began and made little patches of moisture on the windscreen in front of me. They magnified the headlights and made crystals out of the street lighting, and with a shudder, I turned on the heater, feeling the hot air on my feet. Alison sat

139

beside me, looking out.

'He will be there, won't he?'

He will, Alison.

'He will still think I'm beautiful, won't he?'

He will, he will.

The journey seemed short and yet screamingly protracted, and as I drew up at the terminal doors, she snatched at the car handle and jumped out, turning back to me almost immediately.

'Will you wait, just in case he doesn't come?' she asked, glancing around her, frightened to miss him even though he wasn't due for another half an hour. 'If I don't come back to the car in an hour, then he's arrived and I'll see you back at the house later. Okay?'

I nodded, not trusting myself to speak, and I drew the car over to one of the parking bays, from where I could watch who went in and out of the airport. I saw Alison walk up to the doors, her head erect, her figure tall and very slender. She seemed fragile. A porter turned to look at her, but she didn't see him, and the door slammed behind her as she moved on.

After Vivaldi, they played a little of a Mozart concerto, and some piece with a great many violins. It was mournful and I turned it off, settling back to wait, my feet tucked into a rug. I wiped my glasses on a paper tissue and combed my hair in the car mirror, before turning on the windscreen wipers. Back and forwards, back and forwards, whoosh, whoosh, they went against the glass, and every time a few drops settled they were swept aside. I must have dozed because I came to suddenly and looked at my watch to find that forty minutes had passed. Glancing across to the doors I saw only a group of what appeared to be school children — no sign of my sister. He had come, after all. Then, just as I was about to turn on the engine, Alison walked out.

I thought she was alone, that he had stood her up and left her waiting at the barrier in that pretty dress, but almost as soon as I saw her, a tall, middle-aged man followed, his coat slung over his arm.

I had not seen him in a business suit before, and he looked older, but affluent, his charm apparent. They made what is termed 'a handsome couple', and when he kissed her cheek under the fluorescent terminal light, my throat constricted painfully and I turned my head away. When I looked back, they had gone.

She came home at four in the morning, her feet padding on the carpet along the hallway, her dress making a soft swishing as she passed my room. I heard her stop just past my door, and listen. I could imagine her face and the bright eyes open, and imagine her straining to catch a sound. I lay still, not a sinew moving, and after a moment, she moved on.

The morning woke me early, for which I was more than thankful, and I ate my breakfast and got ready to leave before anyone else was stirring. Picking up a piece of paper I scribbled a note to Alison and slipped it under her door before I left.

Alison —
I hope the reunion was a triumph. I have
gone to work, and will see you this evening,
when I want to hear all the news! Nancy
is still asleep and she will probably not
wake until tennish — food in the fridge.
Please get three pints from the milkman, will
you?
  Lots of the usual,
  Jill.

As I backed the car out of the garage, I could just make out the shape of my sister's face at the hall window, but I didn't stop.

Edward was furious when I arrived — which was something of a novelty. He explained that Mrs Wren had rung and said that she was not able to come in that morning, and that she had a bad cold.

'Ridiculous!' he thundered, his pink-rimmed eyes blinking repeatedly. 'That woman treats this place like a hotel — as it suits her.'

I couldn't see what all the fuss was about.

'She's very good, and very reliable usually, and besides, I don't have that much to do in the way of typing this week. I can cope.'

'That's not the point,' he persisted, 'she's too twitchy for my liking.'

I thought that he was being unfair, and I told him so, which made him fall into a sullen silence. He only recovered when I took his coffee in, apologising sheepishly. 'Sorry Jill, it was just that I don't really like new faces. We were doing so well on our own.'

'You suggested getting someone in,' I reminded him gently.

'Yes, I know. But she . . . oh well, it doesn't matter, I'll get used to her in time. Everything changes, doesn't it?'

'The best things go on though,' I replied, echoing Nancy's words from months before, spoken on a windy beach in Cornwall — but I no longer believed them.

Nancy would have to be separated from me from that moment on; she would have to be cut off from my thoughts and my actions, divorced from the closest of my feelings. I could no longer afford to love her as I had previously done, not now. She was the closest to me, and therefore the one person who would know and understand my feelings; she could influence and judge me, and I wanted none of that.

That evening, I came home later than usual, pouring myself a drink and settling down in the lounge in front of the television. I heard Alison come running down the stairs, and I saw the look on her face when she saw that Nancy was with me. I smiled and turned round to face her in my seat.

'Come on, take a pew.' I waved my hand idly at the chair between the two of us. I saw her eyes move to it, and then back to me. 'I've had such a hard day, and my feet are killing me.'

She wanted to talk, that much was obvious in her face; she wanted to share her triumph, and tell me what he had said, and how, and describe the touch and the sense of him. I kept smiling, and puzzled, she sat down.

143

'Edward wants me to go on another exploration somewhere up in the hills of Scotland, for God's sake,' I said, explaining my trip to Nancy, and knowing full well that Alison was watching me. 'Quite a change for me to be the one travelling so far afield.' I continued smiling as I said it, so that the barb need only have been in my sister's imagination.

'When are you going?' Nancy asked, pressing me for details. I was to go that weekend, I told her, and stay over until Monday in some hotel which was near a lake.

'It's terribly high up, and supposed to have spectacular views. I'll ring you and describe it in detail when I get there.'

I turned to Alison and for an instant stopped talking. Her face had taken on the look of a child's — the stunned, uncomprehending expression of someone very close to tears.

'Are you going to go?' she asked me stiffly.

'I'm still thinking about it,' I replied, draining my glass and switching up the volume on the television. For nearly an hour the three of us sat there. Nancy laughed once or twice at something an actor did, the deep boom of humour shaking both of us and making punches into the atmosphere. Alison sat stiffly in her seat, her feet bare, the long line of her trousered legs tucked up beside her, her face staring into and behind the television set. I swear she heard nothing. Then there was me — watching the people moving and talking in some situation comedy; and when one man fell down a flight of steps I glanced across to Nancy and smiled, hearing her laugh again. We were together, like the old times.

When we finally did eat, it was a pleasant meal which Nancy had taken all day to prepare. I asked Alison if she had been shopping and she said something in response, although she was speaking slowly and a little too softly for me to catch everything. Nancy glanced across to her and asked her if she was all right, but she only smiled in reply, and said something about being in late the previous night.

'What happened? Was it profitable?' I asked her, my fork poised between the table and my mouth.

She swallowed hard. 'What?'

'Your business meeting — was it profitable?'

Nancy was watching both of us, her eyes moving from one to the other.

'Yes. I think they'll use me.' Alison managed to stammer out, but she couldn't eat anything else, and left her plate half full.

'You want to get more sleep,' Nancy said to her. 'I know I'm fussing, but I know what's best for you. Get some fresh air and some early nights.'

'Nancy's right,' I added, 'you want to catch up when you can — heaven knows when you'll be off again.'

Her head snapped up.

'I'm not going to be doing so much travelling for a while.'

'Oh,' I said calmly. 'Why is that?'

'There's work in London,' she continued.

'You've never liked London so much before.'

'Well . . . I've been to so many places now, I

145

thought I would spend some time at home, and work from here.'

'It'll be lovely to have you with us,' Nancy chimed in, folding her napkin carefully.

'Just for a while,' Alison said.

'Won't you miss it?' I asked.

'What?'

'The travelling.'

'I've done a lot of it — '

'All the more reason to miss it, I should have thought. You're not likely to settle in London, not when you could go anywhere.'

'I . . . ' she began, and stopped.

'Tea anyone?' Nancy asked us, and I got up and helped her clear away the dinner things. Alison moved a few minutes later, saying she was going up to bed, and I left her for nearly an hour before I followed.

I tapped on her door lightly, using the tips of my fingers, but it was opened immediately as if she had been behind it, waiting for me. Her face was tight with frustration.

'What happened to you?' I asked, looking at her. 'Didn't it go well last night?'

'What the hell were you playing at down there?' she snapped, her cheeks bright with colour, the expression shifting from defence to attack.

'Alison, listen to me — if we are to keep Nancy from interfering in your affair, then we have to allay her suspicions. If I had come in and rushed upstairs with you, she would have guessed that something was up and then we would have had no end of trouble with her. She

146

would want to know who he was, and how much he earns, you know what I mean. Think about it.' It sounded so plausible that she relaxed. 'We'll play it my way, okay?'

'Yes, Jill, you are crafty, I would never have thought of all that. Clever old sister,' she said, sitting down beside me.

'Well, what happened?'

'He loves me,' she said simply.

'Did he say so?'

'Over and over. He said he had missed me and that he had thought of no one else since we had been apart.'

I chose my words carefully. 'When are you seeing him again?'

'Tomorrow. I told you he has a flat in town, well, it's perfect, it means that I can finish work and go back there and be with him.'

'Did he give you a key?'

'No . . . but he will.'

'Did he say he would?'

She looked faintly upset, as if she was being cornered.

'Bloody hell, Jill, you see problems in everything. He'll give me a key if he said he would, and he did.'

'Don't get annoyed, I just thought it would be easier for you, that's all, so you wouldn't be hanging around watching for him.'

She was lost somewhere in the previous evening. 'I love him so much.'

'I can imagine.'

'Oh Jill, you wait until you meet him . . . no, you wait until you meet some man that you can't

147

get out of your mind. There's someone for you, you mark my words.'

We sat for a while in silence and then she began to tell me about her plans for the weekend, and begged me not to go to Scotland.

'What would I do without you, Jill? I couldn't go on without having you to talk to. You won't go, will you?'

She looked so hopeful, her long eyes dark and faintly exotic, the curl of her mouth at that moment very young. I read the appeal for help and support and I nodded and agreed not to go, saying I would remain at home, in the walled house, and wait for her to come home and tell me about her lover.

'Thank you so much. I'll do the same for you, some day.'

The following morning I told Edward that I would be delighted to go on the trip to Scotland, staying at the hilltop hotel; delighted to accept the chance of a journey which he was planning for nearly six months ahead — because by then everything would be sorted out.

'Good, I'm glad about that, Jill,' he responded. 'I think it will be an important event, and I wouldn't have liked you to miss it.'

I smiled and looked up at him from my desk. 'I shall look forward to it.'

He clapped his hands together once, quickly, using the same mannerism he always employed when he was well pleased, and I spent the remainder of the morning returning telephone calls and drafting out articles for a small, specialist magazine.

Alison rang at one fifteen, just as I was having my lunch. I glanced towards the door to check that it was closed and then settled back, propping my feet on the open bottom drawer.

'Go on, there's no one about.'

'He's not rung,' she said, her voice hoarse with anxiety.

'Alison, he's probably busy. Didn't you say he was something to do with archaeology?'

'Yes.'

'Well, take it from me, he probably works odd hours if he gets engrossed in something, and besides if he's busy, he might have forgotten — '

'Forgotten!'

'For God's sake, if he's in the middle of a field, or under a pile of limestone, he's not likely to have a portable phone with him, now, is he?'

Her tone relaxed. 'He'll ring later then?'

'Of course he will. You calm down, as soon as he's free, he'll ring you.'

There was a long pause on the line, during which time neither of us spoke. I chewed one end of my egg sandwich, and waited. It seemed incredible that my sister was behaving like this; I could hardly recognise her. Wasn't it Alison who had always taken men for granted? Laughed at their compliments, and forgotten which man had sent which flowers? Wasn't that my sister? Then who was this stranger on the other end of the telephone, sick with worry about a late phone call?

'Alison?'

'Umm?'

'Are you okay?'

149

'Yes, I'm fine now, you've given me back my equilibrium.'

I bit off another piece of the sandwich.

'Where's Nancy?'

'Downstairs with that ghastly woman. God, I'd forgotten how much I hated her.'

I smiled.

'Which particular woman?'

'Mrs Edwards — the cure for bad thoughts.'

I laughed, nearly choking on the bread I had in my mouth.

'What's she doing?'

'Hoovering under the piano the last time I looked, although I haven't seen her for a bit, so she could be up to anything now. Nancy's following her about like she's attached to her by string. If she doesn't trust the woman she should get rid of her.'

'Alison, shut up! She might hear you.'

There was another pause on the line.

'No, it's all right, I can hear the vacuum going again.'

'What are you doing?'

'Nothing much. I rang the agency and they said that they've got plenty of work for me in London, so that's good news.' She hesitated. 'He will ring, won't he?'

'Not unless I get off this phone he won't.'

'Hell! I'd forgotten that. I must go — '

'Alison!'

'What?'

'What if Nancy picks up the phone and he tells her who he is?'

I heard her laughing down the line.

150

'I would just like to see anyone get to this telephone before I do. Don't worry, Jill, I'll keep it a secret, like we agreed.'

I rang off and in my imagination I could see my sister placing down the receiver carefully in its cradle, so that the call would be sure to come through. I could see her pacing the floor, or wandering listlessly about the house, smiling half-heartedly at the gardener or the odious Mrs Edwards. By three o'clock, curiosity was unhinging me. I phoned Alison.

'Alison?'

I heard her voice come down the line for the second time that day.

'He's just rung!' she shouted, and then whispered, 'We're going out tonight.'

'Good! I just rang to check. See you later.'

In those few days we had spoken more than we had done in years, and our thoughts and conversation centred around one subject, like satellites around a planet. I found that after the first day I was listening for the phone to ring as eagerly as she was; waiting for news as greedily as a night bat searching for insects, snatching at morsels. When she described him, I saw him and heard him and touched him; and when she spoke to him in the dark, it was with my voice, and when he looked into her face, he was seeing mine. I waited for her calls at work, the ones which were hurried and told me where she was meeting him, or the lonely, sad ones which said that he had not phoned, the calls which begged for reassurance, and the happy ones which came chirruping over the line when he told her he

151

loved her, that he would always love her and that he had never cared for anyone else.

We loved him in unison. We got on that tandem and rode on it together, hurtling towards the same man, although she never knew it, and every night when I got back from work she told me about this stranger, this person, describing him with her eyes, and her expressions, although he was still dusty and dirty and hot under a blistering sky in my mind's memory; the same man I had seen months earlier, the one who had kept me awake nights.

'He's so smart, Jill, so careful about his clothes.'

He wore an open necked shirt, and wellingtons, and sun made his jacket look dusty.

'He's handsome, and young for his age — not that he's old . . . mature really.'

His eyes were too small, and his face too long for good looks, and as for his age, he seemed older when I saw him at the airport. Older than I thought.

'You would love him, Jill, I know you would.'

Flies in a dusty car, sandwiches limp in the heat, and a notepad ragged with jottings. I had seen him through a heat haze on a scrubby field dig, heard him over the chuffing of shovels, and turned when he started his engine to leave. I had already loved him.

'Tell me he'll always love me . . . He will, won't he?'

11

Avoiding Nancy was no easy matter; she was too clever not to notice that something was going on, even though she did not know what precisely. We had previously eaten breakfast together, and when I took to getting up before either she or Alison had risen, and leaving for work without exchanging a word, she tackled me.

'What's up?'

'What do you mean?' I replied a little more sharply than I had meant, my guilt making me abrasive.

'You usually eat with me in the mornings, you know you do. You usually wake me half an hour before you go, and I make your breakfast. What's changed?'

She was in her dressing gown, her arms folded across that deep bosom, her hair newly combed, the faint silver streaks beginning to ghost through again.

'I'll do your hair when I get home tonight, it needs doing again.'

She tapped it thoughtfully, although she was not really interested, her attention was focused on her own thoughts.

'Well, so why don't you eat with me now?'

'It's different since Alison came home.'

'How?'

'Well . . . just different.' I smiled across to her, before dropping my gaze. 'We'll have our

153

breakfast together tomorrow, like we usually do. Okay?'

She shrugged and padded softly over to the coffee percolator, pouring out a cupful and drinking it slowly, her eyes on my face.

'I have to go,' I said simply, although I usually left ten minutes later, and knew that she would notice.

'Fine.'

'See you tonight then?'

'Yes, that's fine. Bye, Jill.'

She walked off, without going to the door with me, and was making her way upstairs when I left.

The incident bothered me all day, so that I made typing mistakes and forgot to return someone's call. They rang me at three-thirty, indignant, and it was only after a minute's soothing that they calmed down again. Unsettled, I put the caller through to Edward, and leaned back in my seat, running my hands through the back of my hair.

It was untidy and badly cut, the thickness of it seeming suddenly uncomfortable and ill-fitted on my head. After a moment's hesitation, I rang a hairdresser in Richmond and made an appointment for that afternoon, stressing that I would not be over until five at the earliest. The girl agreed, and told me that they had had a couple of cancellations; a mother and daughter who were supposed to be going on holiday, had cancelled their trip and didn't want their hair done any longer. Just as she was about to ring off, I told her to book me in for a manicure.

'Full manicure?' she asked, and I was too

154

afraid to appear gauche to question what she meant.

'Yes, thank you. A full manicure,' I replied and rang off.

I arrived at the salon a little earlier than I had anticipated, and walked in to find two girls at the reception desk, talking. One of them looked me up and down swiftly before returning to her conversation, although the other one slid off her stool and came over to me.

'Are you the five o'clock appointment?' she asked, all brisk good humour.

I nodded and slipped off my coat, sliding my arms into the overall she was holding out for me. It was pale green and made me look like a docked battleship.

'It shouldn't take too long,' she offered. 'We're not that busy.'

After tying up the tabs on the back of the cover-up she asked me to follow her, and whilst she shampooed my hair she kept talking easily, skipping from one subject to another, like a moth looking for a place to land.

' . . . so they said that they might be taking off the No 87 on the bus route, crazy I call it . . . what do you do? Oh, that's interesting, digging up old bones and stuff . . . is the water too hot? Not in very good condition, is it?' she said, leaning forwards and peering down at my scalp. 'Still, not to worry, we'll have it right for you in a jiffy . . . you live round here then?'

She had a small chin with a dimple in it; cut deeply in, as if it had been stitched there. Her

155

eyes were hazel, the surrounds of the pupils incredibly dark, and her hair was short and savagely cut, making her look like a prisoner of war in an old film.

'Who's cutting your hair?' she asked, pouring warm water over my head.

'Paul.'

'You'll like him,' she said determinedly, tucking a dry towel into the neck of my dress. 'He's very good, trained in Paris . . . or was it Rome?'

She gave me one last reassuring pat on my shoulder and left. She was all of seventeen. I waited for nearly ten minutes, during which time I had the dubious pleasure of seeing my face, with its make-up streaked from the hair-washing, reflected in the mirror in front of me. I had taken off my glasses so the image was unclear to me, and all I could properly make out was a large, pale green trunk, topped by a round pink circle, and a little wet cap of hair. I was so intently trying to focus, that when the girl came back with a coffee, I jumped.

'Oh, I'm sorry,' she said, stepping back so quickly that the liquid slopped uneasily in the cup.

'My fault,' I said, embarrassed, taking it from her.

Paul turned out to be about thirty-five years old, stocky, and rather turgid in his movements. He spoke slowly and methodically, arguing with everything I suggested and pulling up pieces of my hair with two fingers, as if I had something contagious.

156

'Did you have a conditioning treatment?' he asked idly.

'No. I didn't have the time.'

He sighed. 'It needs something really before I can cut it.'

'I can't spare any more time, not today, anyway. Couldn't you cut it and I could come back for the treatment next week?' I asked hopefully, knowing that I would never go back. He rolled his eyes dramatically and then snatched a comb from his top pocket like a magician pulling a bunch of flowers out of thin air. I nearly applauded.

Twenty-five minutes later, the job was done. I could see little difference because it was still wet, but as soon as he began to set it the manicurist arrived and my attention was diverted.

A full massage followed, during which time she pummelled and stretched my fingers, rubbed cream into the backs of my hands and snipped away at the cuticles, and I sat there like an odalisque, and enjoyed every indulgent second. When it came to choosing the nail colour, I picked one I would normally never have chosen, a brilliant scarlet which looked wet even after it had dried, the gloss reflecting all the lights in the salon.

After another hour they pulled me out from under the drier and after some hectic combing, Paul stepped in and applied the finishing touches, pushing the comb back into his top pocket to declare that he had done all he could. I fumbled in my bag for my glasses, careful not to smudge the nail polish, and when I had them

157

on again, I looked into my reflection.

I don't know what I had expected, but it was still me. Still the same face under the new hair. The expression had not altered, and where my fringe ended, the same pair of eyes peered out. Paul coughed twice, and I thanked him, tipping him far more than was necessary, as if I was really pleased. He smiled then for the first time, and pulled back my seat for me as I stood up.

'Will you be able to cope with it?' he asked, as if I was taking a savage dog home.

'Yes, oh yes. It's lovely, really,' I replied, pulling off the green smock and taking the shortest route to the reception desk. The young girl who had washed my hair complimented me, helping me on with my coat and cleaning the collar with a small clothes brush. When I left, she was already talking to the other girl, and as I walked home I could feel the stubbles of hair prick into my skin. By the time I had gone down three roads, little of the new hairstyle remained, and when I finally got in, Nancy greeted me with her eyebrows raised.

'I thought we were doing my hair tonight,' she said accusingly.

'Well, what do you think of it?'

'It's different, but it's a bit too far down over your forehead. It covers too much of your face.'

'In that case, it was worth every penny,' I said tartly, hearing Alison coming out of the kitchen.

She was wearing a plain dress, her hair drawn back with a piece of ribbon, her face shiny and pale now that her tan was beginning to fade. She looked wonderful.

'You've had your hair done,' she said simply, folding her arms and looking at it. 'It's not quite you though.'

'Why?'

'It's too styled,' Nancy blurted out, sitting down by the hall table and looking to Alison for agreement.

'No, it's not that . . . it's just too unnatural for Jill.'

'That's what I mean — it's stiff,' Nancy continued, satisfied.

I turned away from both of them and gazed into the mirror, seeing how the natural waviness and body of my own hair was already lifting the smooth line out of shape. They were right, it didn't suit me. I began to tug at it angrily, frustrated beyond reason. Alison walked over to me.

'Come upstairs, I'll fix it for you. It's nothing much — we'll soon get it right, it just needs a bit of alteration.'

I didn't want her to touch it, I didn't want her to be right, and most of all I didn't want her to put me in her debt; but I went with her all the same.

True to her word, she played with it and after a while it fell into shape easily.

'There you are — nothing to it, and now it shows off your eyes.'

I was ungracious. 'Thanks.'

It was all I could say at that time. I felt somehow beaten by her, as if she had won a point and the knowledge stung me.

'What's news?' I asked her, brushing pieces of

hair off my shoulders. 'Have you heard from him today?'

She sat down, delighted to be talking about her lover, delighted to be invited to confide.

'He wants me to go away with him on Thursday and Friday — he says that he has to do some business and would I like to go with him. What do you think?'

'I think you're going,' I said emphatically.

She laughed, and slid the brush and comb she had been using into her top drawer.

'I think you're right. What do I tell Nancy?'

'Say what you always say — that you have a job on and that you'll be away for a couple of days. I'll back you up.'

So she did just that, and when the phone rang a little later she ran out to answer it, closing the door behind her. Nancy and I sat in the lounge alone, and I kept my eyes fixed to the television like a rabbit mesmerised by a car's headlamps. A little time passed, but it was not comfortable, there was some feeling between us that had never been there before, and we both knew it. Nancy turned on the standard lamp behind her chair, and continued her crossword, trying to fill in two or three empty spaces which remained from that morning. My eyes never left the set.

Alison did not come back into the room, and I toyed with the idea of going upstairs, but resisted, thinking that it would appear too obvious to Nancy that we were hiding something from her. She had known us since we were children and was not likely to be fooled that easily. I watched colours and shapes moving

160

before me, and heard the unending mutter of voices, followed by the familiar chimes of Big Ben.

'Good lord, is that the time?' I said, turning to Nancy. 'Nine o'clock already — I'll go and see what Alison's doing.'

I knew it sounded contrived, but I still said it, getting up and going to the door. Nancy smiled in response, but it seemed a knowing smile, or maybe that was just my guilty conscience. Upstairs, everywhere was quiet, the quick summer having passed and the first warm days of August showing that hint of autumn in the breeze. The heat had gone. There was a bird singing somewhere outside, behind the glass windows which lined the top hallway, and under the birdsong, the slow dribble of traffic sounded from a nearby road.

I paused outside my sister's door and then knocked, hearing her get up off the bed and walk to the door.

'Hi, I was just thinking,' she said, her voice sleepy.

She had the look of a person who had been woken from a dream; that unsteady, slightly bewildered expression which made me feel like an unwelcome interloper. She lay down on the bed again and I moved to the window.

'There's a bird singing its heart out some-where. I thought he was in the apple tree, but I can't see him.'

'Jill?'

'Umm?'

'I've been running things over in my mind — '

161

she began and stopped, her voice teetering on the edge of tears. 'What if he goes back to America?'

I wasn't prepared for his sudden departure — it wasn't part of the plan.

'Did he say he was going?' I asked her, keeping my voice calm.

She didn't respond, and instead went over to one of her drawers and began to tidy it out, folding and refolding jumpers and cardigans, laying them one on top of the other in neat piles.

'No,' she said finally. 'He didn't say it, it was just that I thought he had changed, and that he didn't like me as much.'

'Nonsense, he's hardly had time to get bored with you,' I replied, seeing her look across to me; that slow expression of curiosity and anxiety spreading over her face. That look she wore so often now.

'I can't tell,' she said simply.

'He's over here on business, on a contract, you said?'

'Yes.'

'How long for?' I asked, knowing the answer full well.

'Nine months, supposedly.'

'Well then — what are you worried about? You've only been home for two months, you have another seven months with him for certain, and besides he'll probably stay on when his contract runs out.'

'What if he stops loving me?' she asked, pressing for reassurance.

'Why should he?'

162

'Men do.'

'Oh Alison, they might stop loving other people, but not you.'

She didn't speak for a while, and continued to rearrange her clothes. I switched on a lamp in her room and went back to the window. The daylight was gone then, and in its place smudges of darker clouds lay dragged along the sky. The bird had finished its song, and the streetlamps had just come on.

'Does he seem different?' I asked her.

'No, not really. It's just that I'm so afraid of losing him I suppose I'm imagining things.' She pushed back some hair from her forehead. 'I want him so much, more than I've ever wanted anything before. It hurts,' she said, lifting her hands up and then letting them drop back into her lap. 'I don't ever want to lose him — I couldn't.'

A car changed gears at the end of the street. I heard it first and then saw it pull up outside a house across the road. A young man got out, hardly more than eighteen, acting nervously, and obviously driving his father's car. After a moment a girl ran out to meet him. She was ordinary and unremarkable, wearing a dress which did not suit her, but he smiled when she approached and opened the door on her side.

'Jill?'

'Sorry — I was thinking. Did you say something to me?'

'I asked you how I could keep him.'

'Love him — that's all you can do. Be charming and witty and vivacious, and don't

163

show him how much you feel about him
... that's always the kiss of death to any
relationship.'

She nodded and walked over to me, flinging
her arm around my shoulder and standing
beside me. We both watched the car pull away
from the house opposite.

'They're probably going to a film or the pub.
It's so simple for some people, isn't it?' Alison
said wistfully.

'Just hold on, that's all. He's the man for you,
you'll see.'

She kissed me lightly on the cheek and for a
while we talked about her trip, and when Nancy
called us to say she was going to bed I followed
soon after.

The next weeks passed with numerous phone
calls and secret talks late at night, when Alison
came home. She grew into the relationship, and,
becoming more sure of him, she began to bloom,
opening out like a water lily, her face taking on
that peculiar translucency she had when she was
happy. I encouraged her to love him, encouraged
her to ring him when he forgot, or when he was
late with his mail. I told her to remain cheerful
and breezy, so that he would not think she was
pressuring him, and it worked like a charm. My
envy provided the stimulus and energy I needed,
and it became very simple for me to lie and
express thoughts I did not feel, although I kept
away from my grandmother as much as I could.

Nancy and I did take to having our breakfasts
together again, during the weeks of August and
September, and in a detached fashion we

164

continued our relationship. I believed that Nancy took my reserve as being due to Alison's prolonged stay with us, believing my sister was unnerving me as she had done so many times in the past — and I did not try to dissuade her. She seemed oddly composed, as if she expected every day to be told something, and yet she never asked either of us a direct question. When Nancy and I were alone, we spoke of my work and everyday trivia, and her relationship with Alison continued as it had done previously, probably largely due to the fact that Alison genuinely thought it was better to keep her relationship a secret until things were more settled. Now and again, she would broach the subject with me, but I would convince her to remain silent, saying that it would only upset our grandmother and worry her, and she accepted my logic.

'It won't be long now, and then you will really have something to tell her, but at the moment she would only worry. Believe me, Alison, I've spent more time with her, and I know her better than you do.'

So by making her feel guilty, she would acquiesce and life continued in its strange fashion. Alison came in and out of the walled house like a pretty doll in an old weather clock, rain or shine, and I egged her on until she became so infatuated with Mark that every moment away from him was purgatory.

But I altered also, and I found that Chestnut Walk was no longer as compelling as it had previously been. The insight into Alison's affair, the glamour, the excitement and sheer drama of the whole situation made my work appear odiously dull by comparison, and the fact that I was dealing with dead objects, with no life in them, and no emotion, made the transition between the two worlds stilted and disturbing.

I went from one set of circumstances to the next; veering between the tension of my sister's life to the calm and impassive other-world atmosphere of my office. I found that my mind wandered, that in the middle of conversations I would be thinking of Alison, wondering what she was doing; or whether or not she was with Mark. If she was obsessed, I was possessed, and every normal remark or suggestion made to me, resounded in my head like the banging of a tin drum, tuneless and irritating. Edward went away at that time to give some lectures in Wales. He said he would be gone for a week, but then rang in and told me that he would be staying on because his elusive grandchildren had joined him and he was going to make a holiday out of the trip. I rang off relieved, the strain lifting a little, and the following day I told Mrs Wren that I wouldn't need her for a while.

'That's fine,' she said genuinely. 'I've got so much on at home that it will be a help not to have to come in. You should have a break whilst Mr Worthington's away.'

'No, I don't think so. I'll hold the fort here.'

The lull at work suited me perfectly. It had become more and more difficult for me to keep lying to Alison and Nancy and run the office smoothly, so that now the pressure had been taken off at work I could escape from the house into the relatively peaceful office.

So for the next two weeks I ran the place single-handed, and only Anna intruded into my sanctuary.

'You want lunch?' she asked me one day, her head poked around the door.

'No, thanks, I brought something in,' I told her, surprised at the offer.

She shrugged and instead of leaving, walked in, looking around her slowly.

'Nice. You have it nice in here. Difficult to dust though,' she said, pointing to the table where I had my plants.

'Do you want a cutting?' I volunteered, but she shrugged and moved over to the other side of the room.

'It's quiet with the boss away,' she said, making a long sound of the word 'boss' so that it came out as 'borse'.

'It's a rest for you.'

'No, not so much,' she said, digging her hands into the pockets of her apron, and sidling around like a woman at a market, looking for bargains. 'I like it busy.'

I moved around in my seat and watched her, noticing with a smile that she was wearing her slippers again.

'Has he written to you?' she asked suddenly.

For an instant I was wrong-footed. 'Who?'

'Mr Worthington.'

'No, not yet. He'll probably send a postcard.'

She shrugged again and after a while, moved towards the door, asking me up to tea the following day before she left.

167

It was early October when Edward came back, and he looked older and somewhat changed. 'Geoffrey darling' came with him, holding onto his arm like a drunk, although he was supposed to be helping him. He looked not like the old man he was, but like a wrinkled, beaten-up version of that old man, as if the life had been sucked out of him. 'Geoffrey darling' stayed with him for nearly an hour, and when he had gone, Anna and I descended on Edward like nurses on a terminal patient.

His pink-rimmed eyes looked weepy behind his glasses and his fleshless arms felt even more fragile under the sleeve of his jacket. Anna looked at him and clicked her tongue, disappearing and reappearing later with a snack and some hot tea. He ate it eagerly, hardly speaking, his strange voice more high-pitched than before, the vitality gone.

'You look tired,' I said finally.

'Terrible,' Anna volunteered.

'I feel worn out,' he began, wiping the stray crumbs off his mouth, and leaning his head back against his seat. 'They wore me out . . . those children wore me out.'

'You're exaggerating,' I said softly.

He shook his head. 'No, I'm telling you the truth — they're spoilt and unruly. I went for a rest and I've come back utterly exhausted.'

But he was already reviving, his colour coming back in patches, so that he looked like a badly painted portrait. He asked for his mail and played with it, shuffling the papers on his lap, and when he sent Anna for a glass of whisky she looked at me with an expression of triumph.

'You see,' she said accusingly, 'he's better off here. Children — too rough — they make you old.'

As he came round he pressed me for details regarding work, so we finished talking at seven o'clock, long after our usual time, and it was only after I pulled the front door closed behind me that I remembered I had told Alison I would be home early. I got back as quickly as I could but she had already left, having pushed a note under my door.

8.30 pm

Jill,

I have something very important to tell you — please don't go to bed before I get back. I'm supposed to be meeting Mark for dinner, but he said that he might be delayed so I might see you earlier than I thought.

Lots of the usual,

Yours — sister,

Alison

I wondered what it was that she had to tell me so desperately, and spent several moments calling for Nancy before I found another note on the kitchen table, written in her hand.

Jill —

Your dinner is in the fridge — salad and ham, that's all I could get in time. Angela rang me and asked me over for a game of bridge, and knowing that I can't fail but win, I had to

169

go! Alison's gone out in a fearful hurry — I don't know what's happening to that girl at the moment, but perhaps she'll tell you all about it when she gets back.

If Dorothy rings tell her I've gone to the cinema — don't mention the bridge, or that I'm playing with you-know-who, or we'll never hear the end of it.

Cheerio,
Nancy.

For a moment, total panic set in. What was happening? What had Nancy meant by Alison 'telling me all about it' when she got back? Had she said something to my grandmother? What the hell was going on? Perhaps he had proposed, I thought, and then reasoned that he couldn't have — it wasn't right, and it wasn't the way the plan was supposed to go.

I ate the salad under the kitchen light, on the pine table, and made myself a mug of tea which burnt my mouth when I drank it. I kept reading Nancy's note, and then Alison's, frantically trying to make sense out of them, or read other words written there in their place. Nine o'clock sulked past, and then nine fifteen, and at nine thirty-five, the front door opened. I ran out into the hall to find Alison standing there, the key in her hand.

She was very tired and short of colour, her eyes large in her face, and her lips pale.

'What?' I began and stopped.

'Jill, can you . . . ? No, never mind, I'll do it.'

She was bright and brilliant, her movements

170

edgy, and her whole demeanour jerky and slightly out of control, as if she was being worked by an amateur puppeteer. After pouring herself a large gin, she sat down, her coat falling open by her sides, the line of her dress wet in a patch down the front.

'Is it raining?'

'Well this isn't part of the pattern,' she said unpleasantly and apologised immediately. She refused to confide at first and just kept drinking, making herself another when the first one was emptied.

'Steady on,' I said.

'Why?'

'Because you don't usually drink so much, that's why.'

'I don't usually get pregnant either,' she said flatly.

Unable to speak I merely stood there, watching her. She took it as a judgement and looked away from me.

'For God's sake say something, Jill.'

I swallowed before answering. 'Are you sure?'

She nodded.

'Confirmed yesterday, by a doctor in down-town Harley Street. You know the type — the ones who offer an abortion in the same breath as they're checking your hand for a wedding ring.'

'Alison — '

'I can't think how to tell him,' she continued, busy with her own thoughts. 'I know he'll be pleased, but I just can't think how to tell him.'

'What the hell were you doing?' I asked her

171

angrily, and to my complete surprise, she began to laugh.

'What do you think we were doing? Playing chess?'

'Alison, stop it! This is serious.'

But she didn't seem to think it was, not then. It was inconvenient, but not that serious, not if you were Alison and your man was the reliable kind. Besides, it happened to couples every day of the year, and they got by. I saw my plan fall apart before my eyes, like one of those horribly vulgar ice sculptures, only someone had lit a bonfire under mine and the swan had melted into little more than a spreading stain on the table cloth. I looked at her and forced myself to speak.

'What are you going to do?'

'Go and see him, of course. What else? I thought he might not make it to the restaurant tonight, he said as much on the phone, but I'll call him and go over later to the flat.'

'Why?'

She looked at me with genuine surprise.

'Why? To tell him, why else? I know he'll marry me — he can't do anything but, not now.'

Oh God.

'Marry you!'

'Yes, why not? He loves me and I love him, so . . . why not?'

She was very young suddenly, frightened all at once, and not quite so sure of herself. The bravado was fading.

'Alison — what if he — '

'What?'

172

'What if he doesn't want to marry you?'

'He'll have to marry me, I'm pregnant.'

'You could get rid of it.'

I had said the words before I had thought. Saying them because I was too shocked to keep my thoughts to myself. To Alison it was a betrayal and she banged her glass down on the table beside her.

'Get rid of it! Why should I! I want this child.'

'Why? Did you get pregnant deliberately?' I asked her, watching as she got up and turned her back to me. 'Well, did you?'

'It was an accident.'

'How? *How* was it an accident? You were on the pill, how could it have been?'

'I forgot,' she began lamely and stopped.

'You *wanted* to forget, you wanted to catch him, didn't you? Didn't you?'

She turned around quickly then, her face ash-coloured, the dark smears under her eyes almost purple in the half light.

'What if I did? Why shouldn't I? Other women do it every day, it's not uncommon. I want him,' she said, sitting down heavily, all grace gone. 'I want him and this way he's mine . . . he has to be.'

'Sometimes it doesn't work out that way,' I began, a huge fist balling up in my chest. 'Sometimes it doesn't work like that at all — '

'What the bloody hell would you know about it?' she demanded, her face pinched with fury. For the first time I could see how she would look at fifty or sixty, the savagery of her anger making her ugly.

173

'I don't know — not like you evidently do,' I retorted, stung. 'But then I haven't had your experience!'

'You're jealous!' she shouted. 'You always were. Jealous and envious and grudging. I thought you'd changed, I thought you were genuinely pleased for me this time, but I was wrong. You don't change, Jill, because you can't ever get over the fact that I was born pretty and you were born — '

'Ugly,' I said softly, and she shrugged.

'I didn't say that.'

'You didn't have to.'

She was right. I was plain and jealous and worse, far worse than she knew, or could guess at. But at that moment all I could think of was — what are we going to do? Mark couldn't marry her, but she didn't know that.

'Alison think. What if he won't marry you?'

'Is that what you want? For him to leave me? Is that it?'

She was suddenly quiet again and began to rock herself slowly, just as Nancy had done when we were children.

'Why wouldn't he marry me?'

'He might — '

'What?' she snapped.

'I don't know.'

She got up suddenly and went out into the hall and after a moment I could hear her talking on the phone. She said a few words and stopped to listen, again beginning to talk after a minute or so. Her voice was slightly raised, but more in excitement than anger and as I got to the door,

174

she replaced the receiver.

'Have you told him?'

'No, I'm going over there now. Don't bother to wait up for me, I'd hate to have to tell you the good news — it might ruin your evening.' I moved towards her, but she stepped back. 'No, don't try to pretend — I know what you're thinking, and I hate you for it.'

'Alison, you can't — '

'Oh leave me alone!' she snapped angrily and wrenched open the front door. 'You'll see, he'll marry me and then you'll be sick with envy! It'll burn you up, tear your insides out, and I don't give a damn!' She smiled then, her mouth turning at the corners. 'You're an old maid, Jill, even at your age, an old maid because no one will ever want you. Good night, dear sister, I'll send you an invitation to the wedding.'

I heard the car pull out only a second later, as I walked back into the lounge. I poured myself a drink and left it, untouched. No feelings came to me, not guilt or shame, not concern for Alison, nothing. I felt incapable of thought, and when sense came back to me all I could ask myself was — What would Mark say to her? What, in God's name, would he say?

Oh yes, I had wanted Alison to be hurt. I had wanted her to fall in love with the one man who would be sure not to love her back, the one man who would leave her, and I had encouraged her to that end. I wanted my revenge on her for all the years she had patronised me, and now, instead of triumph, I was sick with fear.

Nancy came home late, and when she saw me

175

she told me some rambling tale about Angela being a bad loser. I think that if I had hung myself from the banisters in the hall she would not have noticed, so wrapped up was she in the evening's entertainment. When she got to the kitchen she saw my unfinished plate and looked across to me.

'Not hungry?'

I shook my head. 'I had something at work.'

She shrugged and shovelled the scraps into a pedal bin.

'Where's your sister?'

'She's gone out.'

'Well, I can see that. Did she say where she was going?'

So Alison had not told her. With relief, and to hide my face from Nancy, I took off my glasses and rubbed my eyes.

'No.'

She snorted quietly and an instant later I heard the sound of the kettle, and the familiar click of the toaster.

'You're eating too much,' I said, propping myself up against the door jamb.

'What's got into you?' she replied, a piece of toast in one hand.

'Nothing. It's just that the doctor said — '

'Damn the doctor, he's not hungry!' she replied, swallowing the remainder of the piece. She looked plump and well-fed, like a fat squirrel going into its winter hibernation. She didn't look her age, she didn't look like a woman with a bad heart; she looked safe.

'That was good,' she said, wiping her hands on

a tea towel. 'I'm going up to bed now, love.'

'Good night, Nancy.'

'Night,' she said, then paused at the door as she passed me. 'Lock up for me, will you? Alison's got her key.'

I nodded and watched her as she moved upstairs. She yawned expansively and then turned the corner on the landing and was out of my sight.

I heard the sound of her footsteps and the noise of the cistern emptying and filling, accompanied by the mumble of the radio from her room. After a while the place was in silence and I moved listlessly back into the lounge.

It was cold in there, now that the October evening had settled in. It smelled damp and the winter scent of mist and wet grass seemed to have seeped into the furniture, so that even the last blaze of the fire was making little impression. I moved the screen away and threw on some logs, watching as they smouldered and then caught, the flames licking the wood and making long tongues up the chimney back.

I kept trying to imagine what was happening, trying to imagine what Mark would say, how he would look at her. I do remember thinking that possibly he would tell her that his marriage was a failure anyway and that he intended to leave his wife, and I don't know if I wanted that to happen, or not. Nothing seemed logical, as if it was happening to another person, in a play. At any moment, the safety curtain would come down and we would get up and have a drink in the bar. Then the first bell would go, and then the second; and before you knew it, we would be back in the theatre seats watching this mess which was happening to someone else. That was how it had to be — it couldn't be real, it couldn't be happening to Alison.

But she didn't come home, and the evening dragged itself into night, and still she didn't return. I wondered, with rising panic, whether she had had an accident, after all, she had been drinking before she left — what if she had been picked up by the police? But no one came, and no one phoned.

At two o'clock, I dozed. Twisted into the chair like a corkscrew, my limbs tight with waiting, I fell asleep, and when the clock struck three I sprang up, listening.

Nothing moved, nothing stirred or made an imprint on the silence, and when I looked out through the curtains there was no one in the road outside, though the lamps beamed against the damp blackness and made skirts of light on the pavement underneath. Still she didn't come.

The fire had finally gone out, there wasn't even a trace of ash left smouldering and instead of relighting it, I pulled on my coat and sat down again. My eyes began to itch, as they always did when I was tired, and my hands felt cold against my face, shaking a little when I took off my glasses. Maybe she had missed him, maybe he hadn't been there I reasoned, but if that was it — where was she now? God Alison, where are you?

Three o'clock banged in the nails of the hours, hammering round the clock face. Each minute marked time; each second was caught between yesterday and whatever would happen when Alison came home. Suddenly I heard Nancy moving around upstairs. I heard her voice from the passage calling out to me, and I heard her go back into her room. She must have thought I was asleep, and she wasn't worried about Alison — Alison could take care of herself.

I could imagine my sister's room upstairs; could see the careful order of her belongings, the little snippets of herself which she brought with her. Hairspray, an ivory comb, a small photograph of Mark which she kept hidden from Nancy under her scarves. We waited, that room and I, for her to return and when almost an hour later the door opened, I was already in the hall as she walked in.

But the woman standing there wasn't Alison; she had gone, faded somewhere into that night, back to when the stone had struck her, or when she had teased me as a child. She was no longer the beautiful sister, certain and sure of her abilities; she was little and broken and stood in the doorway like a dog, not knowing where else left to go. I walked over to her.

'Alison?'

It *was* her, I knew the face, but my sister was somewhere behind the eyes, cloistered and put away for safe keeping, and instead there was a stranger in her place.

'Alison?' I repeated, and put my arms around her.

She didn't move, she just leant against me, the full weight of her limp body against mine. I knew

179

what had happened then, I didn't need to ask her — after all, hadn't I planned and longed for just this? She seemed strangely heavy for her size and it took me a while to get her into the lounge and settled in the chair I had occupied all night. I rubbed her hands in my own and tucked a blanket around her legs, but she didn't speak, and when I asked her to look at me she was somehow sightless, as if she no longer knew how to see. Frightened, I jumped to my feet, seeing her hands drop back on her lap and the slow, staggered breathing only slightly troubling the line of her coat.

I told her that everything would be all right, and began to cry — long after I should have done. I touched her hair and talked about school to her, and about her modelling, but when she didn't move I ran out of the room and up the stairs, arriving outside Nancy's door and banging on the wood panels until she opened it.

'Jill, what's the matter?' she asked, suddenly the matriach, suddenly in control.

'It's Alison,' I said and stopped short.

She moved quickly, pushing past me and taking the stairs two at a time. She was downstairs before I was, pouring a large brandy and holding Alison's head for her to drink it.

'Tell me now, tell me, love. We'll sort it out, don't we always?'

I watched them, the older woman bent over the young girl, the large arms rocking, rocking the cold little body, and the same crooning voice repeating over and over again: 'Whatever it is, it

180

can be mended, you'll see. Don't you worry, love, we'll sort it out between the three of us. Just you, me and Jill, like always. It'll come right, you'll see.'

12

We closed ranks around her from that moment, cutting ourselves off from the world outside, making an island of our house. That was what we did.

When we finally got Alison into bed, she fell deeply to sleep in an artificial, almost drugged way, which left Nancy sitting by her bedside until the early hours. I offered no explanation, and it was close to dawn when Nancy came down into the kitchen, her dressing gown wrapped tightly around her, the strain of the night making dull plains of colour on her cheeks.

'Is she asleep?' I asked, getting up and making some tea for both of us.

'Yes, still fast asleep. She hasn't moved.'

'How does she look?'

'Tired, and very young.'

'She . . . '

I stopped short, uncertain of how to explain, uncertain if an explanation was necessary. My grandmother sipped her tea and said nothing.

'She's been involved with a man . . . '

'Yes, I know.'

She'd known all along, how stupid I'd been to think I could have fooled Nancy, of all people. The tea was too strong, and was already forming a skin on the rim of my cup.

'We didn't want to worry you.'

She said nothing.

'We thought that it would be better not to mention it — not unless something positive happened.'

'How long?'

I was momentarily wrong-footed.

'Sorry?'

'How long has she been seeing him?'

'Since she came home — since May.'

She kept sipping her tea, finally putting the cup down and looking straight at me.

'And you thought that it was better not to worry me for five . . . no, six months? Is that it, Jill? I want to know, just so I get it right.'

'We thought — '

I looked down at my hands; they looked white under the kitchen light. A bird started to sing outside, and daylight seemed imminent.

'We should have told you.'

'Yes.'

'I'm sorry.'

'What happened?' she asked me, tucking some hair behind her ears. 'Did he throw her over?'

'I think so.'

'So she hasn't told you then?'

'No, not yet.' I glanced at her, but she wasn't looking at me, she was turning her tea spoon over and over in her hand.

'But she was seeing him tonight?'

I nodded.

'Well — was she?'

'Yes, she was seeing him tonight, and she was — '

'Going to tell him that she was pregnant,' she finished off for me.

183

'How do you know?'

'I didn't, until a moment ago. You just told me.'

'Nancy, I . . . we should have told you.'

'Yes,' she agreed quietly. 'Who is he?'

I was glad to tell her, eager for her sense, her practicality.

'His name is Ward, Mark Ward. He's an American, over here from New York.'

'What does he do?' she asked, with no perceptible trace of anger.

'He's something to do with archaeology.'

She glanced at me sharply. 'That's quite a coincidence, wouldn't you say?'

I lied as deftly as I could. After all, I had had a great deal of practice.

'It's the same man she met when she was in the States doing that modelling job, don't you remember? The one who was brought in to advise the advertising agency for the series, *Ancient and Modern*.'

Her glance shifted from me back to her tea. She ladled in two spoonfuls of sugar, and then stirred the liquid slowly.

'How old is he?'

'About forty, forty-two. Something like that.'

'That's too old, too old for Alison,' she said, and drank deeply for a moment. 'I suppose that he's married?'

It wasn't really a question, more a statement of fact. 'He's married', she was really saying, with all its dread implications and complications. A married man, getting a young woman pregnant — not exactly the stuff that dreams are made of.

184

'I don't know,' I lied, although she hadn't really asked me for an answer. I was simply trying to cover myself, even then, so that Alison wouldn't be told what I had done; so that Nancy wouldn't find out.

'It would seem likely, I would have thought,' she replied, yawning deeply and pulling her dressing gown around her legs. 'Men of forty are usually married, or divorced. Surely she would have mentioned it to you, though, you've been so close lately.'

I blushed and looked down at the table. Nancy, always wanting to be fair, believed that I thought my loyalties were being questioned, and she apologised.

'Listen Jill, I won't lie to you. I'm hurt that you didn't tell me about Alison and this man. I'm hurt that she didn't confide in me herself — but that's the way it is. You must both have had your reasons, and I don't want you to think that I'm weighing your loyalty towards your sister, against your loyalty towards me. You were children together, and that makes for a very strong bond.'

I kept my head down, because my face was scarlet.

'But the time has come when this mess has to be sorted out — and soon. Alison's in no fit state to think for herself, and I'm in a perfect situation to advise her, being older and a damn sight wiser.'

'She could still decide not to have the child,' I offered.

For a time Nancy didn't respond. I wondered

185

if she was angry, or shocked. She was neither.

'Getting rid of the baby will solve nothing. No, Alison must have this child.'

There was a movement upstairs, and an unnaturally high-pitched voice called out for Nancy. She was on her feet immediately, telling me to make some more tea before rushing out into the hallway.

I did what she asked automatically, expecting to see either my grandmother, or both of them, walk into the kitchen at any moment. But no one came, and it was only when I was about to go upstairs with the tray, that I heard the sound of their raised voices —

'I can't! It's not fair! . . . it's not right . . . he lied to me . . . No, it's not fair!'

When I got to my sister's room the bed was in shambles, covers thrown back and her clothes scattered in and around a suitcase. Nancy was trying to calm her, clinging onto her arms with both hands, her voice even and pitched low, to compensate for Alison's blind panic.

'Listen to me, Alison. Listen to me! We'll sort it out . . . Alison!'

It was impossible. Alison was totally incoherent, and in an instant she threw off Nancy's arms and began to pack, flinging dresses in and out of the case like a child driven to complete frustration.

'I'm going! I'm going, I tell you . . . and you can't stop me.' She began to sob, deep choking sobs which came from her chest. 'He lied to me! Lied! He lied!' she kept repeating, and then finally she threw the half-packed suitcase across the room and made for the door.

Nancy was there before she was, and with a very well-timed aim, struck my sister once, and then again, across the face. Alison rocked back and fell, slipping down the wall and landing in an untidy mound on the floor. My grandmother went over to her, and taking two cups off the tea tray I had brought up, sat down next to her.

'Take this,' she said, offering one to Alison. 'And stop being such a cretin.'

Reluctantly, she took the cup and drank some tea, and when Nancy beckoned me over, I sat down with them. We were three women sitting on a floor, waiting for the night to end, and for daylight to come in on us. Nobody said very much for a while, although Nancy shifted her position a few times, and pulled one of the thrown cushions towards her, tucking it firmly behind her shoulders. Alison rested her head back against the wall, and I watched the light beginning to shine through a gap in the curtains.

'Well, it's nearly another day,' Nancy said finally. 'We'll have to make plans, all of us, and get our house in order.'

I was suddenly six again, listening to my grandmother organising my life; just as she had done the morning she had woken us and said that our parents were dead. It had been winter then, and the frost made patterns on the windows outside, like maps of foreign countries. She told me first, and then repeated it to Alison, because she found it difficult to take in the first time. The frost melted when the sun came out,

187

and trickled down the glass panes in water streamers.

'He lied to me,' Alison repeated again, her face totally immobile; her arms clenched across her middle.

'Men do,' Nancy said briskly, trying to shock her into a response. 'It's the way of things.'

'He lied.'

'Alison, don't — it won't help,' I said, but when she looked over to me there was no expression in her eyes; only a vacuum.

'Jill's right. The best thing to do now is to get ready for the baby coming.' Nancy struggled to her feet. 'We'll need a layette, and some nappies, and a pram.' She stopped and scratched her forehead. 'Where can I get a pram? Gallaghers, I suppose — they have prams.'

'What are you going to tell people?' I asked her quietly.

'Who?'

'Everyone.'

'You mean Angela and Dorothy, and all the other women I know — and the bridge club?' I nodded. 'I'm going to tell them that Alison is going to have a baby, what else?'

'But you can't.'

'Why not?'

'Because she's not married, for one thing.'

I looked over to Alison as I said it, aware that suddenly I was talking about her as though she wasn't there; but there was no indication that she had even heard me.

'So what do you suggest? That we should make her a widow over night? A secret marriage?

Or maybe we're supposed to find the kid on the doorstep a few months from now?' She looked exasperated. 'Do be reasonable, we'll have to brazen it out.'

'But it's a child, and it's a whole life . . . I mean, it's not something that has a beginning and an end to it. Once a baby comes, it'll be here permanently, and it might ruin Alison's chances later on.'

'She should have thought about that beforehand,' she replied briskly. 'I can't think how she could have been so stupid. Still, I'm not going to get angry with her — she's got enough on her plate just now, and she won't know what's hit her when this baby comes.'

'Will she have the baby here?'

'Where else?'

So it was settled. As a result of my blind jealousy, I had succeeded in being responsible for my sister's condition, and for her obvious desperation. I realised then that she had obviously loved Mark, although the possibility had not occured to me before. I merely thought that she would be fascinated by him, as I was, and then get over the affair in time. I had not reckoned on Alison seriously wanting to marry him; neither had I thought her capable of setting out to trap him in the oldest way known to mankind. To say I felt sick with guilt is an understatement: I felt ashamed, and horribly aware that I could never, never confide in either Nancy or Alison. That was to be my punishment: I was to watch Alison carry a child whose father would not marry her, and when that child was

189

born, I would see it grow, and remember how, and in what manner, its very existence had begun.

I went to bed for a couple of hours, and slept fitfully, dreaming of Mark and Alison and a field dig, only this time the sunny day had clouded over and my sister began to uncover little pottery figures which, when she lifted them, came alive and began to cry. I woke exhausted, and made my way towards Nancy's room, peering in on Alison as I passed.

She was fast asleep, although it was then seven o'clock. Her arms were out of bed, and lay on the pillow above her head. All around her, there were signs of last night's chaos; scattered cushions, the suitcase with its hinges broken, and a selection of clothes all thrown around in complete disorder. By the side of her bed was a glass of water, and her small reading lamp was still switched on.

I moved to turn it off, and she stirred.

'Jill?'

'Yes, it's me.'

Her eyes filled quickly. 'He was married, you know . . . he lied to me . . . he said he couldn't . . . wouldn't marry me . . . he said he didn't want to anyway.'

'Sssh, I'm sorry. I'm so sorry,' I said, sitting beside her on the bed. She played with the edge of the sheet.

'I was so happy when I got to the flat . . . I rang the bell and he answered, and when I told him . . . he just said that he was leaving anyway, and that it was for the best because he was

190

married.' She began to cry softly, not wrinkling up her face, but talking as the tears poured down her cheeks and fell onto the pillow. 'He said that we had had a good time, and that was all . . . he said that he could put me in touch with someone who would help me to get rid of the baby.'

She stopped and listened, as though she expected someone to come in.

'Was that the phone?' she asked pathetically, sitting up in bed. 'Was it? Go and listen, Jill, it might be him.'

'It wasn't the phone, Alison.'

Her expression faded and she slumped back.

'No, it wouldn't be, of course not. He said he was going back to New York today anyway, and that he was going to tell me he was leaving last night . . . He lied to me, you know.'

She never reproached me. She never asked why I had led her wrongly; she never implied that I was in any way to blame. She took it all on, every bit of the whole sad, sorry mess, and it beat the heart out of her.

'Alison — '

'I thought he loved me. Isn't that silly? I did so love him.' Quick movements of her hands disturbed the white blindness of the sheets. 'Will he come back to me?'

For the first time I did not lie to her. 'No, Alison, no, he won't come back.'

She nodded twice and then turned away from me, crying. I left her soon after and found Nancy in the kitchen. She was dressed and already frying bacon, the usual rounds of toast on the table.

'How can you eat?' I asked her.

'Someone's got to keep their strength up, and I suggest you do the same.'

She slammed three slices onto a plate and pushed it across to me. 'Eat it.'

I did, slowly, helping it down with some tea and watching the clock face turn from seven to eight o'clock.

'I must get ready for work,' I said finally.

'Yes, do that, and in your lunch hour book an appointment with the doctor for Alison. She'll need proper attention now, and treatment. I don't want this child to start life badly.'

I could have laughed. Here was a baby entering the world without a father, or a name, and here was my grandmother worrying about vitamins.

'Did she say when the baby was due?' I asked.

'June. Which is good, because it means that the weather will be warm, and that's right for the child — we can pop it into the garden in a pram and let it get all the sunshine.'

She was so practical, so utterly in charge of the situation.

'So Alison has agreed to have the baby then?'

'Of course, she was only worried about how I would take it, that's all.'

'And you don't mind?'

'Yes, I mind!' she said suddenly, banging down her hands on the kitchen table. 'I mind because I wanted my two granddaughters to have large, white weddings, and I wanted son-in-laws, or whatever I would have called them. I mind because I wanted you both to be loved and hopefully have children, somewhat later than nine months after the wedding. Do you seriously think I will enjoy knowing that everyone is talking about my granddaughter? That everyone will be saying that she was dumped by some man who wouldn't marry her even after he got her into trouble?' She was angry, her face taking on the expression of another person. 'I've loved you both too much, perhaps, but I thought that I taught you some common sense, enough at least to warn you not to get mixed up with that type of man, and enough to know how not to get pregnant.'

'Nancy — '

'Yes, I know before you say it — I'll bring on an angina attack. Well, I'll tell you something, Jill, there is no way that my heart is going to be affected any longer, because it's taken such a beating now and survived, that nothing else will even make a dent in it.'

I got up and hugged her, and for a second she squeezed me tightly before pushing me away and sending me off to get dressed. She was back in control, and both of us knew it.

In the office I was busy all day, the phone ringing constantly, people needing my help every few minutes. It was only after Edward had mentioned it that I remembered the trip to Scotland, the one about which I had lied to Alison, six months earlier.

'This weekend?'

'Yes, this weekend. Had you forgotten, Jill?'

He looked confused, blinking behind the thick

193

glasses, his hands shuffling the papers on my desk.

'No, no I hadn't forgotten,' I lied, trying to sound convincing. 'It's just that it's come up so quickly.' My voice was calm, although I was shaken badly. If I was away for the weekend, it meant that Nancy and Alison would be alone, and that my sister might just let something slip about my part in her disastrous romance. She might mention how I had encouraged her, and Nancy, being Nancy, might detect my motives. She, of all people, knew how jealous I was.

If I had been a braver and more honest person, I would have told my grandmother. I would have admitted what I had done, and tried to make amends — but I was too much of a coward to face her, and too frightened to lose her love, to risk a confession. So I kept quiet, and swore that I would help Alison as much as I could until she had the baby — after which she could continue with her own career, and go back to her old way of life. That was how I rationalised the circumstances; that was how I lied to myself.

When I got home that night, Alison was in the lounge, a fire banked high in the grate in front of her, a book by her side. She greeted me when I came in, and then turned back to the fire.

'Do you want anything, Alison?'

'No, thank you.'

'Do you remember how we used to watch the flames when we were children?' I asked, sitting down in the chair next to hers. 'You used to see dragons and birds, and I always thought that there were goblins who lived in the ashes. Do

194

you remember that?'

'I wish I was a child now,' she said simply, and my heart turned.

I waited for a moment, and then walked out into the hallway, resting my head against the banister rail, and wondering how I was going to watch Alison carry a child whose very existence reminded her constantly of the man who had left her. A sick wave of anxiety began, as I tried to assess how strong Alison was, and whether or not she was capable of coming to terms with her situation.

Nancy had already got the pram that morning, and told me that when she bought it, the woman in the shop asked her if it was for a grandchild.

'Do you know, I felt *proud*. I'd probably have snapped her head off if she'd asked me about its parents, but just thinking about having a child in the house again, made me happy. Damn funny how things work out.'

She was cheerful, already making plans for the future.

'I made an appointment for Alison at the doctor's — ten fifteen tomorrow.'

'Good, I'll take her.'

I glanced over to the doorway. 'How's she been today?'

'Quiet,' Nancy said, pausing as she wrote on the pad in front of her. 'What else does a baby need?'

I had no idea.

'I'm not sure . . . Nancy, how do you think my grandfather would have taken all of this?'

'Who knows? Let's just thank God that he

isn't around to cause any further complications.' No, he wasn't. Neither was there a man around who would willingly provide the child with a name. There were no men in our lives — not mine; not Alison's; not even the baby's. From then on, free from any male presence, the house reverted to what it would remain for generations — a house of women.

13

Within days, Nancy was treating us like children again — not in the obvious ways, but in the important areas, so that decisions were made for us, not with us. I did not oppose her, and Alison never attempted any resistance, reverting instead to her usual, placid self. From the evening she returned after seeing Mark, she had altered, and day by day, shrank back from the world. We both watched her carefully.

I went on the weekend trip with Edward, staying at the hotel I had described to my sister, perched high over a pewter lake, but all the time I was there my mind kept creeping back to Alison and the walled house. When I returned, Nancy was in full control, and because of that I genuinely believed that we would be all right — that we would come through.

Yet with Alison's easy compliance, an altogether more sinister side began to emerge. I was watching her from the lounge window as she walked around the garden, her coat buttoned up to her neck, her gloved hands plucking at the bare branches of the apple tree. Under the blunt daylight, her face looked pale, the eyes dark and shadowed underneath. No one would have known she was pregnant; she looked only like a young woman in a winter garden — but she looked older.

Nancy was tidying the room behind me,

197

beating the cushions with her hands.

'Don't you think it's odd that Alison won't talk about the baby?' I asked her, keeping my eyes on my sister.

'Just give her time to get used to the idea.'

'But she seems so . . . unfeeling.'

Curious, Nancy walked over to stand beside me at the window. Alison was sitting on the bench then, her head slightly bowed. I was watching her, and trying to find some part of the confident girl I had so despised; trying to uncover that luminous, brilliant creature, who had dazzled and dazed us over the years; trying to resurrect from the still, little figure a flutter of her huge beauty. She was still lovely — but she wasn't Alison.

'Give her time,' Nancy repeated, moving away.

I doubted that time would bring her back to us.

It was a Tuesday evening when Alison and I talked about the baby. Nancy was out playing bridge, and I was sitting next to my sister in front of the fire.

'It'll be lovely when the baby comes,' I began.

'Yes,' she said slowly, 'when it comes.'

'What are you going to call it?' I asked her, glad that she was at last responding, and taking an interest.

'I'll have to ask them,' she replied, frowning.

'Who, Alison?'

'The child's parents,' she said.

I swallowed hard, and tried to keep my voice steady. 'Alison, this is your child. The baby you're carrying is yours.'

She smiled at me brightly; her beauty breathtaking again. 'Oh no, I'm having it for a friend.'

'Alison, be sensible! This is your child. This child that you are going to have is *yours*.'

Resolutely, she continued to watch the flames.

'No, I'm having it for a friend.'

The flames in front of us burned up quickly with a sudden flurry of red and gold, accompanied by a sharp hiss of smoke up the chimney. A log collapsed, and from its broken pieces, sparks scattered upwards, some clinging to the black soot of the fire back.

'Who is this friend of yours, Alison?' I asked quietly.

'I can't tell you.'

'Well, is it someone I've met?' I pressed her.

'No, it's no one you've met.'

'Has Nancy met them?'

She smiled that deep, secure smile she used when we were children.

'No, but she will.'

It was an unhealthy conversation, which left me panicky and light-headed. Alison appeared to be talking quite reasonably, yet what she said was strange and made no sense. For the first time I glimpsed her slipping into that twilight world of her own making, letting herself fall backwards into a safe retreat from reality.

'What are we having for dinner?' she asked me suddenly, and for a moment I thought she might turn round and wink, to tell me that she had just been pretending — to frighten me. But when I looked at her she was unchanged, and I had to

199

force myself to answer.

'Didn't Nancy make you something to eat before she went out?'

She paused to think.

'Oh yes, I'd forgotten. We had steak,' she said lightly, pulling the rug tighter around her legs, although the room was warm. 'It was good too, very good.'

'What did you have with it?' I asked, wanting to know if she could remember. She was terrifying me.

'Potatoes and beans. Why?'

'Oh nothing, just curious.'

I heard the front door open soon after, and the sound of Nancy throwing her umbrella into the stand. I rushed out into the hallway and pointed to the kitchen. She nodded, and called hello to Alison as she passed the lounge door.

When we were both in the other room I closed the door, and began to explain, even before my grandmother had had a chance to take off her coat.

'Nancy, something's wrong with Alison. Something badly wrong.'

Patiently, she put down her bag on the table and undid her jacket.

'How?'

'She's talking about the baby as if it's not hers. She told me she was having it for a friend.'

'You misheard,' she said confidently, and began to set the table for breakfast, something she did every night before she went to bed.

'I didn't mishear, she said it very plainly, and repeated it later.'

Nancy paused, and jiggled the forks in her left hand.

'Well, she was all right earlier. Perhaps she's having you on.'

'Alison?'

'I'll go in and have a word!' she said, glancing towards the door. 'You finish off in here.'

She was away for nearly ten minutes, and when she came back into the kitchen she looked anxious.

'She's sick, that much is certain. It's probably because she's still in shock.' Idly, she began to drum her fingertips on the table top, the dull sound repeated over and over again.

'Perhaps she'll be better tomorrow,' I suggested, praying that she would; praying that she might return to normal, to Alison again.

'What have you been saying to her?' Nancy said suddenly, a tone of suspicion in her voice.

'Nothing! Why should it be my fault?'

Why indeed?

'Sorry dear, it's just that it's happened so quickly, that's all. I can't understand it.'

Alison went up to bed soon afterwards, talking perfectly normally about a book she had been reading, and about a plane crash which had been on the news. She appeared to be coherent and sensible, and I wondered if she had merely suffered a form of mental block which might not recur. She slept untroubled, although Nancy looked in on her several times, as I did.

'She's fast asleep. Maybe we ought to mention this evening's conversation to the doctor,' she said when I came downstairs.

'Perhaps it would be for the best.'

'My God, I'm glad your mother isn't here to see this — it would have broken her heart.'

She slumped down in the chair next to me and began to pluck at the loose covers with her fingers.

'Nancy, what *would* you have done if this had happened to my mother? I mean, if it had been your daughter, instead of your granddaughter?'

She turned to me and raised her eyebrows. 'Who knows?'

From then on we watched my sister avidly, spying on her movements and conversations, so that Christmas came and left us, tense and stiffened with anxiety. Alison seldom left the house, and made no further references to the baby, although a chance remark on New Year's · Eve brought the matter into very sharp focus.

'Well, Alison, here's to the child who will come this New Year and be another part of this family,' Nancy said, lifting her glass. 'To the baby!'

Alison stopped short, her glass of wine held stiffly in her right hand, her expression wooden.

'But it won't be here this time next year. It will have gone then.'

For an instant, Nancy looked at Alison, dumbstruck.

'Alison,' she said finally, 'don't be silly, this child is here to stay.'

'No,' replied my sister calmly. 'It's only a temporary thing.' Then she smiled and raised her glass again. 'Here's to *our* New Year!'

We swallowed the wine as if it had been Paraquat. I dared not look at Nancy, although

202

she was too preoccupied to notice my reaction. Wordlessly, she drained her glass and went off to get the dinner, tapping Alison lightly on the head as she passed her chair.

We ate and drank that dinner like robots, Nancy and I, and at twelve o'clock we had another toast to let in the New Year, although no one mentioned the baby that time. And Alison, my beautiful sister, Alison, threw back her head and conned both of us into believing that she was normal again. By one o'clock in the morning she was pale and tired, her deep red dress creased round the waist line. Lazily she kissed both of us good night, and went up to bed.

Nancy and I drank the remainder of the wine with our cheese. We picked at pieces of bread and fruit which neither of us really wanted, and talked as people do in dentists' waiting rooms, when their minds are elsewhere. I longed to confide in her, and have her comfort me; longing for her comfort and security, but I spared her that. I had seen the first signs of Alison's deterioration and knew that I had been the cause of it — and I could confide in no one.

The whip hand I had had momentarily over my sister had turned out to be a bitter victory, and had meant nothing. If they found out what I had done there would be no safe harbour, no loving Nancy, no security; only a ruin of what I had prized so much, and jeopardised for my own envy. Alison was the underdog, from then on, people would talk about her and laugh at her, seeing her brought down and deserted. She had been amongst the angels, and had fallen from

203

heaven. And they were bound to enjoy her story even more because she had been the girl with everything.

If she ever found out that her sister had wanted her destruction as much as the rest of them did, it would destroy her.

She had loved Mark; but she had trusted me.

14

Finding my coolness hard to understand, Nancy presumed that it was due to Alison's prolonged stay in the house.

'You don't begrudge her being here, do you?' she asked me. 'It's just that I have to spend a good deal of time with her at the moment. When the baby comes, you will be more involved, but at the moment I have to fuss over her.'

'It's all right, honestly. You have to look after Alison.'

She appeared unconvinced. 'But you seem so . . . withdrawn. I don't want you think that I don't care about you.'

'Oh, Nancy, I know you care about me.' I touched her arm lightly. 'You take care of Alison, that's the right thing to do.'

'If you're sure — '

'I'm sure.'

As I said it, I drew back from her, although it was impossible to pull away from Alison. She was too much a part of me. She teetered on the edge of a wall which I couldn't see, but I knew was there, for her. The wall was high, and very narrow, not unlike the wall which bordered our house, and she ran up and down it every day, sometimes losing her balance, sometimes wobbling, but never, as yet, falling off. It was a wall without an end to it, and on either side there was nothing, only a deep expanse of emptiness. When she got on it she was going nowhere and when she ran along it, there was no finishing post. The wall existed solely in her mind, and the only way I believed that she could not fall off, was if either Nancy or I were holding her hand.

We lived with her imminent breakdown throughout the winter months, the New Year having blown in with wind and hard frosts, making black ice on the roads and deep drifts on the common across the park. The weather sharpened its claws on us, and hissed throughout the long, dark, evenings and bitter nights. Nothing struggled up from under the smouldering snow, and early winter sunlight soon faded beneath a ceiling of low cloud.

I went in and out of Chestnut Walk like an automaton, doing my job efficiently, and leaving on time for home. Edward noticed no change in me, although Anna collared me one evening as I was about to leave.

'You okay?' she asked bluntly.

'I'm fine, why shouldn't I be?'

She shrugged and gave me a letter to post for her husband, but the following morning there was a cake on my desk, which was her way of saying that her thoughts were with me.

So we staggered through January and into February, when Alison began to change suddenly, turning from an amenable person into a difficult, truculent woman. Within weeks the situation became intolerable, and after one particularly uneasy evening when she hadn't uttered a single word to either Nancy or myself,

I rang our doctor and asked that Alison be referred to a psychiatrist for help. He seemed momentarily surprised, and then said that he had thought of suggesting the same thing himself after their last meeting. I let him think I believed him.

He was as good as his word, however, and the following week I took Alison to see a Dr Leggat, who practised in the middle of London's 'medical mile'. My sister was thankfully calm that day.

'I never liked driving, you know,' she said idly, as we stopped at some traffic lights. 'Too many cars on the road, and it's worse here, in the middle of London.'

I turned into Wimpole Street, and luckily found a parking space quickly, getting out and feeding the meter before I helped Alison out of the car. She was dressed in light grey, her long legs looking incongruous in the flat shoes she was forced to wear because her feet swelled. A passerby glanced across to her, probably thinking that this beautiful young woman would have an equally beautiful child. Possibly he thought she was happy.

We walked up to the dark blue door together, and I rang the bell. When it was opened Alison jumped, and appeared to hesitate when she was invited in.

'It's all right. Come on,' I said to her.

She looked at me, smiled, and then followed.

Dr Leggat was tall and well built, with a slippery, easy voice I found difficult to hear. His suit was tight across his stomach and under his

207

chin he had a large brown birthmark. I found him quietly smug.

'Well, now that I've got all the boring, everyday details,' he said, having written down Alison's birth date, and previous medical history, 'we can have a little chat.' He glanced over to me. 'I think you could wait outside. How would that be?'

The words sounded slick, as though they had been well oiled by countless repetition, but I got up obediently and walked out, waiting nearly fifty minutes before Alison reappeared and settled herself down happily with a magazine. When I went back in to talk to Dr Leggat, he was washing his hands, and turned to smile. I wondered why he needed to wash after merely talking to someone.

'Come in, come in,' he said enthusiastically, pointing to a chair opposite his desk. 'Now that I've had a chance to talk to your sister, I think I can say with certainty that she is perfectly well.'

I waited for him to carry on.

'As I was saying,' he continued finally, as though he had expected me to say something, 'she seems a little confused, but then she's had a bad experience and some personalities react in this fashion — blocking out the unpleasant aspects of life in order to avoid facing up to them.'

He stopped, and again I said nothing in response.

'That is my opinion,' he said crisply.

'Will she stay like this?' I asked, and then explained myself further. 'You said she was 'confused' — will she stay confused, or will she get better?'

He smiled confidently. 'She will return to normal after the baby is born.'

'But she keeps saying that it isn't hers, and that she's carrying it for a friend.'

He pulled down the bottom of his waistcoat.

'That is only what she believes now, but when the child is born and it's there in front of her, after she's gone through the birth process — she'll soon respond and take to the baby. It's normal.'

I had a vision of the 'birth process' — almost as though she was going in for a service. One fat young woman popping in one end, and then out the other with a baby. Two for the price of one.

He continued smoothly, 'Your sister is a very beautiful young woman. When she has had the child she will probably return to work and put all these unhappy memories behind her. Is she going to bring up the infant herself?'

'No, the three of us are going to bring it up.'

He looked surprised.

'You and who else?'

'Myself, Alison and our grandmother.'

'Your grandmother?'

'Oh, it's not what you think. Nancy's not old, and besides, she copes better with Alison than anyone else, and she wants this baby.'

'That could cause problems later on between the three of you.'

'Frankly, Dr Leggat, that is the least of my worries. I merely want to get Alison back to normal. Otherwise the rest is academic.'

He looked stung and got up from his seat to indicate that the interview was at an end. 'I think that you have nothing to worry about,' he concluded, holding the door open for me.

Dr Bennington and Dr English thought the same, and told me so, using virtually the exact words that Dr Leggat had. Everyone seemed convinced that Alison was merely in shock and would return to normal as soon as the baby arrived. Even Nancy seemed eager to accept their opinions. Only I remained doubtful.

'They're doctors, Jill, specialists in these matters — If they say she's going to recover, then that's fine by me.'

But if Alison was going to recover after the birth, it left four months until June for her to hover on the brink.

The two of us had repeated rows over little trivial matters, which left Alison tearful and almost childishly apologetic. Nancy coped with her perfectly, being supportive and loving when she was calm, and ignoring her when she was in one of her all too frequent rages. Unless we were visiting doctors, my sister never left the house and never referred to Mark, or to my part in the affair.

Yet when March ended, the bleak and frustrating anger left her also. She became calm again, although she still ignored any reference to the child she was carrying. In other ways, she was practically normal.

'Alison, I thought I'd go to a film tonight in town. Do you want to come?'

She frowned automatically.

'No thanks, Jill. I don't think so. I'd rather stay home. Anyway, it's cold.'

I pushed her.

'Not if you put on some warm things and wrap up well. Come on, Alison, the change will do you good.'

She smiled, her mind made up.

'No honestly, not just now.'

Meanwhile, Nancy was preparing for the child. She bought matinée sets and nappies in their dozens, stacking them up in neat piles in the spare room. She knew that people talked about us, and her reaction was to carry on as normal, putting on a bold face.

'That bloody Fenwick woman! I met her in the chemist's and she said that she'd heard that Alison was pregnant. 'Really' I said, 'I am surprised, she's been pregnant for six months now, you should have heard sooner.''

'They expect you to be ashamed,' I said.

'Well, hell can freeze over before I'll be ashamed of one of my grandchildren.'

But gradually her friends dropped off one by one, or made feeble excuses as to why they couldn't make up bridge parties.

'I couldn't care less,' she said, more times than was necessary. 'If that's the kind of shallow, pea-brained types they are — I'm well rid of them!'

And as the weeks passed, Alison and I spent more and more time together, almost children again. She told me about modelling jobs she had done, and I told her about Chestnut Walk, and Edward, sharing them for the first time. When I repeated the story about the woman who had left her jewellery in the Ladies loo she laughed, throwing back her head as she usually did, her neck smooth and very fragile. But she found after the sixth month that she was physically uncomfortable, and complained bitterly about her back.

'I'll never get used to it, not in a month of Sundays. I can't bear the discomfort.'

'Rub this into your tummy,' Nancy told her, passing some cream. 'And stop moaning. If you use that, you won't get stretch marks.'

She was all commonsense, whilst I provided the mental stimulus for Alison, as bit by bit she rallied, seeming to want to please us more than herself. Then one morning when I got up to get ready for work, I caught her crying. From down the corridor I heard the muffled sounds and made my way to her room. She was sitting up in bed, rocking herself slowly, her arms clenched tightly around her body.

'I love him . . . what am I going to do?' she said softly, her face swollen with long crying. 'Oh God, what am I going to do?'

We had thought she had forgotten him; that she had put him out of her thoughts. We were wrong. She turned to me and wept, clinging onto my arms and sobbing for minutes at a time.

' . . . I still love him . . . I love him.'

She was back on the wall, and falling.

15

When I told Nancy, she was indignant.

'If that bloody man ever comes within ten miles of this place I'll gut him and castrate him — in that order.'

'I thought she'd forgotten him,' I said, more to myself than to my grandmother.

She shrugged and rolled up some pastry savagely. 'No chance, not yet, it's too soon, and besides she's carrying around a constant reminder of him,' she concluded, slapping the top onto a steak pie, and cutting around the edges with a small knife. I glanced away from her, an irrational anger boiling inside, against myself and against Mark. I found that by hating him I could come to terms with my own guilt, and I deftly chose to consider him the more guilty of the two of us.

Nancy looked across to me, her two plump hands round the pastry dish.

'You resigned, or something?'

'Huh?'

'Are you going to work today, or not?' she asked, jerking her head towards the kitchen clock.

'God, is that the time?' I said, getting up and kissing her on the cheek. 'I'll see you later.'

Then a strange coincidence occurred, although in a way I was expecting it, Edward had been in Cambridge, giving a lecture, and had stayed overnight, returning the following morning, just as I arrived at the office.

'Well, good morning, you going out early, or coming in late?'

He smiled a welcome, his weak eyes blinking against the sunlight. 'I gave that talk last night, and it went very well. Come through and I'll tell you all about it.'

I made us both coffee and after he had opened his mail he began a long and very funny account of the previous evening, describing various people and their various wives, several of whom had attended the lecture.

'Then a couple of quite reasonable middle-aged men began to argue at the back of the hall. I couldn't see them clearly, but I could hear them. I stopped and asked them to continue their discussion outside, and they seemed to settle, but after I finished they apparently came to blows in the road.' He clapped his hands together with pleasure, and smiled at the memory. I was sorry I hadn't gone.

'Was anyone we know there?' I asked him.

'No, apart from Cox — you remember him, whippety man with a sweaty upper lip. Talks — very — slowly,' he concluded dragging the words out. 'But I did meet a very interesting newcomer, an American called Mark Ward, he's over here doing some research.'

I kept my voice steady. 'I know the man you mean. You remember when I went to that field dig on your behalf? The one near Oxford?' He looked puzzled. 'Oh, it's quite a while back now, but he was there. He only stayed for the day

214

. . . I wrote about it in my notes.'

'Yes, that's right, I remember now — he came over and found something pretty interesting straight off. Yes, that's the bloke.'

'I thought he had gone back to America,' I said flatly.

'Apparently he comes and goes as he pleases. They give him a free hand, and he's a lucky devil — one of those people who are always in the right place at the right time.'

I wondered if Alison would have agreed with him.

'How long is he staying this time?'

'A few months, I think. He said that he'd just come over from the States, and that he wouldn't be going again for some time. I thought he'd be worth cultivating.'

I couldn't answer, and he continued almost immediately onto another topic. So Mark was back, and I didn't know what to do about his return, whether I should tell Alison, or whether, for once, I should let sleeping dogs lie. My sister was rid of him, and even if she did still love Mark, what was the good of reopening old wounds? The more I thought about it, the more I decided that he should be made to do something — I wasn't sure what, but he should at least know that Alison was carrying his child. He should be told how she had changed; he should be made to face up to what he had done to her.

Finally I had someone onto whom I could transfer all my own anxiety and guilt. A man I could point to and say that he was the one who was really responsible. Mark became my

215

scapegoat, and I decided that he should be made to account for his actions. I was that much of a hypocrite.

So when Edward left that afternoon, I found Mark's telephone number and dialled it, checking first to make sure that the door of my office was shut. There was no answer. Frustration welled up in me — after having steeled myself to ring, he wasn't even there. I waited for another half hour, playing with letters, reading and rereading the print which jumped about in front of my eyes, and then dialled again. He answered on the fourth ring.

'Hello?'

I couldn't think of anything to say.

'Hello? Hello?'

He didn't sound angry, only amused, almost like a person who had expected a trick to be played on them.

'Mark Ward?' I stammered, my mouth chalky with fright.

'Yes, this is Mark Ward,' he paused. 'Can I help you?'

'You should. I mean, yes . . . do you remember Alison Henly?'

There was silence on the line. He said nothing. I said nothing.

'Who is this?' he snapped, all humour gone. 'Is this Alison?'

'Does it sound like her?' I snapped back.

'No. Is she okay?'

'Why? Would that matter to you?'

He toughened instantly. 'Who the hell are you?'

'She's ill,' I replied, ignoring the question.

'Alison?'

'Isn't that who we are talking about?'

He breathed in sharply. 'What's the matter with her?'

'She's ill, because of you,' I said, shovelling all my guilt onto him quickly; my voice rising with indignation.

'Now, just a minute — '

'No, you wait a minute! You left her, dumped her, and she's . . . ill.'

I wasn't prepared to tell him everything over the phone — I wanted to see his face when I told him about Alison's mental state.

'This is hardly any business of yours, whoever you are.'

'I'm her sister.'

'Jill?'

So he had remembered me, or maybe only the name, maybe he only recalled that Alison had a sister named Jill. Maybe he had forgotten the sad, hopeless little lunch we had blundered through, on a blistering summer afternoon.

'Yes that's right, it's Jill,' I replied softly.

'Where is she now?'

'With me and Nancy.'

'Who's Nancy?'

I shook my head at the end of the line.

'That's not important. What matters is that my sister is ill, and you've got to do something.' My voice was rising again.

'Calm down,' he said smoothly.

'Don't tell me to calm down! Have you any idea what it's like to watch someone you love

217

going downhill — day by day?' I didn't give him time to answer. 'She's so beautiful, and you've spoilt her . . . she's frightened and unhappy now, not like she used to be . . . and it's all because of you.'

I was blaming him for what I had done, and all my own anxiety was coming out as I spoke.

'Where are you?'

I stopped suddenly, wondering what he was going to say next.

'At work. Why?'

'Maybe we should meet and talk about this. I mean — what to do about Alison. I can explain.'

I laughed into the phone.

'That's a joke! Or are you being serious, Mr Ward? Are you really going to say something which will explain everything to me?'

His tone was cool; almost arrogant.

'All right, have it your own way — '

I cut in quickly.

'You owe her something.'

'Are you asking for money?'

'My God, you're unbelievable!' I pushed back the hair which had fallen over my forehead. 'No, I'm not asking for money . . . but I will meet you, just so you can explain everything to me.' I took in a deep breath. 'Where?'

'Do you know the pub in Gerrard Row, off Regent's Park?'

I knew it.

'Yes.'

'Meet me there in half an hour.'

With that, he put the phone down.

From Chestnut Walk, it was only fifteen

218

minutes to the pub, which left me exactly a quarter of an hour to compose myself. I looked into the mirror in the cloakroom, and saw that my face was red, that the collar of my dress was creased, and that my make up had almost completely worn off. Carefully I rubbed in some new foundation, and reapplied my lipstick, but when I had finished I merely looked hot, and somehow faded. Collecting my things together in my bag I left the office, calling out to Anna as I closed the front door. I should have taken tea with her that day.

The weather was breezy, even for April. Pieces of paper and old underground tickets blew up from the pavement as I walked, and dry sticks and twigs collected in gutters. The sky clouded over in patches, making little timid threats of rain which never amounted to more than a few drops on the ground in front of me. I walked with my eyes down, my head bent against the dull sky.

The pub was busy, the early evening office staff taking up all of the chairs, and a row of businessmen leaning against the bar rail. The landlord was thick-set and surly, with a face more suited to a bouncer in a strip club than the owner of a fashionable drinking place. Around the walls there were several photographs of well-known personalities, alongside the colours of a much fancied racehorse, and in the corner a log fire blazed cheerfully under a copper hood.

Looking round, I didn't see him immediately, as the chatter and smoke drummed into my ears and eyes, and a low growl erupted from beneath a small table. I bent down and found two amber eyes looking back at me. Obviously, the dog felt as out of place as I did. Stroking his ears, I promised myself that I would stay for only another ten minutes and then if he had not come, I would go. I was just getting to my feet when the barmaid collided with me.

'Sorry!'

'You gave me such a fright,' she began, 'coming up from under that table.' She glanced down. 'Talking to the dog, were you? Well, be careful, he bites.'

She rattled on for a while and I nodded at intervals, watching the door from over her shoulder. It was then that I saw him, his tall figure comfortable and almost arrogantly healthy. At that moment, I wanted to leave — wanted to run out before he saw me — or I wanted to look like Alison. Clamping a smile on my face I moved over to him and wondered if he would recognise me, but when I touched his sleeve and he turned, there was only the faintest hesitation, before he greeted me as a stranger.

'Jill?' he asked me, and smiled.

My heart shifted uneasily; all the old trauma resurrected itself in an instant. His eyes were sharp and very clear, and when he asked me what I wanted to drink, his voice was muted and intimate, for a new acquaintance. He found us two seats in an alcove, well away from the fire so that after a minute or two I was cold, my hands numb. He appeared not to notice the chill and took off his overcoat, draping it idly over the back of his seat. There was an evening paper in the inside pocket.

'I'm glad we met to have this chat,' he began, well used to talking to women, with the easy patter of the man-about-town. 'Now tell me, how is the lovely Alison?'

I wanted to shake him, to knock the complacent smile off his complacent face.

'She's pregnant.'

The smile didn't fade, it stuck, like a bad photograph taken when the subject didn't expect it. He looked nettled.

'Alison?'

I nodded.

'How long?'

'The baby's due in June. Only two and a half months to go.'

'So she's going to have it,' he said stupidly.

'It would seem that way.'

I wondered then why I had been so enamoured of him, and why Alison had been too — he looked so bemused, so uncertain of himself, his hair combed back neatly from his face, his eyes lustreless now that the smile had finally gone.

'I'm married.'

It was a statement which actually said 'I'm not free, sort yourselves out.'

'Oh yes, I know, and so does Alison. If you remember, you told her on your last meeting.'

'I love my wife. We're devoted to one another.' He was floundering, his heady confidence going down the drain like foam after a bubble bath. 'I told her that I could put her in touch with someone who . . . could have helped her out.'

I frowned and put down my glass.

'Experienced as you no doubt are in these matters, my sister wants this baby,' I lied. 'I just wanted you to know that she was in a mess.'

The colour was coming back to his face — he had a very fast recovery rate.

'Does she need anything. I mean, when you said that she was ill — did you mean pregnant?'

'No. I meant that she is really ill. Mentally ill actually — she thinks that she's having the baby for someone else. The doctors said that it's the only way she can come to terms with the circumstances, and that she will return to normal after the baby is born. That's what they said.'

He was paralysed into immobility, which was exactly why I had told him Alison's condition in such a flat, offhand manner. I wanted the full force of the situation to hit him, not through dramatics, but through a quiet statement of the facts.

'You should admit that the child is yours,' I said finally, not expecting him to do anything at all, but merely wanting to frighten him. 'You should pay for its upbringing, at least.'

Then suddenly his expression altered. It was odd — like watching a glove being turned inside out. It was still the same shape, but changed; still a glove, but a different version of that same glove. He shifted his tactics deftly. 'Are you very close to her?'

'Yes, why?'

'She's lucky to have someone like you to depend on.'

He was smiling again, the wide mouth

222

uptilted, the eyes brimming with sympathy. 'You don't look alike.'

I was stung by the remark. 'No, I was always the plain one.'

He sipped his drink slowly. 'No, I wouldn't say plain, more . . . natural looking. I almost feel as though we've met before.'

I felt the full force of the words, and sat unmoving as he rested his hand next to mine on the table, but not touching it.

'You have lovely hands.'

I should have got up then and left, how easy it would have been. Instead I stayed, hearing the voices and the laughter of the other people in the pub hammer inside my head, whilst the man in front of me told me about the various projects he had been on, and made me laugh, which is perhaps the most dangerous ability of all, and within an hour I was caught, hooked, and landed. He appeared to be interested in what I said, and what I thought, although his mind might well have been elsewhere, and he paid me compliments I had waited over twenty years to hear. I was grateful to him — and he knew it.

After we finished our drinks, we went to eat dinner at a place he knew which was quite small and full of people, none of whom were with their legal partners, and it had a heady, faintly disreputable atmosphere. The waiter knew him well, and soon after we arrived a couple came in and stopped to talk to Mark, the woman slim and well-dressed, with a small, nervous mouth. She seemed threatened and uneasy, and when they finally moved away, she looked over her

223

shoulder to him, although he had already continued to eat.

He was glamorous and hopelessly exciting, and when he touched my hand and smiled, I was light-headed and almost giddy with achievement. I wanted to shout out and say 'Look at this wonderful man, who's with me.' I wanted to show Nancy and her friends, and all the other people who had dismissed me as clumsy and incapable of inspiring any feeling other than pity in a man. I wanted them to know — and that was the last thing I could do.

As the evening drew to a close I was sick with misery — one part of me wanting to be rid of him, and the other hopelessly attracted. I understood that he was manipulating me, to try and smooth his path with regard to the baby, and I even suspected that he remembered me from the previous summer, but was too astute to mention it and double the insult. I knew what he was doing, and yet I didn't break away from him, whilst I still could.

At eleven, I told him I had to go.

'No, don't go so soon. Come back for a drink.'

'What did you say?'

'Come back to my flat for a drink, I said.'

He was smiling, his confidence soaring again.

'No, I don't think so,' I said stiffly, and began to collect my things together. 'It's been a pleasant evening, but I only came to tell you about Alison.'

He leaned forwards and clutched my hand. 'Really?'

I turned away, embarrassed, as the waiter

arrived with our coats. Mark paid the bill and I walked on outside, gulping in the night air to steady myself. When I heard his footsteps behind me I did not turn and when he drove me home I asked him to drop me at the end of the road, getting out of the car without saying goodnight. He had understood me better than I understood myself, and I resented the fact. Inside, Nancy was in the lounge waiting for me.

'What happened to you?'

I pulled off my coat and sat down, staring in front of me at the fire. I could have told her the truth, and for an instant I almost did.

'I was working late . . . and then I had dinner with Anna.'

She believed me, and looked back at her newspaper. 'You should have rung.'

'I'm sorry,' I said, tugging at the hem of my skirt. 'How's Alison?'

Pointedly, she ignored the query.

'You girls, honestly I can't keep track of you. You should realise, Jill, that I worry about you, especially since Alison's been ill. I only want to know where you are, and that you're safe.'

'Nancy, I've said that I'm sorry, I won't do it again. Okay?'

Angry, she looked away and continued with her crossword puzzle.

When I went upstairs to see Alison she was already asleep, and I went on into my own room without talking to Nancy again. It was the first time we had argued without making up again afterwards. Once more, the balance had shifted.

In order that this does not seem too fatuous, I

225

have to say that I did try to make an effort not to get involved with Mark; I did attempt to put him out of my thoughts, and tried to resist the temptation of daydreaming about him, I tried to force myself to see him for what he actually was, to realise that he was using me, as he had used Alison. But when the phone rang three days later I was still not prepared.

'I would like to speak to Jill, please.'

I was collecting some files together at the time and as I struggled to answer the call, several slipped onto the top of my desk.

'Speaking.'

'It's Mark. Mark Ward. How are you?'

The files fell haphazardly, some sliding off the far end of the desk and making untidy patterns on the floor. I said nothing in response.

'Are you there?'

'What do you want?' I answered stiffly.

'What should I want? God, you are suspicious.'

'Maybe I have reason to be,' I said quietly. 'Well, what is it?'

'I'd like to take you to lunch, that's all.'

We met a little while later, and I waited until he was sitting down before I began.

'Well, what's all this about? I'm no beauty, so you can't possibly be attracted to me, and I know that this is your way of trying to make sure that there is no unpleasantness about your child. Is it a question of 'Butter up the sister, and all will be forgiven?' Is that it?'

'You are so distrustful,' he said, obviously amused.

'Haven't I a right to be? Look at me — I'm plain, with glasses and legs like a grand piano. What is your game?'

'You interest me,' he answered, smiling.

'Well, you sicken me,' I retorted, seeing him momentarily discomforted.

'Don't say that, I meant what I said. You fascinate me.'

He spoke for a while longer and when he had finished talking I was convinced, or rather the irrational, gullible girl was convinced. He opened up the door on that lovely woman I was inside, making all my fantasies come true within the space of a few sentences. If I had been loved before, I would have been immune, or at least cautious, but as it was, I was too tired of craving for affection to even attempt to resist.

Alison never entered my head, neither did Nancy. I shut them out because that was the only way I could cope with what I was doing. I committed a Solomon's judgement on myself; cutting myself down the middle, so that one half of me slept and lived in the walled house, and the other loved Mark, or perhaps I should actually say, idolised him. But I was not a complete fool, I knew that every time he touched me, he would soon be touching someone else, and that he would leave me also in time. I was watching my sister fall apart in front of my eyes, and if I had ever derived some pleasure from that fall, it was short-lived. After that I slipped down with her.

Many times I tried to call a halt to the affair, and on a couple of occasions I actually rang him

227

to cancel a meeting.

'I can't come tonight.'

'Of course you can, I'll see you in half an hour.'

'Mark — I can't meet you . . . really.'

He breathed in deeply on the other end of the line. 'You want to come, and I want to see you. Jill please.'

And of course, I went.

We met frequently in the afternoons for lunch, and then more often in the evenings, so that I had to begin to make excuses to Nancy for my late returns home.

'Edward wants me to do some cataloguing work for him — for his research — and I thought I'd stay on in town and get it done when the office is quiet in the evening. I'll be back when I've finished, but it might be late.'

Had I been a pretty girl, no doubt Nancy would have been worried. But I was Jill, and therefore she never thought of me in those terms. It was the only time in my life when my plainness was an advantage to me, and I fell into the affair with a willingness and a ruthlessness which would have astonished me, only weeks before.

Meanwhile, Mark was enjoying the piquancy of the situation, and was also let off the hook with regard to Alison's child. He set out to charm and dazzle me because the situation appealed to his vanity, and at first he was thoughtful and considerate, but after a while his attitude changed and he became offhand and thoughtless, knowing that I was committed to him, and that he no longer needed to make any effort to win me over.

We agreed to meet one evening in the same restaurant where we had gone that first night, and several times since. I arrived punctually and, after exchanging a few words with the waiter, sat down expecting Mark to arrive at any moment. Fifteen minutes passed, then half an hour, and that exquisite embarrassment of a person kept waiting crept up on me, and made me first uncomfortable and then acutely distressed. Around me, many couples were talking and laughing, and when I noticed the waiter glance over to me and then turn away I was sick when I saw the look of pity and cynicism in his face. Mark appeared seconds later.

'Where have you been?' I snapped, losing my usual caution. He ignored me and sat down, smoothing his hair with both hands.

'Late at work,' he explained finally, glancing across to a pretty woman on the next table. 'What's the matter with you? You knew I'd be coming eventually.'

'I felt so conspicuous,' I said, already trying to appease him and swallow my own discomfort. 'It doesn't matter now that you're here, forget it.'

He leant back in his seat, and smiled slowly. 'Sometimes, my darling girl, you can be quite a bore.'

I felt the insult and flinched inwardly, although I smiled back at him and coaxed him into telling me about his day. Gradually he unwound, but it was apparent that the novelty of our situation had worn off, and I had too little experience, or beauty, to hold him for long. In those minutes, I began to lose my self-respect, and that, allied to the crushing guilt I was experiencing with Alison, dragged me down inch by inch into some kind of queasy and unsteady limbo. I turned to Mark for the comfort and support I needed from a man, but he was the wrong man.

So in the weeks which followed I tried to mould myself into the perfect companion for him. If I said anything which made him frown, I was immediately contrite; if he asked me to get him things, or find out details for his work, I did it willingly. If he had asked me then to jump off Nelson's Column, I probably would have — because nothing made sense any longer, and besides, I was tired of the struggle.

16

'Do you love me?' I asked Mark for the thousandth time.

'Yes, yes, of course,' he said, and moved away from me quickly.

'Really love me?'

'Jill, I've just said so, haven't I? Stop being so . . . demanding.'

I knew I was irritating him, and yet I continued, ignoring all the warning signs in a rash bid to find out his true feelings.

'But they're only words — '

'What do you want?' he said suddenly, spinning round to face me. 'Should I open a vein or something?' He calmed down quickly, and sat down on the edge of the bed. 'Listen, maybe we should let this rest for a while, and see how things go. We've been seeing a lot of each other lately, and besides I was thinking about going back to the States for a while.'

I sat up.

'When? You never said anything about this before.'

'It's been on my mind for a time.'

'And suddenly this is the right time?' I finished more quietly. 'Don't go, Mark, please — I'll get off your back, honestly.'

'We'll see,' he answered evasively, and left it at that.

Hours later I was back at the walled house,

231

pushing open the gate which led up to the house, and unlocking the front door. Suddenly, I leant back against the wood to steady myself and breathed deeply a few times, until Mark's image had faded and the reality of where I was, and with whom, sank in. Inside, I called out for Nancy.

'In the kitchen,' she replied.

I walked through and put my bag on a chair beside her.

'Sorry I'm so late, the man came to repair the gas cooker at Chestnut Walk, and because Anna is away, I had to stay on.'

She was reading a recipe, and merely nodded to indicate she had heard me.

'Look, I can't talk whilst I'm doing this. Go up and see how Alison is, will you?'

When I got upstairs, Alison was sitting by the window in her room, a pale pink smock covering her large bulk. My stomach shifted uneasily and for the first few moments I could not look at her, although she glanced over to me and smiled.

'Hi.'

'I got you some oranges,' I said, beginning to peel one, and passing the segments to her, one by one. The sun fell through the window and made auburn patches on her hair, although as she moved, the effect faded and the light struck the wall beside her.

'How do you feel today?'

'Not too bad. Okay really.'

She ate daintily, the orangey smell smothering us.

'Nancy's cooking again,' I said, 'though God

232

knows who's supposed to eat all this food. We could be cut off for months and still have enough to feed half of the Russian Army.'

Alison smiled.

'Maybe she knows something we don't,' she began, 'maybe she knows that there's going to be another flood and that the water will fill up outside the house, all around the walls, like a moat. Maybe we'll be stuck here and have to send out pigeons, or doves, to get help.'

'No,' I said, joining in, 'we'd have to borrow Mrs Alder's budgie from down the road, and send him off with a note tied to his leg.'

'If that bird flies anything like she drives, we'll be walled up for life!'

She swallowed the last segment whilst she was still laughing, and began to cough. In the sunlight then, she looked very young.

'Are you working at the office late again tomorrow?' she asked me as I tipped all the orange peel into a bag and crumpled it.

'I'm not sure, it depends on Anna.'

'Is she on a course, or something?'

'Why?'

Alison shrugged.

'She seems to be out so much in the evenings, that's all, and I just thought she might be doing an evening class somewhere.'

I smiled as I lied to her. 'Oh, I see what you mean. No, she has some members of her family over from Malta, and she takes them out in the evenings to see the sights.' I changed the subject quickly and after a moment, relaxed again.

And this was how life continued for weeks; no

one came to see my sister, neither did Nancy invite any of her few remaining friends into the house. We were the only ones who occupied those walls, and we became totally absorbed in one another, as Nancy and I watched Alison for any sign of instability in her. Then my grandmother noticed a difference in me, and tackled me about it one morning before I left for work.

'You look strained.' She peered into my face harshly. 'I think you're feeling the strain more than any of us,' she said, moving away. 'Don't worry too much, everything will turn out fine in the end.'

'I worry about you coping,' I said woodenly.

'Never worry about me, Jill, I can look after myself.' She glanced over to me again. 'Perhaps that boss of yours is overworking you. Maybe you should tell him that you're under some strain at home, and then he wouldn't pile the work on you so much.'

I wanted to tell her everything then, and for a minute the impulse was so strong it was almost physical, a deep ache of unhappiness.

'Nancy — '

'Pass me that spoon, thanks,' she said, and then looked over to me absent-mindedly. 'Were you saying something?'

The moment had gone.

'No, nothing,' I said, and turned away.

At night, when the house was quiet, I walked around downstairs, opening windows and breathing in the cool air, letting it chill me. I seldom turned on the lights, and at those times I thought of Mark. Then, one evening as I sat by the window, the phone rang.

'Hello?'

'Jill? It's Mark, how are you?'

I dropped my voice, listening for sounds upstairs, or for the click of the extension phone in Nancy's room.

'Mark, I've asked you never to ring me at home. It's not fair.'

His voice was peevish. 'Suit yourself. I just wanted to talk to you, that's all.'

But that wasn't all. He was actually testing his hold over me, because I had been less than loving the last time we had talked. He knew how difficult it was for me to explain away a mysterious phone call in the middle of the night — and that was why he was doing it — to make sure that I understood the rules of the games. If I wanted him, I had to learn not to be irritating, otherwise he could make life very unpleasant indeed.

How I kept my sanity it is impossible to guess, or maybe I was so committed to all three I could never have been parted from any one of them. I missed Nancy's warmth and her closeness, and suffered bewildering guilt about Alison's mental state — but even these reasons did not give me sufficient incentive to leave Mark. I longed for the man I thought he was, for that figure I built and breathed life into in the early hours; I longed for the concern I pretended he could provide; for the gentleness, the love, and the stability. I gave him kindness when he was cruel; and thoughtfulness when he was selfish, and developed a

235

second form of short-sight, an emotional blurring of vision which prevented me from seeing him as he actually was. I could even forget that he was married, sometimes, if I tried very hard. So blinkering myself from the present, I lived day to day.

Then, with the first days of May, the heatwave began, making the garden parched within a week, the ground baked and cracking under a high sun. Every night, Nancy and I watered, talking as we used to, only this time there was no closeness — that much had gone. Cuttings she had planted only weeks earlier, shrivelled and dried up in the hot air, and by afternoon the sky was heavy with insects and white light. People said the weather was freakish and wouldn't last. Journeys home in the car left me breathless and red-faced, the heavy frames of my glasses slipping down the bridge of my nose. Hot air from the engine rose up to form a peculiar heat haze in the traffic jams, and under the noon sky, people jostled for shade and drank from beer cans.

I arrived at Mark's flat, just as the sun had gone down and the air was mercifully cool. He opened the door and smiled his professional smile.

'Welcome, come on in. I was just thinking about you,' he said, stepping back to let me enter.

He had opened all the windows, so that the smell of night air and moisture came into the room and hung around us. The apartment was not large, it had no need to be, and consisted

236

merely of a kitchen, bedroom and bathroom, with a large reception room looking out onto an enclosed square below. If I stood on the balcony, I could see straight across the square to the houses on the other side. There was a harp in one window, a huge, gold harp which no one ever played — it just stood there, day after day, as incongruous as a ship's figurehead in a desert.

'Are you well?' Mark asked me, kissing my neck lightly. He never asked about Alison any more. We never mentioned her.

'Yes, I'm fine.'

I laid my head on the side of the wooden window frame, expecting it to be cool, but the paint was hot and felt strange against my skin.

'I've been busy at work,' he volunteered, pouring himself a drink. I refused one. 'Come and sit here, next to me.'

I can't remember what else he said, only that for a split second then I no longer loved him. Oh yes, I was still besotted by him, still fascinated, but the love had gone. I wanted to leave, but the effort was too great, and instead I stayed and pretended to myself. From that moment on, I needed Mark not as a prop, but as an excuse. I needed to kid myself that I loved him deeply, otherwise how could I have done the things I had? How could I have lied to and betrayed Alison, and deceived Nancy. How? Unless I loved the man.

So when he talked, I listened, and when I left later that night, much later, I waved and looked up to his window from the square outside. He stood on the balcony and smiled at me, and I responded, tilting my face up to the street light before turning away briskly, the tears burning behind my eyes.

17

The weather continued to bleach us; smouldering under roofs and making furnaces out of parked cars. The birds grew listless also, and hung about in little discontented groups in the branches of trees, the leaves only offering indifferent shade from the early summer frenzy.

Alison took walks again in the evenings when the worst of the heat was gone, her large body on its fine legs, shifting from wall to apple tree, from apple tree to house, as she hummed to herself, in that tuneless, discordant fashion children adopt. Her refusal to talk about the baby continued and her mental state veered from silent rage to a happy, almost giddy light heartedness, which was not natural. We watched her constantly, and now and again, I talked to Nancy about the child.

'What about its education?' I asked her.

'It will go to school, what else?'

'Under which name?'

She frowned. 'I see what you mean — my name or yours?'

She hadn't understood what I meant at all.

'It will be difficult for the child without a father,' I persisted.

'Oh, I don't know,' she said, pushing me out of her way in the kitchen. 'It'll have three mothers, after all.'

I kept asking questions in order to force her to reassure me, and although she didn't understand her function, she fulfilled the purpose constantly.

'But what about the christening? Will they let it be christened in church?'

'Why ever not?' she replied, genuinely surprised.

'Because it's got no father.'

'So what does that make it — the Anti-Christ?' She smiled at me, genuinely amused. 'You worry too much about everything. When the baby comes all this will fall into place. Alison will come to her senses, and the child will settle with the rest of us, and the pressure will be off you.'

'And you? You're the one we all lean on — who looks after you?'

'You will, when I get old.'

She seemed to get all her energy and strength from the simple fact that we needed her, just as we had done as children. It was no effort for her, this continuation of her role, she was only hurt by other people's attitudes, and when she could no longer stand Mrs Edwards' unsubtle remarks, she fired her.

The woman left with a great deal of muttered complaint, saying something about having been with us for many happy years, although that was merely a figment of her imagination. She pulled her apron off the back of the cupboard door in the porch, and ripped the neckline as she did so. I think she felt cheated, having been thrown out before the baby came.

'I couldn't stand her a minute longer,' Nancy explained, 'she was always behind me, or watching Alison. I'm sure it must have got on her nerves.'

'Nothing seems to get on Alison's nerves,' I said quietly, wishing something would force a response out of her.

'Oh, I don't know about that. It's in her expression more than anything else, the look in her eyes. It's tiring, though, having to think for her.'

If Nancy found Alison's mental state tiring, I found it terrifying. I came home and sat by her as she watched the television, or listened to music, and when she did talk I held my breath and almost prayed that she would be coherent.

'I've been thinking,' she said suddenly, heaving herself upright in the chair, her fine arms straining with the weight.

'About what?'

'About Nancy. It's her birthday next week and I think we should give her a party, or something.'

I was stunned that she hadn't noticed that no one came to the house any longer, that Nancy's friends had dropped off like November leaves. Tactfully, I tried to explain. 'She's spending most of her time with us, at the moment.'

'That's all the more reason why we should give her a party.'

'I think that she would like to have a big meal with us — just the three of us.'

'No.' She frowned. 'That would be like every other day.'

'Not if we made it special.'

'Like how?'

I had her interest at last: she leant forward, her face animated.

'We could eat outside, with umbrellas and

241

exotic foods, and I could get some lamps for the garden.'

'Yes, yes,' she said eagerly, her eyes following mine. She was caught up in the idea and her plans for the big party vanished.

From that night on, until Nancy's birthday, we plotted, deciding what we would do. I came into the house each night with packages which I rushed upstairs much to the annoyance of my grandmother, whose curiosity was eating at her. There was something in the attics I wanted and, after seeing that Alison was asleep, I climbed upstairs to find Nancy there, heaving at a stack of boxes.

'What are you doing?'

'It occurred to me today that this is the ideal place for Alison and the baby. It's two separate rooms, after all, and private from the rest of the house, and it has the best views.'

I looked round. 'It's also dusty and in need of decorating.'

Nancy straightened up.

'I knew you would say that, so the decorators are coming in after the weekend.' She smiled and put her hands on her hips. 'Now what do you think?'

I moved under the slanted roof and thought back to when Alison and I had been children there, smelling the familiar scent of wood and dust. Above my head, the skylight shuddered under the heat, and the handle hung down haphazardly, casting its shadow on the floorboards below. There were some fragments of old curtain left from our time, faded and eaten with

sunlight, their pattern obliterated under countless summers, and when I glanced across I could
see the faint mark of the witch, still there in the
wallpaper, although it had not rained for almost
two weeks.

I turned back to Nancy. 'It needs some bright
wallpaper to cheer the place up.'

She sat down on the edge of a tea chest,
making it creak ominously

'It's as hot as hell up here,' she said, dabbing
at her face with a handkerchief. 'Yes, you're
right, something yellow or pink would be nice.'

Sunlight exploded on the floorboards, and
made patterns in the early evening air. The dust
throttled me.

'Can't we open some windows?'

Nancy shook her head. 'All glued up with
paint years ago.'

The sun caught the side of her face, and on
her top lip was a faint trace of perspiration. Idly,
she yawned and flapped a hand ineffectually in
front of her mouth. 'I'm exhausted, it must be
the heat.'

After a few moments we began to move the
remaining boxes, stacking them neatly so that
the workmen could move around more easily. It
was nearly ten o'clock when I finally pulled the
door closed behind me, a wave of nostalgia,
homesickness even, flooding me. I believed that
after the men had been, nothing of our
childhood would remain, that the rooms would
take on other lives, and somehow obliterate
mine.

Then later, as Nancy did her crossword

puzzle, I longed so much to touch her hand, or move closer to her, knowing that if I did so she would hug me and restore us to where we had previously been. But I couldn't let her close to me, because if I did I would weaken and confide in her. I missed her.

The following weekend, Mark went away, telling me at the last moment, when his plans were made. He said that the trip was for work, and I was too terrified to press the matter. I had learnt to keep my place; and when he returned his mood was cheerful and intimate, acting as though he was genuinely pleased to see me again. When he touched me I was almost dizzy with relief, and at the end of the evening I was reluctant to leave him and return home. When I did get back, I was silent and uncommunicative, so much so that Nancy snapped at me.

'And you can stop sulking, girl, I've got one in the house and that's enough. Get a grip on yourself.'

'I wasn't sulking.'

'Well, I don't know what you call it, but to me it's sulking.' She stopped shouting and passed me a pile of nappies. 'Count those for me.'

The attic rooms had been finished, and were resplendent in pale pink. Pigeons flapped on the roof outside, and in the smaller of the two rooms the bars on the windows had been painted with shockingly white gloss paint. Even with the windows open, the smell of it cloyed in the hot atmosphere, and peeled down the stairs into the rest of the house, making excursions even as far as the kitchen. In my room I had hidden the bits and pieces for Nancy's birthday, and that night I made the final preparations for our meal the next day.

The following morning Alison and I laid out the table in the garden carefully, drawing all the curtains around the back of the house so that Nancy couldn't see what we were doing. Alison was almost herself again, and when I heard her chatting I could imagine her as she used to be — until I turned around and saw her bulky figure with its uncomfortable, unsteady walk. Guiltily, I moved away from her.

We called Nancy out at eight in the evening, the huge umbrella over the table providing shade from the still-present sun. She flung her arms around each of us in turn, squeezing us hard, her face hot with pleasure.

'What a treat! What a wonderful surprise!' She turned to Alison. 'Did you help Jill with all of this?'

My sister nodded and loaded herself heavily into her chair, the fine material of her summer dress shifting slightly as she moved.

'Well done!' Nancy said again, winking at me. 'Makes a change — not having to cook for once.'

The daylight dimmed gradually, and a red sky pooled under a bank of turquoise cloud. Birds settled in the trees and bats hovered over our heads, making dives into the still air. I lit the candles in the garden, the large, upright candles which burned brightly and threw their light over the black lawn and up to the foot of the wall. It was warm until late, and we chatted easily and comfortably into the still air. I wanted so much

245

to hold onto that evening, to clamp down a huge glass dome over the garden and the house and the three women who were sitting there, talking under the trees.

Slowly the night settled in on us and made us indolent, and when the first hard drops of rain fell onto the table we all looked up before gathering together the dishes and dashing for the shelter of the house. Within seconds, the candles were extinguished and the water banged on the roof and rushed in through the open windows before we had time to close them.

'Go on up, Alison, I'll look in on you later,' Nancy called out, over her shoulder.

'You sure? I should help you tidy up,' she replied quietly, her face deadly pale.

'I'm sure, go on, I'll see you later.'

After Alison left, there were just the two of us, hurrying from room to room, banging windows against the thunder and lightening which had followed the first rain. When we finished, Nancy moved back into the kitchen and I followed her.

'You are not to wash the dishes tonight. That's my prerogative,' I said, taking the dishtowel from her hands.

For a long minute she looked at me, and I read something in her eyes which was a plea for my confidence. Unsettled, I glanced away and in response she pecked me silently on my cheek and left.

And of course, I was still seeing Mark. For a time he behaved kindly, after his trip, seeming refreshed and invigorated, and presented me with a pair of earrings which I wore constantly

246

when I was with him, and slipped into the zip compartment of my handbag when I went home. I tried to improve how I looked to please him, spending money on clothes which didn't suit me, or trying to alter my hair to make something out of the face and figure I was born to.

'You have lovely hands,' he said, turning them over in his own, and I knew that he meant it, but they were just hands, and only such a little part of a whole person. I still longed for the exaggerated compliments men pay to their women, and I learnt how to cover disappointment — the fine art of smiling when I felt as though I had been kicked in the teeth; or feigning indifference when he said something hurtful; flattering him to make him the good companion — the man of every woman's dreams.

'You look tired,' he said to me, staring hard into my face. 'You should put some more make-up on . . . do something.'

My face reddened with embarrassment and hurt.

'I do . . . I'm tired, that's all. Don't nag me, please.'

He smiled sardonically, no humour in the expression at all.

'I don't nag you, that's your speciality,' he said spitefully and leant back in his seat.

'I love you, whatever you say,' I told him, and the dull, hard look on his face altered, softened perceptibly.

'Sorry, sweetheart. You look just fine.'

It was absurd to let myself be bated and

thrown from one mood to another, I should have had more sense, more self respect, but I didn't. I had him, and that was enough, and I clung on.

In the mornings I set off for Chestnut Walk and Edward, filing papers and making phone calls about various digs. It was peaceful and serene there, and very safe. Later I returned to the walled house and Nancy, to Alison who was disturbed and tense, now that the birth was no longer that far away. And in the back of my mind, constantly, unerringly, was Mark.

Three different places; three different sets of people; three different ways of behaving for three different reasons. I spun around them all like a painted horse on a carnival merry-go-round, only the music had stopped a while back and I could no longer get off.

The rainstorm had been only an intermission and as May left us, June blistered in, full of hot sun and long, dry days. The atmosphere in the house altered too, becoming calm and impassive, and Alison remained mostly in her room, her cheerfulness on Nancy's birthday now replaced by a disjointed, detached attitude. We tried to encourage her to talk about the baby but there was no response, and every mention of it saw her sliding further away. Doctors, health visitors and every other expert said she would return to normal, but the days yawned out towards the birth and we tightened inside ourselves, each one of us, and waited.

If I had stopped and thought for a moment, if I had possessed that much sense, or love in me, I could have shocked myself into normality.

248

Perhaps on one of those breathless, airless evenings when I lay beside Mark, I might well have stepped back and seen him for what he was, and loathed him as he deserved. But by loathing him, I judged myself.

'Alison?' I said to her when I got back, pushing open her bedroom door a fraction. 'Are you awake?'

I knew she wasn't. I could hear her steady breathing in the quiet room.

'Alison, I'm sorry, so sorry . . . I'm so sorry.'

Outside, an owl hooted.

18

'Mark, I care about you so much, so very much . . . ' I said stiltedly, hoping that the words would have the desired effect, and pull his attention back to me. He turned round, smiled and touched my face with the tips of his fingers. He had the look of a man who had been told the same thing many times.

We knew that Alison's pregnancy was nearing its end, and neither of us had the courage to mention it. Oddly, the situation between us changed, and Mark became the more tormented, and needed me because my presence absolved him of some of his own guilt. Looking at me, he appeared less bad, and we existed together like two thieves, lacking in both love and honour, and because of that a deep bond cemented us.

'What would I do without you, hey, funny face?' he said.

I smiled back in response, pretending at some cosiness, and leant my head against his shoulder.

'You'd be lost,' I replied, not knowing if I really meant it.

He had changed. Now when I met him, he got up and kissed me openly, making a statement of his affection, and our complicity. He was not curious about the child itself, but about this continuation of himself, and it fed his vanity. I saw the alteration in him, and found that our meetings were less exciting than before, and that

250

the overhanging threat of the birth did what I found impossible to do — it relegated Mark to second place.

I longed for the baby with a passion, believing that Alison would return to her normal self and go back to modelling after a little time had elapsed, leaving Nancy to do most of the child rearing. As for Mark, I never expected him to step forward and provide for the child, even though he had no other children, and plenty of money. It was too much of a commitment for a man like him to make. It implied that he was dependable, trustworthy, and reliable — all the things he was incapable of being. His charm lay in the fact that he was outside the domestic restrictions of other people, and could circle the globe like some ageing Peter Pan, until age, or illness, caught up with him.

The heat persisted, and at work flies droned against the windows, and wriggled on the warm ledges when they fell. Plants withered and died in the windowboxes, and inside the office, the air hummed with the sounds of traffic. Edward took on less and less work, disliking having to travel in the heat, and continued with his various theses, so that there was little for me to do, and less for Mrs Wren.

'I wonder how long this will last?' I asked her, jerking my head towards the sunblasted window.

'Not long, it can't at this rate. It'll burn itself out soon,' she replied with total conviction, her hair making damp patterns on the back of her neck.

And in the walled house, we all waited for the

251

child to be born. Sometimes the temperature in the rooms reached the high eighties, and Alison lay on her bed, moving around slowly, her face a little bloated in the heat, her skin shining. I drew the curtains for her, and put a fan by her bedside, but she appeared not to notice.

Those days seemed endless; beginning hot and ending in a welter of insects and dust stirred up from the garden. Clocks wound down the interminable minutes, and even the trees began to flag and wither under the overblown sun. Nancy and I built a fire, and burnt a pile of rubbish, watching as the smoke columned upwards, not a breath of air to disturb its passage. I glanced across to her, noticing that she looked strained, her skin slack and reddened by the fire.

'Are you all right?' I asked.

She straightened up immediately.

'Fine . . . Do you know what everyone will be saying about us?' she asked, and I glanced at her, alarmed. 'They'll be saying that we're mad to light a bonfire on a night like this.'

I laughed with relief, and watched as the papers ignited, the white leaves curling and browning where the flames touched them.

'Nancy, do you think the baby will be a boy or a girl?'

'A girl, I think,' she answered, wiping her face with a handkerchief. 'Go and look at Alison, will you? I'm going for a shower.'

When I got to my sister's room, she was lying on her right side, so that her back was towards the door. Although she must have heard me, she did not move when I walked in.

'Hello, Alison.'

She turned slowly, the heat making her clumsy.

'I was thinking about a job I did in Florence. The shots were so good they used most of them, and said I was the best model they had ever had.'

'It was the truth,' I responded, unsettled.

'Yes, probably, although people don't always tell you the truth, do they?' she said, turning away from me and back to the wall. After a moment I left, a deep thumping of unease sounding in my stomach.

All the curtains were drawn in Nancy's room, making the place look like an old sepia photograph. She had just showered and was wrapped in a yellow towelling robe, her radio playing from the bathroom. The atmosphere was strange and heady.

'It's hot,' I said flatly.

'Have a bath then, it'll make you feel better,' Nancy suggested, brushing her hair back vigorously. 'Are you going to work tonight?'

I looked down at the carpet; there was a fly walking over the pattern.

'No, not tonight.'

'Good. You know, I do sympathise with you, having to work in this heat. It must be murder.'

I wanted to leave because I knew that if I stayed there any longer I would tell her everything. Yet oddly, I stayed, and tempted fate.

'You must spend some more time with us when the baby's born,' she said, still fiddling with her hair. 'I'll need some help.'

253

'Yes, yes, of course.'

'You're not still worried about your sister, are you?'

'She's so young,' I said stupidly, desperate to confide, to tell her and have done, and accept the consequences.

'Don't worry, I'll take care of her,' Nancy said. 'Besides, I was a year younger than Alison when I had your mother. She will be okay.'

Without warning I began to cry, and Nancy, thinking that I was crying for my sister, got up from her dressing table and comforted me. 'Now stop that. I've told you that everything will be fine. Would I lie to you?'

The words were already on my tongue, the words which were about to tell her everything, when the door swung open and my sister walked in. Nancy released me, and went over to her.

'How's things?' she asked, putting her hand on Alison's forehead.

'I feel terrible.'

'Any pain?' Nancy asked, her face anxious.

'No, nothing like that. I just don't feel well.'

Gently, Nancy slid her arm around my sister and helped her back to her room. After a moment I heard the sound of running water and the hum of their low voices. It was ten minutes later when Nancy reappeared. Ten minutes in which I had not moved.

'She's not too bad, but I'll ring the doctor in the morning, just in case. Now,' she said quietly, 'what were you going to tell me?'

I hesitated for only an instant. 'Nothing. Nothing important, Nancy.'

She patted my arm and smiled, and I left for my own room. Later, I tried to sleep but it was no longer possible — Alison had unnerved me. I was certain that she knew something, and if she knew, Nancy would soon. I stared up at the ceiling and for a time I dozed, suddenly jumping up, my heart banging. I was sure something had woken me, and yet as I strained for the sound of voices, I heard nothing and turned back into sleep, the covers fell off my bed, and around the bedside light, moths battered and bruised their wings on the silk shade.

I dreamt I was a child again, and that the high wall which surrounded the house was falling down, stone by stone. My grandfather ran out, holding up his hands against the crumbling stonework which remained. I called out to him to stop, but he couldn't hear me, and when I ran to get Nancy I found that she was already in the garden trying to help him, and that the stones were falling on both of them.

I woke quickly, my mouth dry with fright; and from far away I could hear the sound of someone screaming. I thought I was still dreaming, but then with horror I realised that the noise was coming from down the hall — from my sister's room.

19

It was the nineteenth of June and the baby was coming early. Nancy rang for an ambulance and it came within minutes, the men lifting Alison onto a stretcher and then into the back of the vehicle, where we joined her. Her face was stiff with fear, and she grabbed Nancy's hand and held on, her knuckles white.

When we got to the hospital, two nurses descended on Alison and wheeled her into a room off the main delivery room, telling us to wait in the hallway.

'I'll do no such thing,' Nancy began firmly. 'She's on her own and she needs some moral support.'

'Are you her mother?' the nurse asked, eyeing her with ill-disguised impatience.

'I'm her grandmother.'

She sighed audibly. 'We don't usually like people to sit with the mother, unless it's the father, of course. It would be better if he was here.'

'That's what we've been saying for months,' Nancy responded drily.

The nurse blushed as the inference sank in and, wrong-footed, she agreed to let my grandmother sit with Alison. Nancy came over to me before she went through.

'Now listen, if I can get you in there I will, but don't rely on it. Alison needs me because I know what she's going through.' She stroked my hair gently. 'Don't worry, or try not to, at least. Wait for me here.'

Then she walked off, her large figure erect, the full impact of her personality dwarfing the nurse. I sat in the hallway and waited.

It was five o'clock in the morning and the wards were quiet. Now and then someone coughed, although from where I was sitting I couldn't tell if it was coming from the nurses' room, or from the wards. On the right, there was the maternity wing, and on the left, a large room in which there were two rows of cribs, like a massive nursery. A young nurse was sitting and writing at the far end. She wrote constantly, only glancing up every few minutes before continuing. A large clock hung on the wall over her head, the second hand circling the white face evenly. Not one of the babies cried.

After a while I couldn't sit still any longer and walked down the passageway awkwardly, like one of those stiff, wooden ducks in a shooting gallery. The double door which led to the delivery room was closed and although I glanced over frequently, Nancy did not reappear.

The silence became oppressive and somehow unnerving, so that my imagination soared as the stillness and warmth of the hospital soaked into me. I kept running over what Alison had said, terrified that she might tell Nancy, terrified that my sister was suffering. Then suddenly, the hospital curled into life, and large trolleys with tea materialised from the kitchens, coming out of lifts and clanking down the passageways with a huge explosion of sound. It was six fifteen. The few nurses who had been on night duty were relieved by the influx of the day staff. A baby began to cry.

Spotting me in the corridor, a small, very dark nurse came over to me. She was part oriental, and spoke slowly, her smile fresh.

'Good morning. I believe it is your sister in the delivery room.' She glanced down at her notes. 'A Miss Alison Henly — is that right?'

I nodded and wondered why she had to mention the 'Miss'.

'She came in just before five,' I told her and then realised that she already had the details. 'How is she? I mean, no one's told me anything since then.'

There was a label on her uniform which said 'Nurse Cho,' and a small watch hung from her top pocket.

'First babies take their time, I shouldn't worry too much,' she said kindly. Everyone was telling me not to worry. 'I'll pop in for you and see how she's doing.'

I thanked her and she moved off down the corridor. She had a doll's tiny body, and slim, slightly bowed legs.

It took her ten minutes to return, and when she did, she looked apologetic.

'I'm sorry I was so long, but I've been in now and your sister is doing well. There's still a long way to go,' she added. 'Have you eaten this morning?'

'No. I never thought — '

'There's a café downstairs, or a machine at the

258

far end of this ward, through those swing doors.' She pointed out the way for me. 'You could get some coffee and a sandwich perhaps.'

I nodded and set off, although I wasn't too hungry. I did it more for something to do, rather than a genuine need. On either side of me, people were milling about, mothers were yawning and getting themselves to the bathrooms, and a few hovered in the corridor, looking through the window into the nursery. A tall coloured woman, obviously pregnant, passed me and smiled, and as I pushed open the swing doors, a porter was coming in with a patient in a wheelchair.

The coffee machine gobbled up three of my coins and gave me nothing in return. I glanced round, and then thumped it vigorously on its side, hearing a dull thud and the slow grinding process of coffee being made. Whilst I sipped the coffee, I noticed there was a public call box in the corner, and walked over. After finding some more change, I dialled and waited for the call to be connected.

There was a muffle on the line, and I had to strain to hear.

'Anna, is that you?'

'Who's this?'

'It's me. Jill.'

'Jill? Why you ring so early?'

I looked at my watch — it was six-thirty. I had thought it was much later.

'Sorry, Anna, I'm a bit mixed up . . . Listen, can you give Edward a message from me? Tell him I can't get in today, and that I'll explain when I see him.' I paused, but she said nothing. 'Anna — have you got that?'

'Sure, sure.'

'Tell him I'll ring later.' I added. 'Sorry if I woke you.'

'It's okay, I was already up. I tell him — don't worry.'

She rang off without saying goodbye, and I hesitated for a while wondering whether or not to make the next call. I drank the remainder of my coffee and threw the plastic cup into a large, green bin which was full from the previous night. I dialled slowly, Mark answered on the third ring, his voice thick with sleep, the American accent more pronounced.

'Hello?'

'It's Jill.'

'Are you okay?'

'I'm fine, but Alison's having the baby.'

There was a long pause at the other end.

'Which hospital?'

'Why? Are you going to send flowers?' I snapped.

'Is she . . . coping?'

'If that means 'is she back to normal?' I can't tell you. They brought her in at five and I haven't seen Nancy since. She's with her. The nurse just said what they always say — 'doing fine, don't worry.' I can't tell you anymore.'

'How are you feeling?' he asked softly, all the old concern flooding back.

'You can imagine.'

I hung onto the phone and said nothing else, and for a time he was also silent. Neither of us had anything to say, and neither of us wanted to sever the connection. I spoke first. 'I'll let you know how things go.'

'I love you,' he said suddenly.

'What?'

'I said that I loved you,' he repeated patiently.

My eyes filled with a mixture of anger and frustration. 'So why tell me now? Why?'

'Jill, listen to me — '

I slammed down the receiver and walked back to the corridor, and after ten minutes I was calm enough to think rationally. Mark had obviously been half-asleep, or caught off-guard — he must have been, otherwise he would never have said something like that, especially at such a time. He was not the type of man who told women he loved them, not spontaneously, at least, that led to commitment and promises for the future — a future he tried consistently to leave open. He had threatened his own freedom, and I couldn't understand why.

When Nancy re-emerged, she was chalky with tiredness, and sat down heavily beside me.

'She's terrified, they've given her painkillers and tried to calm her, but she's bordering on the hysterical.' She pushed back her hair with both hands. 'I just thought I'd come out and have a word with you.'

The material of the thin summer dress she was wearing was badly creased across the front from where she had been sitting for so long. I got her some coffee and a sandwich, which she ate fiercely, and then heaving herself to her feet, she went back to the delivery room.

261

The early morning escalated into a summer day and by nine, the cool corridors were warming up quickly, the steady increase of heat snaking along the passages and up the stairwells. Light poured through the windows, so that the nurses drew the blinds half way down, making the hospital look cooler, although the temperature remained the same. A few flies idled around the high ceilings, and the sister in charge turned on some fans in the corridor. They hummed tunelessly.

'Miss Henly?'

I spun round to see the Chinese nurse smiling at me. 'Your sister is in the last stages of labour. I thought you might like to know.'

I thanked her and waited.

The time swelled, just as the heat did, and a few babies cried out loudly into the spellbound air. I thought of ringing Mark again, and decided against it. I understood then why he had said he loved me — he was frightened. He was utterly and completely terrified that he might lose his hold over me, that someone else — like Alison's child — would take over the premier role in my affections. I knew he was manipulating me again, and yet still at the base of my heart I wanted to believe that he genuinely loved me. I was still that much of a fool.

Suddenly behind me, there was a crash, and a large trolley with various types of equipment was rushed into the delivery room, closely followed by an empty incubator. I jumped to my feet and paced the corridor, whilst a man in a gown hurried out and knocked me aside, apologising as he rushed back. I began to sweat.

The dial on the clock face in the nursery pulled itself round the hour, and in my imagination I thought I could hear ticking. Suddenly it became the clock at home, the old one which worked only intermittently; and under the sound of the ticking was the voice of Mark, telling me that he loved me. I shook my head but the noises remained, and as I staggered towards my seat I could see Nancy in the kitchen, and Alison, turning to smile, as she watched the firelight.

The Chinese nurse was sympathetic as she helped me to my feet. 'It's the heat, you know. So many people faint in this heat, and besides, you must be worried about your sister.'

I struggled to get my bearings, and then knelt down, fumbling for my glasses on the tiled floor.

'Here you are,' the nurse said, handing them to me, 'I took them off for you. It would have been a pity to break them.'

I accepted them from her gratefully, putting them on and bringing her face back into focus, before standing up very slowly.

'You should eat something, that would help,' she suggested, walking away and coming back in a moment with a sandwich. I rummaged in my bag for the money with which to pay her, but she shook her head. 'No charge — someone gave them to me in the kitchen.'

The bread was very white and looked almost blue in the hospital light, but as I ate, I began to feel better and thanked her again.

'You see, sometimes all it takes is a bite to eat.

Even from the hospital kitchen!'

She moved away then, and I was just beginning my second sandwich when I heard a short scream, a quick, deep stab of pain which I recognised as being a distorted version of Alison's voice. I pushed the food inside. The first cry was not repeated, and as I sat there I begged God that she would be all right, that she would survive, making impossible promises to heaven, clenching my eyes shut, and holding my breath for seconds at a time to try and stop the mounting panic. From out of a side ward, a woman came over and sat beside me. She was wearing a suit which looked too hot for the time of year, and her hair was greasy and lay flat against her head.

'Are you waiting for news as well?' she asked, her voice low pitched, the trace of a faint Edinburgh accent apparent in the vowels.

'My sister's having a baby,' I replied tonelessly.

She opened her handbag and took out a bag of sweets, offering me one. I refused. She unwrapped her own quickly, screwing up the brightly coloured paper and pushing it into her pocket. The toffee made a lump in her cheek.

'You been here long?'

'Since this morning,' I said, and crossed my legs, trying to imply that I didn't want to continue the conversation.

'I saw you faint,' she confided, and then corrected herself. 'Well, I didn't actually see you — I heard. The foreign nurse said you'd passed out.'

'It was the heat,' I said uncomfortably.

264

'Well yes, it would be, wouldn't it?' she said, sucking on her toffee thoughtfully. Her bottom teeth were darker than the top set. 'Is this her first?'

'Sorry?'

'Your sister — is this her first child?'

'Yes, her first,' I said and turned to look at the delivery room. The doors were still closed.

'Always a trial, the first one.'

I ignored her.

'I've had three. Quite an expert now. Is she wanting a boy or a girl?'

'It doesn't matter.'

'But I bet the father wants a boy — they all do.'

'He doesn't care,' I said stiffly.

The woman stopped chewing and shifted round in her seat to face me. 'Doesn't care? What sort of a father is that?'

'The absent sort,' I said rudely and stood up.

Faintly, I could hear the sound of a woman moaning, followed by several quieter voices and the strong tones of Nancy rising above the rest. She was talking to Alison, and encouraging her, although I couldn't make the words out clearly. There was another flurry of movement and then a baby crying, followed by a vast bellow of laughter echoing from the other room. Nancy was laughing — so everything must be all right. Alison must be all right. A doctor walked over to me.

'Your sister is well,' he began.

I looked over to Nancy, who had also come out into the corridor.

'And the baby?'

'Some complications,' he explained, and I saw Nancy's face stiffen and her eyes grow sharp. 'She's very tiny and we've placed her in an incubator. There should be no reason to suggest that she won't survive and become a pefectly healthy child.'

'What's the matter with her?' I asked, surprised at the calmness of my voice.

He responded evenly. 'She has some respiratory problems, so we've put her on a ventilator, a machine which breathes for her.' He was explaining carefully. 'When she gets stronger we can take her off it and let her breathe for herself.'

'When will that be?'

'Possibly days, possibly weeks. It's up to the baby really.'

'I see, thank you.'

He walked off and Nancy hugged me.

'She's beautiful,' she said, holding me at arm's length.

'How could she be otherwise?' I said, 'being Alison's child.'

'Wait until you see her, she's not looking her best, but she's wonderful.'

Nancy was euphoric; in her eyes and in her voice she was decades younger — the child could have been her own. When I asked her if I could go in and see Alison, she nodded and tactfully, let me go alone.

My sister was lying in a small, narrow bed, prior to being taken down to the ward. Her face was shiny and white, and her hands gripped the bed covers. As she heard me, she turned her head and smiled.

'Well done,' I said softly, and as I held her hand she fell asleep.

Nancy and I hung around the hospital for several hours until Alison woke. When we went in to see her again, she looked refreshed and astonishingly like her usual self, her beauty almost overpowering in the small room.

'You look wonderful,' I said, bending to kiss her cheek. 'How do you feel?'

'Fine,' she replied calmly.

'Have you seen the baby?' I asked, arranging some flowers on the table beside her.

'No.'

Nancy's face set hard. 'Haven't you asked to see her?'

Alison turned to face our grandmother, her expression impassive. 'Why should I? She's not mine.'

Exasperated, Nancy pushed back her chair and walked out.

'Alison — ' I began, but she interrupted me.

'Will you do something for me, Jill?'

'Of course.'

'Bring in my make-up, and a clean nightie, there's a love.'

Stunned, I agreed, and after staying with her a little longer, I joined Nancy in the corridor outside. She was eating a sandwich, and looked enraged.

'Well, what do you make of that?' she said finally, flinging the crusts into the waste bin. 'I've just spoken to the doctor, and he said that she will return to normal and accept the baby in time.' She snorted in disgust. 'Meanwhile we aren't to do anything to upset her, or to force her to take to the child.'

'Well, they know best,' I said, half-heartedly, my own anxiety making me a poor comforter. 'I'll just go and see the baby and we'll go home. Okay?'

Nancy nodded and sat down, her hands drumming on her legs, her face almost pinched with annoyance.

The baby was in the intensive care unit, almost hidden in an incubator and surrounded by tubes and equipment. She looked tiny and fragile, her slender arms waving silently, her little head almost birdlike. She wasn't beautiful, except to her grandmother and her aunt, she was merely pathetic, and helpless and I loved her instantly. I laid my hand against the glass of the incubator and although it was only a random action on her part, she moved until her own fingers brushed the other side of the machine which separated us.

'Welcome, little one,' I whispered. 'Welcome home.'

20

We returned to the walled house to freshen up and change, and as I paid off the taxi driver, Nancy unlocked the front door, going upstairs immediately afterwards to run a bath, whilst I went round the house opening windows because the heat was building up, and the air was thick with heat and the smell of dry earth. I was making some coffee when I heard a tapping at the back door.

'What are you doing here?' I asked, incredulous, as I saw Mark standing in the glass porch, his face unshaven, his eyes slightly puffy.

'I had to see you.'

'If Nancy comes down — ' I began.

'Then come out to the car, I'm parked out front. I have to talk to you, Jill.'

He didn't wait for my answer but walked off. After I had checked that Nancy was busy in the bathroom, I joined him. The heat in the car was intense and Mark was sweating, his shirt sleeves rolled up, his hair sticking to his forehead.

'You look awful,' I said bluntly.

He smoothed his hair half-heartedly. 'How's Alison?'

'She's fine, and the baby is a girl. They've got her in an incubator at the moment, because she's having trouble breathing for herself.'

I was stunned by the change in him. All his polish had gone, like smoke on a windy night.

He seemed older and thinner, and tired. I looked at him and tried very hard to see him as I had done only the previous day, because I wanted to love him and need him, and feel that tremendous passion and commitment which for so long had made him more important than my family.

Instead, I saw a middle-aged, married man, who was looking for comfort.

'Mark,' I began quietly, 'your child has just been born. Your child, and Alison's. I can't see you any longer . . . I feel so bad about what I've done . . . so ashamed and guilty.' I turned away and looked out of the open car window. A woman was working in a garden opposite us. 'I betrayed my family, and I won't do that to a child. It's finished — we've done enough.'

'Don't — ' he began.

I stopped him the only way I knew how. I got out of the car and walked back to the house. After a moment, I heard him start up the engine and drive off.

It was hardly nobility which made me act that way. I had been too long a traveller on that devious road which promises to take the traveller to new and exotic places, and instead, weaves and curls around on itself and ends up in alleys and hovels. I had blinded myself to all the things I had prized for so long, and weighed them against one man, and I had done all this for what is laughingly called 'love', and is in reality, physical desire. He gave me the status of being wanted, and because I was plain and unlovely, I had taken that to be the finest compliment one human being could pay to another. And with the affair, I had finally laid the ghost of my sister's towering beauty. I had taken her man, and had even managed to get him to tell me he loved me — as if it was worth something. I saw Mark blown up with ego and conceit, like a huge, brightly coloured balloon at a child's fair, until he became massive and grotesque. I could have wept at my own stupidity.

There and then I decided that I had to make it up to Alison, that I had to atone in some way. I already missed Mark, missed the excitement and understood that it was unlikely to come my way again. I already longed for him — for the sound of his voice, and the touch of his hand. I knew that in the future I would turn when I saw a man who walked like him, or saw a car like his, and understood that every day something would remind me of our time together.

I stood by the side of the back door and wept. I had been prepared to deceive my grandmother and my sister, but not a child. That was how much I loved her — even then.

Slowly I went upstairs, showered and dressed in a cool print suit. I polished my glasses and looked at my reflection in the mirror, seeing a heavy girl staring back at me — because the image had gone, and reality had taken its place. I came back down to earth with a fall of which Icarus would have been proud.

'Are you ready?' Nancy said, walking into my room, and glancing round.

'I'm ready,' I answered, and together we walked out to the car.

Alison was delighted that I had remembered

271

her make-up and began to reapply it and comb her hair as we talked to her. She did not mention the baby.

'When can you come out?' Nancy asked her, eating a handful of the grapes she had brought with her.

'In a few days.'

'The baby's lovely,' Nancy persisted, spitting out some pips and putting them into the brown paper bag.

'When are you going to see her?' I asked Alison, and immediately her face closed up, and she laid her head back against the pillows.

'I think I'd like to sleep now, thanks for coming,' she said, and reluctantly, we walked out.

In the corridor, Nancy fumed. 'I could have knocked her bloody head off! Fancy not even asking about the baby.'

'You know what they said — Alison has to come around to the idea in her own time.'

Nancy snorted. 'In her time — what about the baby's time?'

We went home in silence. Nancy, annoyed because of Alison's attitude, myself, because I was already missing Mark, and still horribly anxious about my sister's mental state. They had said at the hospital that although she was greatly improved, we had to be careful what we said to her, or how we treated her. They warned us that although she was improving, the situation was still precarious, and that only time would fully cure her. We were not out of the wood yet.

It rained when we got back to the house,

pouring down in great gasps, and when it stopped the garden hummed with birds and insects, whilst the slow drip of the water off the gable ends splashed down and made pools on the concrete underneath. The earth came to life again, and under the deep smell of the rain, the scent of roses and stocks swelled up and perfumed the warm air. A low sun dipped behind trees, and where the last light shone through, the garden blinked back as the shade deepened up against the stone wall.

I stood there and believed that my life had altered, that I could begin again, that a new episode would follow — but that was too simple, and too convenient, and besides, it was probably more than I deserved.

The following morning I did not wake Nancy, thinking that a lie-in would do her good, and I backed my car out of the garage quietly, making as little noise as possible. At the crossroads I stopped, only to hear someone pipping their horn behind me. It was Mark. I drove a little further, trying to ignore him, but he kept sounding his horn, so that eventually I pulled over and turned off the engine. He walked over to the car.

'Jill, we can't leave it like this.'

'You'll have to get used to the idea,' I replied sourly, glancing in my rear mirror to check the street behind.

He was agitated and wrenched open the door, sitting down in the passenger seat next to me. His appearance was immaculate and my heart shifted uncomfortably.

'I've left my wife,' he said, without a trace of expression in his face, or in his voice. 'And I want you to come away with me.'

Only a week earlier I would have done anything just to hear those few words, and now, now it was too late, and too little.

'Is this some sort of joke?' I said, my tone cold.

'Come with me . . . please.'

His face was calm, the eyes almost willing me to say yes.

'You're using me, you know you are, Mark,' I said, glancing away. 'All this talk is just so you can find out how much control you have over me, to check what I'll give up for you. I know that's all it is.'

'Can't you trust me?' His tone was persuasive.

'No. Why should I? Could Alison? What do you really want from me?' I said, turning back to face him. 'My devotion — you had that; my complete absorption in you — well, you had that too; what the hell else, Mark, you tell me, because I don't know any more.'

'We were happy together. We're alike.'

'But I don't want to be like you!' I said loudly. 'I don't want to be as greedy or as selfish or as . . . unloving as you. You cheated on your wife, and Alison, and next it will be me. No, I don't want you, and I don't want to be like you. I don't love you any more, Mark, if I ever did.'

'Don't be stupid, you're feeling guilty because of the child, that's all.'

'That's just it — I can't go on acting the way I did, it's sickening.'

I put my head down.

'It didn't seem to bother you that much before,' he added spitefully.

'No, but I'm not going on with it. You think I could leave them now, after everything that's happened? Simply to run away with you? You're mad, you must be . . . it's too ridiculous to even consider seriously.'

He continued as though he had not heard me. 'Come with me, Jill, you'll forget all of this when we're away from it.'

I laid my head back against the headrest of the car seat.

'That is not the point. I don't want to forget them, or what I did. I want to stay with them now and get my life back to where it should be.' I moved my head to face him. 'If I went with you now, how long would it last? A month? Two months? And then what? I'll tell you, you would pick someone else up and I'd be left, God knows where, unable to to go home and face my family again. You would have spoilt everything. No, Mark, if I stay I can make amends.'

'I left my wife for you,' he said bitterly.

'I never asked you to.'

'I can't go back to her now.'

'Well, maybe she's the only one to get anything out of all this,' I replied acidly.

But he carried on wheedling and persuading me, so that after a few minutes I was convinced. Maybe I was too easy to persuade, maybe I knew only too well that I might never again be in the position of having a man want me. Perhaps I believed that it was my only chance of happiness,

275

of a sort. I wanted to go with him, because I was afraid that I might never find another man, and the thought of middle age, and a long old age welled up in front of me. What happened when Alison married, and the child grew up? What happened when Nancy died? I would stay there, in that walled house, and crumble, just as the wall had done in my dream. What did it matter whether he was using me? What mattered any longer? That he would return to his wife? That he would leave me? I saw it all so clearly, but in the end, I could not resist that chance of maybe finding happiness, no matter how short-lived.

'All right, Mark, I'll go with you.'

He snatched up my left hand and kissed the palm.

'I'll make you happy,' he said, so convincingly that I almost believed him.

'Wait for me, I have to go back to the house and pack some things.'

He nodded, smiled at me, and I got out of the car.

As I unlocked the front door, I listened for the sound of Nancy moving about, but the place was silent. The clock ticked in the hallway, and several letters lay on the front door mat. I threw some clothes into a case, and pressed down the lid, remembering how Nancy had strained with her suitcase in Cornwall, and when I had finished I went down into the kitchen and wrote two letters, one for Nancy and one for my sister.

I began the letter to Nancy three times, and then left the last version, inadequate as it was, on the kitchen table. Taking up another sheet of paper, I began my explanation to Alison:

Alison —
When you read this I will be out of London,
even I am not sure where, and I will be with
Mark. It seems very cruel to set it out like that
— in black and white, but I didn't want to
make excuses first and then tell you the facts
— it wouldn't have been fair.
In all honesty I can't say that I love him,
only that he is the nearest thing to love that I
can hope for. I met him before you did, and
we had lunch together — an uncomfortable
little meeting which he forgot with an almost
indecent haste. I fell in love with him, and
when you came back from America and told
me that you had met him, and loved him too
. . . well, my jealousy erupted, and I
encouraged you in the affair, knowing that he
was married. It's not something that anyone
would be proud of, and I'm sorry. You see, I
never thought you would get pregnant — I
only thought that he would leave you, and that
you'd feel the humiliation I've felt so many
times in the past, when I was the 'also ran'.
That sounds as though it's all your fault, and
that's not true. I am the one who should be
making amends.
Alison, I can't excuse what I'm doing, and I
know that in your position, I could never
forgive what I am about to do. I don't know
how it will end, but there is a child, at least,
and that child is a part of you.
I need him, you see, and I'm too frightened

277

to be left alone . . . that's why.
Jill

I sealed the envelope and wrote her name and the ward number on the top, so that I could give it to the nurse in charge to pass on to my sister later. I turned around and looked at the kitchen, and stood in the hallway, still listening for sounds of my grandmother having woken. But she was still asleep, and as I pulled the door closed behind me, I was glad that I didn't have to confront her and see the look in her eyes.

I didn't know what she would do when she read the note, neither could I imagine that my action might finally push Alison off the edge of that narrow wall, and this time, there would be no one to catch her.

21

Mark was waiting for me in his car. Sunlight shone in through the windscreen and along the dashboard there was a fine tracing of dust. When he heard my footsteps, he leant over and opened the door on my side, and after throwing my case onto the back seat, I got in.

'Did you see your grandmother?'

'No, she was still asleep,' I said, wondering whether or not to offer any further information. 'I left a note for her in the kitchen, and I want to take this one to the hospital for Alison.'

'Are you sure?'

'Yes, I'm sure.'

He nodded silently, and started the car.

The traffic had begun in earnest, and hundreds of cars were heading for London. Mark drove well, his eyes fixed on the road, and when a couple of times I glanced over to him, the situation seemed oddly unreal. In profile, he was almost perfectly handsome, and when he turned his head to watch for traffic, he was so attractive that I was alarmed, and wanted suddenly to leave. We were mismatched and mistaken, irredeemably reckless and selfish, and we didn't even have the excuse of love on our side.

'Why did you finally leave your wife and ask me to come away with you?'

A car came out of a side street without

279

looking, and he blasted his horn, too loudly and too long.

'I need you.'

'Is that it?'

'That is usually enough for most women.'

I asked him nothing else, and we drove to the hospital in silence.

When I arrived at the ward where Alison was, I asked to speak to the sister in charge.

'How's the baby?'

She smiled warmly. 'She's holding her own, and making a little progress.'

'That's good,' I said, rummaging in my handbag, and handing her the letter for Alison. 'Will you give this to my sister in about an hour?'

She took it from me, frowning slightly. 'Don't you want to see her? She's awake.'

Easily, I lied. 'No, just give her the letter, will you? I'll see her later.'

She accepted it then, and pushed the envelope in amongst several others on the top of the desk.

'Thank you,' I said, and left, my feet making squeaking sounds on the tiled floor.

Almost out of the hospital, I remembered the baby, and suddenly realising that I might never see her again, made my way to the intensive care unit, and was shown into a small anteroom where she lay in the incubator, her little body breathing laboriously. A monitor bleeped on the table beside her, and a chart hung from the side of the machine, its curves and peaks mapping out the first few hours of her life.

She was fast asleep, the tinyness of her almost absurd amongst the amount of machinery around. A respirator breathed for her, in, out, in, out, and as she slept she moved a few times idly, her minute limbs delicate. There were blue smudges of colour under her eyes, and where her mouth fell open around the tube, her lips were pink and well formed. I loved her immediately, and selfishly I wanted her to wake, to know that I was there. I wanted her to look at me, and see me, just once, before I left. Otherwise we would never know each other.

But she slept on undisturbed and I walked to the window, and looking out was surprised to find myself over the car park. Instinctively, I glanced around for Mark's car, and found it, parked under a tree. He was there, smoking a cigarette, and leaning against the bonnet in his shirt sleeves. He looked like another woman's man, another woman's husband — he looked wrong for me. But as I saw him, I wanted him, and only a slight alteration in the rhythm of the monitor made me turn.

The baby was still asleep, and the monitor continued to bleep resolutely as downstairs, Mark ground out his cigarette with the sole of his shoe. Sunlight fell through the blinds and made regular slats of light on the polished floor, and after a time, a middle-aged nurse came in and looked at me.

'She's a nice little thing, isn't she?' she said, glancing down at the baby.

'She's beautiful,' I agreed.

'Her mother must be very proud of her. Children can be such a comfort,' she added, and walked out, leaving the words ringing in my ears.

281

I thought of Alison then, imagining her lovely face and how her eyes would take on all that pain when she read my note. I wondered if she would cry, and think back to the night when she had first told me about Mark. And I wondered if she would despise me. Hate me, for what I had done to her. Even Alison, my sister, Alison. Or maybe she would take another of those long steps back when the world grew too huge, too fierce, for her to cope with. And what would Nancy think of me?'

One thing was for certain, my grandmother would never forgive me. Alison might, she might even find some explanation for what I did — but not Nancy. I had broken her code of ethics, and understood that when I pulled that front door closed behind me, I could never open it again.

I returned to the window, and looked out to see Mark pacing up and down on the tarmac. From such a distance, he seemed small and out of place. Watching him, I realised that he might stay with me for a couple of months, and then that would be it, or maybe a year — possibly there was enough between us for a year. Certainly no longer — even guilt was exhaustible.

The sun was warming up the room, and when the nurse returned, she opened a top window.

'The baby won't be in a draught, will she?' I asked.

The woman smiled patiently. 'Not at all. She's very well protected in there.'

She moved over to the incubator and looked at the chart.

'We haven't decided what to call her,' I said stupidly.

Replacing the chart, she looked over to me. 'When you get her home, you'll know. Children usually pick their own names, in a way. You look at them and realise that they look just like a Claire, or a Jenny.' She tucked some hair into her cap as she talked. 'That's what usually happens anyway.'

But I could never be part of that choosing of names, I could never see this baby grow up, or watch her develop. Her life was divorced from mine. I would never know if she might be pretty and successful, or if she might remain sickly and need a great deal of care. None of this I could know, because I had excluded myself, and the knowledge knifed me, and made me glance away from the baby.

'Would you like a cup of tea?' the nurse asked me, and I shook my head, hardly trusting my voice to speak.

The machine bleeped constantly, monitoring her heart beats, and tracing a green pattern across the dark screen. I heard the doors open again and turned, expecting the nurse, although a young doctor stood there, a file in his hands.

'Miss Henly?'

I nodded.

'You should be pleased, the baby is doing well. If she continues in this fashion, she should be off the respirator by the weekend. Have you seen your sister this morning?'

'No, she was asleep earlier.'

He drummed his fingers lightly on the side of

the monitor, and watched the baby. He was only twenty-six or twenty-seven, slightly built and so very blond that his eyelashes were almost invisible in the sunlight.

'She's not seen the child yet,' he said, making it a statement, not an accusation.

'My sister has had a bad experience . . . things didn't work out for her as she expected.'

I was sorry he had come in. It seemed as though he was passing judgement on her. I dreaded his next words.

'You'll need to give her a great deal of support.' A slight smile spread across his face. 'Your grandmother will help too — she's a remarkable woman.'

I wondered if Nancy had found the letter yet, whether she was then sitting in the kitchen, reading it as we spoke.

'She's always been very determined, very strong minded,' I said, half-heartedly.

'She brought you both up, I believe?'

I nodded.

'Since we were children. My parents were killed, or rather, I should say, our parents, were killed. Alison and I came to her as children, and she looked after us from then on.'

'So you still live with her?'

I nodded again.

'And your sister?'

'When she's not travelling, yes. She has a very successful career, and travels a good deal, so she doesn't spend that much time with us.' I looked at him carefully. 'Why?'

'I just wondered. So you think she'll continue

to live with you and your grandmother after she takes the baby home?'

'I suppose so.'

My mind kept shifting back to the car outside, and to Mark, who was waiting for me. I wanted to leave then, I didn't want to talk about a future in which I could have no part. The doctor was unnerving me.

'Perhaps she'll go back to work, after the baby's grown up a bit,' I offered.

'Is that likely?'

Irritation welled up in me. 'I don't know my sister's plans.'

He glanced up from the piece of floorboard he had been studying. 'But would that seem likely? I mean, if she knows she has you and your grandmother to support her, and help look after the child, she might take to the baby gradually. In stages, so to speak.'

He was trying to make life easier for Alison — just as everyone had always done.

'She's not my child,' I said ungraciously.

'No.'

'I shouldn't have to look after her child, her mistake,' I snapped without thinking, wanting to get out of the room and down to the car park, and Mark. 'She'll meet someone else, she's beautiful and has never been short of admirers.'

Was there really a look of disbelief in his face, or was I imagining it?

'But with your support — '

I interrupted him. 'With my support she can make a new life for herself? Is that what you mean, doctor? With the support of an old lady,

285

and a plain sister, who will obviously never marry, with that support she can be released to follow her own life again, knowing that she will have us to look after her child?'

'I didn't mean — '

'Well, what did you mean?' I said, turning round and walking over to the window again.

'I just thought that you might want to help her. I'm sorry, I had no right . . . '

'No, you had no right, doctor.'

I expected him to go, but although he looked young and inexperienced, he was surprisingly determined, and continued, 'You see, if she doesn't have your support, we could consider putting the child up for adoption,' he said, and for an instant I could not reply. Thinking that I was seriously considering the matter, he pushed his advantage. 'She hasn't even seen the baby yet, and appears to want nothing to do with her. There are a good many couples who want a child badly.'

I kept staring out of the window. Mark was out of sight, although his car was still there. I had to get out fast.

'Alison won't give the child up for adoption,' I said finally.

'Miss Henly, she has already discussed the matter with a social worker.'

I was too shocked to speak, and noticing my hesitation, he continued carefully, 'She talked to them half an hour ago, and said she would think about it.'

I turned from the window, and moved over to the incubator. The little body was still moving,

286

the limbs waving idly, her hands wrinkled and old-looking.

'How dare she,' I said hoarsely.

'As you said — it's her child,' he replied.

'Don't preach to me, doctor! You don't know what you're talking about! This child is as much mine as it is hers, perhaps more so. She has no right, no right at all.'

His face coloured, a red stain spreading from his neck to the top of his forehead.

'Miss Henly, I only thought that you might like to talk to her about it.'

Panicking, I turned from the incubator to the window, from the window to the incubator. Downstairs, Mark appeared from around the corner of the adjoining building, his tall figure relaxed, the ease of his movements contrasting strongly with the discomforted, unattractive man in front of me.

'She has no right,' I repeated numbly.

'We'll see.'

He gave me no chance to reply and walked out, the double doors closing softly behind him.

My head was banging. How could Alison think of letting the baby go? How could she even consider that part of her be cut off, and given to other people, so that she would never know how her baby was, or where? How could she do it? Then I thought back, to the pliant, pleasing Alison who was perfectly charming unless something upset her, after which she could be ruthlessly, wholeheartedly, cruel. Obviously, she saw the child as an embarrassment, something to be rid of as quickly as

287

possible. She had to be stopped.

Walking to the doors, I looked at my watch. Had Alison read the letter already? It was possible, I had been with the baby almost an hour. And if she had read hers, then so had Nancy.

The heat curled round me, and under the weight of my hair my skin was sticky. Outside, Mark was waiting for me, and only feet from where I stood, was Alison's child. As I looked at her, she opened her eyes, and although she found it hard to focus, I bent down and talked to her through the glass of the incubator.

'I have to go. I have to. It's my only chance. Your mother will meet other men, but I have only this one chance.'

She looked at me, and in that instant I saw myself — the old defiance in the eyes, all the world's anger. I knew then that she would grow up with all the same jealousy, only this time it would be the envy of a beautiful mother. Later, she would probably run off with the first, hopelessly unsuitable man who ever whispered love to her in the dark. In her — I saw myself.

I flung open the doors and ran down the stairs, hurtling out into the car park. I reached Mark just as he was getting out to greet me, and grabbing hold of my case from the back seat, I slammed the car door closed. He looked confused and handsome, and he smiled that small smile which meant very little.

'Go, Mark, go now, please. I'm not coming with you.'

'Jill,' he said simply, his expression bordering on irritation.

'Go! I don't love you, and I'm not going. Go back to your wife and leave me alone!'

He looked at me for a long moment, and frowned, his eyes taking on an expression of humour, and then defeat. Finally, inexplicably, he touched my cheek and nodded.

As I rushed back to the hospital, I heard the car start up and leave, and as I came under the shadow of the building, I turned back only once briefly towards the parking space where he had been only seconds before. Then dry-eyed I turned away and made for the stairs, taking them two at a time, and arrived at the maternity ward, breathless. At the desk I saw the nurse I had entrusted with the letter for Alison.

'Did you give my sister that note?' I asked her quickly.

She looked embarrassed.

'Oh God, I'm awfully sorry . . . we've been so busy here, I forgot. I'll go now — '

I could hardly stop myself from laughing, and took the letter from her, ramming it into my jacket pocket.

'It's not a problem, forget it,' I said, rushing off and running out of the hospital to hail a taxi on the street corner outside.

As I sat in that hot cab, I could only pray that Nancy had not found her letter. If she had, everything was finished, and worse, I no longer had Mark to run to. The miles stretched out and every turning and bend in the road threw up obstacles which held us back. Each traffic light was red; each crossroad busy. The journey tortured me, and the sun burned through the cab windows and made the seats hot, the air heavy with the smell of leather. I had the money ready in my hand as he drew up outside the walled house, and when he called me back for the change, I didn't stop.

Struggling, I couldn't manage the lock on the front door, and had to try twice before it opened. Inside, I could hear the sound of water being run — Nancy was up, she must have risen and gone downstairs, as she always did, to make herself a cup of tea to begin the day. She must have read the letter. She knew.

I had lost. I had lost my family and my home and could never return. Tears ran down my cheeks as I leant back against the door for support, and waited for Nancy to come down the stairs and find me.

The footsteps started briskly along the top corridor, and then turned at the head of the stairs. I saw her walking down with the newspaper in her hands, already turned to the crossword page. I tensed myself for her reaction when she saw me, for her anger, and when she paused two steps from the bottom, I waited for her to speak first.

'Jill?'

She looked surprised, her face serious, the expression calm.

'Get me a cuppa, dear, will you? I haven't had a chance to make myself one this morning, what with Angela ringing and wanting to know all about the baby.'

My voice sounded tinny, and a long way off. 'Haven't you been in the kitchen?'

She glanced up, and then back to her crossword. 'No, not yet. Why?' she replied, and then walked over to me slowly. 'What's the matter? Why aren't you at work?'

Without answering, I moved away and rushed into the kitchen, pocketing the letter before she had a chance to catch up with me. I was putting on the kettle when she took hold of my arm.

'You're crying, what's the matter? Is it Alison?'

I replied evenly, the excuse ready on my tongue. 'She wants to have the baby adopted. Alison wants to give the baby away.'

Furious, Nancy threw down the newspaper on the table and pulled her dressing gown tightly around herself. 'Over my dead body — that child's ours.'

22

Without another word, Nancy went upstairs and dressed, calling down to me when she was ready to bring her some toast and tea. When I got back upstairs she was putting the final touches to her make-up.

'Before you say it, I know what you're thinking — that we should leave Alison to come round to the baby in her own time. Well, frankly, you can keep that suggestion. If she doesn't want the child, we do, and we'll look after her. Poor little sod,' she finished sympathetically.

I could have hugged her, but instead I moved the breakfast tray and went back downstairs with it, and then shoved my suitcase under my bed so that she couldn't come across it unexpectedly. I felt as though I was moving around inside a bubble, the impression of relief was so strong.

Only minutes later I was driving us back to the hospital, and when we arrived at the maternity ward, Nancy turned to me. 'I'm going in for a word with your sister. Wait for me here, and don't worry.'

I nodded and sat down obediently.

Ten minutes passed, and then twenty, before she re-emerged, looking grim-faced and grabbing hold of my arm as she passed.

'Well, the adoption idea's off, so that's one little problem sorted. Now all we have to do is to get the stupid girl home with her baby.'

'What are we going to call her?' I asked, wanting her to have a name, a real identity.

'Rachel,' Nancy said without hesitation. It had been my mother's name.

So that weekend Rachel and Alison came home, the baby bundled up in white blankets, my sister holding her awkwardly, her face tense with strain. Already the baby's eyes were darkening from blue to navy, and her little hands seemed less wrinkled, the skin pink. I opened the door for them.

'Oh, Alison, she's lovely — can I hold her?'

'Sure,' my sister replied, anxious to be rid of her. 'She's very quiet, you'll have no trouble.'

I loved her totally, whether from guilt or instinct I can't say, but within a couple of hours she felt more mine than my sister's, and when Nancy settled them in upstairs, I missed Rachel, and longed for the sound of her crying, or for Alison calling me — any excuse so that I could run upstairs and hold her.

It took my sister only three weeks to become restless.

'Listen, Nancy, I know it's only a little while after the birth, but I do feel I would like to go back to work. It brings in loads of money, and besides, I don't want to become a hausfrau.'

'And are you sure you want to leave Rachel with us so much?'

The answer was written all over Alison's face.

'Oh, but I couldn't leave her in better hands! I know that you and Jill will look after her for me, and I know that she will be happy.'

'But you'll miss so much of her growing up,'

293

Nancy persisted, trying in vain to resurrect some kind of maternal feeling in Alison, because although she now admitted that the child was hers, and her mental state had returned to normal, she seemed disinterested and detached from her daughter.

'No, honestly, that's all right. I can get all the details from you two . . . it will be better for me to get back to work.'

She rang the agency the following day, and a week later she was in Amsterdam on a modelling job, kissing Rachel goodbye with an almost palpable sense of relief. When she was away, she sent her a couple of presents, with little stilted notes attached to them — 'to my baby' — or — 'to dearest Rachel' but the handwriting stammered on the paper. The night she left, I moved into her room at the top of the house, next to Rachel, and when she cried I got up and fed her, and in the morning Nancy took her into the garden for a walk in her large, coach-built pram. If Alison was ashamed of her, we gloried in her.

By the time several months had elapsed, an unspoken agreement was reached. Alison wanted to go back full time to her modelling and she wanted us to look after Rachel. We accepted easily and never considered our situation unusual, although it might well have seemed so to outsiders. Only weeks after the birth, some of Nancy's friends began to drift back, and the even tenor of our lives was restored, albeit with an extra addition to the family.

'Nancy, we should have Rachel christened,' I

said to her, as she prepared a bottle.

'You're right — move out of the way, I can't get round you.' She pushed past me good-naturedly. 'When and where?'

'As soon as possible, and why not in the local church?'

She clamped down the teat adeptly.

'Your grandfather's buried there.'

'So is my mother. Rachel's namesake,' I added.

Squeezing a drop of the milk onto the back of her hand, Nancy smiled quietly. 'It's a good idea, can you fix it for us, and make sure Alison's in the country then?'

I made the arrangements and telephoned Alison who was in Brussels. She sounded only politely interested and agreed to the date, saying that she wasn't working then.

'Only don't alter it, because I can't afford to refuse work.'

Her tone was indignant, and I bit my lip to stop myself snapping at her. I still felt guilty.

'I won't. We'll see you then, Alison. Bye.'

It was a perfect morning, and the few people we invited turned up in their best clothes, and generally oohed and ahhed over Rachel. Nancy dressed her in one of our christening gowns, and put a tiny, laced bonnet on her head. She looked enchanting, although Alison never saw her, making a last minute phone call instead to say that she was stuck in France.

'I can't help it, things just happen that way,' she pleaded.

'Alison, it's your child.'

'Oh, do shut up, Jill, and stop being so patronising! I can't get there, and that's that. Give Rachel a kiss from me.'

Nancy was outraged when I told her.

' 'Give her a kiss from me' — I'd like to get my hands on that girl, she's going from bad to worse. She should take some responsibility for Rachel, or love her, at the very least.'

'Perhaps she does, in her own way,' I offered, trying to placate her.

'In her own way — that's the story of Alison's whole life — doing things her own way.'

As a gesture of defiance, Nancy had the photographs of the christening developed and a large print made out of a close up of Rachel, framing it and putting it on the top of the piano, beside ours, but when Alison returned home on her next visit, she didn't even comment on it.

Her reaction to her own child was peculiar, and faintly disturbing. When she picked her up, she did so awkwardly, passing Rachel back to us as soon as she could, and smoothing her clothes as though contact with the child would leave her somehow contaminated.

'Don't you think she's getting prettier?' I asked my sister, watching her as she bent over the cot.

'I suppose so.'

I glanced around the nursery. 'I'll move out now that you're home.'

A look of genuine panic filled her eyes. 'Oh no, don't do that on my account. Besides, you're used to the baby and I'm still a beginner.' She smiled warmly. 'You're a lot better at this than I am.'

Suddenly, I wanted her to know how grateful I was.

'Alison, I'm the one who benefits from looking after Rachel . . . thank you for letting me have her so much.'

My sister looked away, embarrassed.

'Any time,' she said breezily, and walked out.

The atmosphere between us was cordial, if not warm. She never referred to Mark directly, or if it comes to that, indirectly. She seemed to obliterate her child's father from her mind, as she had hoped to do with the child herself, and lived her life away from us as much as she decently could. I felt guilt still, with a grinding anxiety that one day Alison would know everything, and because of that I felt I owed her, and on every occasion defended her against Nancy's anger, or other people's tactless remarks.

'Still away?' Angela said, her bland face turned towards mine.

I pretended that I hadn't understood. 'Sorry?'

'Your sister, is she still away?'

'Yes, Angela.'

'Spends a lot of time separated from the child, doesn't she?'

'The child is called Rachel, and, no I don't think Alison spends a lot of time away, she has a job to do, that's all.'

'Sorry I spoke,' she said, lapsing into an uncomfortable silence, until Nancy returned and I made a bolt for the nursery upstairs.

I have to say here that I still thought of Mark. That I remembered his voice and the little, trivial things which don't matter, like the way he hung up his coat, or poured a drink. He didn't ring, although for several weeks after we parted I woke often, thinking that I heard the phone, and I waited for the post with a deliberate, masochistic routine, although no letters ever came. He had gone on to another woman, I knew that, but it didn't make the loss easier.

I saw him in Rachel, of course, even as a baby, and as the months passed, I remembered Alison's words; 'I'm having it for a friend', she said, and in a way, she was right, and fulfilled her own prophecy.

I took over Rachel more and more, as the months passed, whilst Nancy, with her typical generosity, stood back and let me. I loved her and looked after her, taking her for walks and feeding her, although the discipline I left to Nancy.

'Stop it, or I'll slap you!' Nancy said, watching as Rachel reached towards the fire. 'I'm warning you!'

Rachel still continued to put out her hand, and my grandmother smacked her. A look of bewilderment spread across her face, and then she started to cry.

'Oh, Nancy, don't be so hard on her, she's only a baby.'

'She's not a baby any longer, and if she burns a hole in herself, or pulls down a pan of boiling water on her head, she won't forgive me for that.'

298

It's better that she's hurt now, before anything worse happens.'

She was right, of course. To me, Rachel was simply a plaything, a lovely, little creature who took away all the disappointments of my own life; she was my safeguard against the future. To her, I was the adult who loved her unconditionally, who played with her and bought her toys. Looking after Rachel, I had a purpose, and so we needed each other.

Gradually, Alison stayed abroad for ten months a year, returning home for Rachel's birthday or for Christmas, when she brought toys with her. But after a few days she was back in the garden, walking on her own, longing for the excitement of her usual life.

'Alison, come on in, Rachel's playing with that doll you brought her.'

She turned, her face agitated. 'She's not interested in me . . . she won't notice I'm not there.'

I walked over to her.

'She won't, if you don't spend some more time with her. She's only three, Alison, she doesn't understand.'

My sister moved away, back towards the house. 'For an unmarried, childless woman, you are quite an expert,' she said softly, making me glance over to her in surprise, although her face was impassive and it appeared as though she had not meant the remark unkindly. We walked back without another word.

In the lounge, Nancy was playing with Rachel, her face bent down low over the child, her hands offering her a dress which Alison had brought that morning.

'Look at this, darling, look what your mummy's got for you.'

Rachel hesitated, looking from Nancy to her mother and then at the dress.

'Here you are,' my grandmother persisted, laying it in her little hands.

The child sat, unmoving, and then with a look of utter determination let the dress fall onto the floor in front of her.

'No,' she said simply, and looked away.

Alison's face flickered with annoyance. 'Don't be tiresome, Rachel,' she said, sitting down in a chair in front of the fire. 'Come to me.'

'Won't.'

'Rachel,' Alison repeated icily, the threat implicit in her tone. 'Come here.'

Reluctantly, the child got to her feet and walked unsteadily to her mother. Alison smiled triumphantly, her thick, rosewood coloured hair falling across her face as she bent down. 'There's a good girl, a very good little girl,' she said softly, although Rachel rested only momentarily in her arms, and was soon struggling to get free and return to Nancy.

As she moved from two to three, and then four years of age, Rachel changed from an unremarkable baby into a very attractive child. In no way as beautiful as her mother, she was still enormously appealing, and sometimes when she looked towards me, a turn of her head conjured up an image of Mark which was uncanny, and left me light-headed, my heart banging uneasily in my chest.

She learnt quickly, and by the age of four was attending a small primary school which Nancy and I chose, Alison being away at the time. I took her on the first day, and left her at the school doors, her face bright with misery, her hair tied neatly into two small plaits.

'Now you go in there, and make some new friends, and when I come back for you later, you can tell me all about it.'

Her bottom lip trembled.

'Go on, Rachel. It's only for a little while,' I said firmly, and pushed her slightly with my hand. She stepped forward awkwardly, and stopped. 'Go on,' I repeated as she glanced over her shoulder at me before finally walking in.

I felt as though someone had crushed me between two walls, and for nearly an hour I hung around the playground with tears in my eyes, before setting off for work. At three, I left to collect her, expecting the same wan figure to greet me, but when she rushed out with two small companions I was inexplicably disappointed, and it took a few minutes for me to come to terms with the fact that she had made the first of her own journeys into the world.

I wrote to Alison frequently, long cheerful letters about Rachel's progress, with the inevitable, scrappy footnote added by Nancy, although if something exciting happened I telephoned her long distance.

'Alison?'

'Jill?'

'Yes, it's me. I rang to tell you that Rachel's

been chosen for the lead in the play at school, and she's thrilled.' There was no response. 'Did you hear me?'

'Yes, oh well that's lovely,' she replied dully.

'Don't you want to know what part she's playing?'

'Tell me.'

'She's Alice In Wonderland, and she's trying to learn some of the words now, although it's not for weeks,' I continued, hoping to elicit some response.

'That's splendid. Give her a kiss from me, and tell her that I'll be wishing her luck.'

'But you haven't asked when it is . . . you might be home, and able to see her.'

'Yes . . . but it's busy at the moment . . . let me know. Thanks for ringing, Jill.'

I put down the receiver angrily, wondering whether it was worth the effort. But my guilt insisted that I make amends, and so I did, constantly, hoping that one day the frail chord between Alison and Rachel might strengthen, and a real bond grow between them.

'Rachel, look, here's a postcard from your mummy,' I said, passing her a brightly coloured card one morning.

She looked at it disinterestedly.

'Isn't that nice? Isn't she kind to send it to you?'

She looked at me sullenly, the obvious threat of tears imminent, although she seldom cried. 'It's not from mummy! You're my mummy!' she shouted, and ran to me, hugging me tightly with her small arms.

302

'Listen to me, darling, I'm not your mummy, I'm your aunt, and you know that. You can't go around saying those things, because it would hurt your mummy if she knew.'

'I don't care,' she said, her voice muffled by my jumper.

'You do, you do really,' I said, cuddling her for a minute longer and then releasing her and making her get ready for school. As I turned to see her go, Nancy walked into the kitchen.

'Did you hear that?' I asked and she nodded. 'She insists on calling me her mother. She thinks of me as that.' I cleaned my glasses on a handkerchief. 'I keep trying to explain, but I don't think that she's really come to terms with it.'

'I'm not suprised, Alison won't win any prizes for child rearing,' Nancy said.

'But it's not fair on her, Rachel is her child,' I said magnanimously.

'On the contrary, I think it's exactly what she deserves.'

'Why?'

'Because she's a bloody awful mother, that's why,' she said briskly and walked off.

By the time Rachel was six, Alison was reduced to a glorious figure who came into our lives very occasionally, and made little impression on our existence from day to day. I wondered to myself if she denied her child, or if she simply never alluded to her, keeping her a secret, as I had done with Alison at Chestnut Walk. Her life was back on its old tracks, although she kept her male admirers secret, and her love affairs well under wraps. Neither of us mentioned Mark.

At work Rachel was made very welcome, although Anna did express some surprise that I had never mentioned having a sister.

'You never say anything about your family,' she said reproachfully. 'Very strange I think.'

'Alison and I never got on,' I said, by way of explanation.

'But you bring up her child?'

'That's different.'

'How?'

I shrugged. 'It's just different, that's all.'

Both she and Edward loved Rachel because she was quiet, good-natured, and affectionate. Chestnut Walk became a second home to her — Edward a grandfather, and Anna a kind of aunt. They provided her with the relatives she did not have, and filled in the areas of her life which should automatically have been filled by her family.

But I worried constantly about Rachel, and about how the other children at her school viewed her illegitimacy, because that was the blunt truth of the matter, and I dreaded that she should be made to suffer for Alison's error and my vindictiveness. However, it was apparent that she felt at no disadvantage, and seemed to possess her mother's unswerving confidence when it mattered.

But if the ties from birth had been strained between Alison and Rachel, time did not help matters. There was no love on either side, and although I tried to bring my sister into her

304

child's life as much as I could, Rachel was already wise enough to understand that she had been left with Nancy and I for safe keeping, and that her mother had chosen to live without her. She decided that she would hate her for it.

'She left me,' she wailed, after we had had a brief argument. 'You keep talking about her, and saying how kind she is — but she left me, she left me . . . and she doesn't love me.'

'Rachel, that's not true. She does love you. You know that. She has to work to make money and so you can have pretty things.'

'I don't want pretty things!'

I watched her carefully.

'Do you miss her?'

'She left me!'

'Rachel — do you miss your mother?'

She glanced up at me, puzzled. 'I hate her,' she said simply, and hugged me, her arms round my neck. I wanted to scold her, to get angry and tell her never to say anything like that about her mother again, but instead I clung onto Alison's child, stroking the top of her head, and rocking her, as Nancy had rocked us.

Then the day came when she asked me who her father was. I was in the garden, weeding; Nancy was in the kitchen and Rachel was following me around purposefully. I knew that she wanted to say something that was important, and after a few tentative starts, she launched forth.

'Jill — who's my father?'

'My father', she had said. My father. My lover, I thought. One and the same man. A tall,

305

handsome man who was shallow and thoughtless and very, very much alive in his child.

'What did you say?'

She repeated the question evenly, giving me no time for thought. 'I asked you who my father was.'

I wanted to say that I loved him, that I had loved him once and still did, even though it was pointless, and futile and hardly worth saying. I wanted to tell her that he was with me every day, and every night, and that he had told me he loved me — but I couldn't.

'He loved your mother very much,' I said, keeping my head down, my trowel working at the soft ground.

'But who was he?' Rachel persisted, sitting on the grass beside me.

'Rachel,' I said, straightening up, and shielding my eyes from the sunlight. 'Haven't I always been honest with you?'

She nodded.

'Then believe me when I say that I can't tell you. You have to ask your mother for that information.'

She digested the words and nodded, although her eyes looked disappointed.

'I'll ask her,' she said simply.

I was not prepared to let Alison escape this one unpleasant duty.

I need not have worried. When my sister came home the following week, her daughter tackled her almost as soon as she arrived, sitting in the chair next to hers in the lounge, her legs swinging.

'Who is my father?' she said confidently.

Alison's eyebrows raised, and she looked over to me. I shook my head.

'Why, Rachel?' she answered, glancing back to her child.

'I want to know.'

'Why now?' Alison countered, her exquisite face genuinely puzzled.

Rachel looked away.

'Cause someone asked me who he was,' she said quietly, her small head down, her dark hair brushing against the collar of her school dress.

My sister sucked in her breath and then smiled. 'He was called Mark.'

'Mark what?' Rachel asked, her head still bowed.

'Mark Thomas,' Alison replied evenly, making me flinch where I was standing by the window.

For a second Rachel didn't move, and then, without another word, she ran out of the room and into the garden where I could soon see her on the swing under the apple tree.

'Thomas?' I repeated, looking over to Alison.

She shrugged her shoulders. 'So what? If I told her his real name she might look him up later, and then we'd have no end of trouble.'

'But it's a lie,' I said quietly, watching as Alison turned her head and looked over her shoulder to me.

'Yes. Isn't that awful? Still, sometimes a few lies are better than the truth, wouldn't you say?'

Suddenly she was older, very much older than her years, the light marking out the line of her cheek like a cameo cut into the side of a shell.

She was actually saying something else — something *under* the words — but when she moved the impression vanished.

Soon after I went up to bed, but slept little. I dreamt that time had gone backwards, and that I walked into Alison's room and found her sitting by the window, where she used to sit before her child was born. Before Rachel. All the years I had tried to make up for what I had done to her seemed like a sham — as though she had known all along, and had waited until now to tell me.

Alison was going to have her revenge and, for an instant, I was frightened of her.

23

I realised how much Rachel loved me, and I treasured that love as much as I treasured the fact that she chose to love me. Nancy stepped back, and let me take over my niece as much as I wanted to, as she settled into what must have been a welcome calm in her life. Rachel held her in some awe, seeing her as an old woman with a sharp temper, and a great deal to say on any matter.

'She keeps nagging me,' Rachel said on her eighth birthday, her hair cut short for the summer, the mass of it surrounding her pale face. She didn't look like Alison. 'She just keeps on and on.'

'It's her way. Don't worry about it,' I assured her, trying to get some papers for Edward into order for the next day.

'But she's so . . . cross,' Rachel finished, content that she had found the right word.

'She's not cross, it's just her manner. She's always been that way as long as I can remember.'

'Is it because she's old?'

The words stunned me momentarily — to think of Nancy as old was like thinking of the Albert Memorial as being out of fashion.

'She isn't old,' I said, defending her.

'My friend says so,' Rachel responded, ladling some honey onto a piece of toast. 'My friend says that her mother said that Nancy was old.'

Irritated, I slammed the papers down on the table top.

'Your friend's mother is an idiot!' I said. 'Nancy is not old, and is a damn sight more active than most people half her age. Go and tell your friend that.'

Rachel looked at me, surprise written all over her face.

'I didn't mean — '

Apologetically I smiled at her, and tapped her head with a sheaf of papers. 'Yes, I know. Go on now or you'll be late for school.'

I had not thought of Nancy as seen through Rachel's eyes; I could not stand back and see my grandmother as anything other than the very forceful, practical woman that she always had been. She couldn't get old — not Nancy, not the woman who had stood by us through everything, who had taken on both Alison and I, and then a child. Perhaps I had underestimated her, I thought, perhaps I was too used to her capabilities to see them for what they really were, and now perhaps I couldn't see that she was old, and tired.

The insight made me thoughtful for the remainder of the day, and when, that evening, the doorbell rang, I got to my feet reluctantly to find Alison standing on the doorstep, a suitcase in her hands.

'Hello, Jill,' she said, pecking me on the cheek and calling for Nancy who materialised almost immediately.

'Well, hello. How long this time?'

'What do you mean?'

310

'How long are you staying?'

Alison eyed me suspiciously. 'As long as Jill will let me have my child,' she said peevishly.

Nancy's patience erupted. 'Your child! Since when have you been so interested in your child?'

Behind us, Rachel ran out, her hands pressed over her ears. Alison watched her go and then turned back to Nancy.

'Rachel *is* my child, and I want her to know that. Obviously Jill has been taking her over since I've been away, so now she hardly knows me.'

'I'm not surprised, seeing how little time you spend here,' Nancy replied, and then lowered her voice. 'Listen to me, and listen good, Alison, you can't pick up a child and expect it to love you automatically, and then, when you're bored with her, give her back to us. Children need constant love and attention — not some sort of fair weather mother.'

Alison's mouth tightened at the corners, and spinning away from Nancy, she rounded on me.

'It's all your fault! All your fault! I've lost her because of you, and she's my child — not yours!' she shouted, and then calming herself, sat down on the chair beside the fire, her voice softer. 'She hates me — I can see it in her eyes. God knows what you've been doing to her.'

'Right! That's enough!' Nancy said, exasperated. 'You've no right to talk to Jill like that. She spends all her time with Rachel, and is the first one to tell her who her mother is. She makes excuses for you all the time.'

White with anger, Alison replied spitefully, 'Maybe it's her guilty conscience.'

311

A cold feeling slid down my back, like leaning against the tiled wall of a swimming bath.

'And what is that supposed to mean?' Nancy asked her, folding her arms across her chest.

'Ask your granddaughter.'

'Well?' she said, turning back to me.

'Alison . . . '

And then just as I was about to try and appease her, the phone rang and Alison went out to answer it, banging the door behind her as she went. Nancy sat down heavily, her legs splayed out in front of her.

'That blasted girl! What on earth is the matter with her now?' she said, glancing over to me. 'We'll have to watch all this arguing, Jill, it's not good for Rachel.'

I said nothing and sat down, waiting for Alison to return and resume the quarrel, although when she finally reopened the door, she was smiling.

'Well, I'm off out for dinner. So if you'll excuse me, I'll get dressed.'

Neither Nancy nor I said a word.

She left an hour later, turning at the door to tell us not to wait up for her.

'Alison, what about saying good night to your daughter?' Nancy said smoothly.

'Oh, kiss her for me, will you? Night.'

The argument was a turning point for Rachel, who from that evening on regarded her mother with little short of loathing. She never mentioned her unless we referred to Alison, and when I spoke to her teachers they told me that she insisted that I was her mother, although they had tried repeatedly to explain the truth to her.

'It's no good, Miss Henly, she won't accept it, no matter how often we tell her,' one particularly harassed teacher told me when I arrived early to collect Rachel. 'She just doesn't want to know about her real mother. I'm sorry.'

'I'm sure you tried your best,' I said reassuringly. 'Maybe she'll come round to it in time.'

Secretly, I hoped Rachel didn't. I hoped that she would turn to me more and more and regard me as the focal point in her life, because through her I had some purpose, I felt important; and besides, being a surrogate mother to a child was less dangerous than trying to compete for a man's affections. She needed me, I reasoned, and anyway, I owed it to Alison — didn't I?

But when Alison rang us from America late one night and told us she was coming home the following day, I was unreasonably alarmed.

'What for?' I asked her, raising my voice so that she could hear me over the muffled line.

'To see you all — why else?'

I wasn't convinced. 'But you sound so . . . lively — is everything all right?'

She laughed, the sound making tinny echoes on the phone.

'Everything is perfect, just perfect. I'll tell you all about it tomorrow.'

My curiosity was unbearable.

'Can't you tell me a little now?'

'And spoil a lovely surprise? No chance, Jill, I want to see your faces when I tell you.'

She rang off soon after, leaving me with the phone in my hand, and a very queasy feeling in my stomach. I was sure that Alison's idea of a surprise might turn out to be something unpleasant and disturbing, something which might rock the steady rhythm of our lives in the walled house. I dreaded her appearance the next day.

She arrived just as I drove in after collecting Rachel from school, standing on the path, her hair blowing slightly in the wind, an expression of intense pleasure on her face. The smile she was wearing was her secret one, her childhood smile of triumph.

'Hello, Alison,' I said, getting out and opening the back door of the car for Rachel. She hung back sullenly.

'Hello, Jill,' my sister responded, bending down towards Rachel who was still sitting in the back seat, having made no effort to greet her mother. 'What about a kiss for me?'

She still didn't move, and Alison, irritated, walked away towards the front door. Nancy was already there, drying her hands on a tea towel.

'My, don't you look well?' she said, smiling.

Alison smiled back and walked past her into the lounge, turning on the reading lamp and both bars of the electric fire because the room was chilly.

'Well, go on,' I said, watching her as she reorganised us.

'I'm getting married.'

'What?' Nancy said, her hands twisting the cloth round tightly.

'I'm getting married,' she repeated, turning her attention to Rachel who was hovering by the

314

door. 'Well darling, you're going to have a new daddy.'

'I've never had a daddy,' Rachel said defiantly.

'Well, you will have . . . very soon.'

I was too stunned to speak, although it wasn't that surprising, we knew that Alison would marry sometime. But to tell us like this, and to break the news to Rachel in such a harsh way . . . it was cruel.

'Alison — perhaps you would like to talk to Rachel on your own for a while?' I began, hoping she might pick up the hint.

It fell on deaf ears.

'Oh no, that's fine . . . and I know that my little girl will understand. How do you feel about all this, Rachel?'

Rachel was apparently struck by the same dumbness as Nancy, and said nothing as she edged her way towards me, to put the greatest distance between herself and her mother. Alison was genuinely bewildered.

'Well — are none of you going to congratulate me?'

I turned to Nancy, and watched as her face took on a look of resignation, as though she was finally seeing her granddaughter as she was, and understood that she couldn't change her.

'Who is he?'

'Matthew Reynolds, he's in banking and very rich.' She was confident of our approval. 'We'll be living in California, and you'll be able to have a pony, Rachel — won't that be nice?'

But her daughter still remained silent, catching hold of my hand, her fingers pressing into my

315

flesh. With a lunge of pity, I looked down at the back of her bent head, where a few strands of hair lay, as though painted, on the pale skin of her neck. I realised then that Alison was going to take her. She was going to take Rachel.

'But it's so far away . . . ' I began stiltedly. 'We won't see Rachel much.'

'You can visit,' Alison said sharply, implying that the matter was already settled. I felt my hand stiffen in Rachel's.

'Perhaps you ought to see how you settle down first, and then send for her.'

Nancy said nothing, she merely watched us both, her head moving from one to the other.

'No, Jill, I don't think so. I've said it before, and I'll say it again — Rachel is my daughter, not yours, even if you would like to pretend otherwise.'

'Alison, I'm not trying to take your child. I just thought that it might be too much of a shock for her, everything happening so suddenly.'

'You thought! You thought! That's all I ever hear — what you thought for *my* child. How dare you! When have I ever got involved with your life?'

'You never wanted to,' I said coldly.

'Well, are you surprised? You've got nothing I want — you never had. I can understand that you must be envious of me, all the things I have, but you . . . whatever have you got that I would want?'

Nancy stepped forward. 'This has gone far enough.'

'No, no, it hasn't,' Alison continued, 'it hasn't

316

gone nearly far enough. I've got something to say, and I'm going to say it.'

'Alison! I'm warning you. You show some respect and stop now, you're upsetting the child.'

Alison swung round to face her grandmother. 'Nancy, this is not your fight.'

Snatching hold of Rachel's hand, my grandmother walked to the door with her.

'Anything which involves this child is my fight. You aren't a fit mother and you don't deserve to have her. I never thought I would live to say this about one of my own, but I'm ashamed of you.'

She walked out and closed the door behind her. I could hear her footsteps, and the lighter ones of Rachel, as they went upstairs. Alison poured herself a drink and turned to me, her face impassive.

'Round one to you, I think,' she said, sipping her gin and tonic.

'What is it? What's the matter with you?' I asked.

'I want my child, that's all, — what every mother wants. But then, you wouldn't know, would you?'

'Why are you being such a bitch? It's not like you,' I said, stupified.

'I'm making up for lost time. I'm sick of being the nice one, the pretty one — I want to act as I feel, and that means that right now I could slap your face and take my child back to America with me.'

'You're jealous,' I said softly, watching as her face hardened.

'Yes, actually I am. Jealous of Rachel's love for

317

you. Seems incredible to think that I could envy you, doesn't it?'

I smiled slowly. After all these years I had the upper hand. I had actually won.

Soon afterwards she left, staying at the airport hotel before flying out the next day for California. Three days later we received an apologetic letter admitting that she had been impossible, and saying that we should put it all down to over-strained nerves. Nancy was unimpressed.

'She is not having Rachel until she deserves her,' she said adamantly.

But if we could talk about the matter amongst ourselves, Rachel remained absolutely silent on the topic, her attitude taking on a supreme calmness which was not natural in a child of her years. I left it a couple of days and then tackled her, determined that she would tell me what she really thought.

'You want me to go,' she said without a trace of emotion.

I was baffled.

'Rachel, whatever do you mean?'

'My mother gave me to you when she went away, and now you're giving me back.'

I caught hold of her and hugged her to me tightly. 'That is not true. I love you and I want to care for you always — but I'm not your mother, and I can't stop my sister from wanting to take you. She's your real mother.'

'She hates me,' Rachel said, her voice flat.

And I couldn't deny it. I couldn't look into her eyes and lie to her. So I hung onto her and

318

rocked her, and after a while, she slept.

The wedding took place only three weeks later, in a register office in the middle of London. There were only six people present, including Nancy, myself and Rachel. Alison wore a cream suit trimmed with brown, and a large hat with its brim turned back, so her face was shown to its full advantage. When the photographs were taken, she smiled professionally, whilst I smiled at the camera uneasily, half hiding myself behind a pillar. Her husband was a rather plump, balding man, with a deep, slow voice, and he hovered around her arrogantly with the air of a market trader who had made a good bargain. They looked ill-suited and on edge.

But her triumph regarding Rachel had been short lived. After my initial shock, I decided that she was not going to have the child I loved, and lived for. So carefully, artfully, I suggested that Rachel might become a difficult, withdrawn child, a child whose presence might well aggravate a new husband, and a high-flying lifestyle. With her usual pliancy, Alison turned the tables to suit herself.

'You know, you might well be right, Jill. I've thought about what you and Nancy said, and reread your letters, and decided that possibly it would be best to leave Rachel where she is happy. She has her schoolfriends here, and she might find it difficult to adjust to American life.'

'You are sure?' I said, knowing that she would not back off. She was thinking of her own comfort.

'Oh no, I mustn't be selfish. Thank you, Jill,

319

you've really been a great help.'

I smiled at her, and was still smiling as I watched my sister in the small room at the Dorchester where her reception was being held. The table was opulent with food and flowers, and Nancy tucked in vigorously, whilst Rachel picked at the edges of dishes and screwed up her napkin in her hand. She wore pink, and across her chest was a thick layer of smocking. She had chosen the dress herself, and hung around Alison in the hope that she might comment. When she finally paused to say that her daughter looked 'sweet', I could feel my own heart turn, and read the disappointment on Rachel's face.

As the afternoon wore on, Alison turned from an immaculate bride into a slightly tipsy woman. She was amusing and intelligent and made everyone laugh, but she was bordering uneasily on drunkenness. At the first opportunity I stepped in and steered her to the Powder Room where she sobered up quickly and adjusted her hair in the full length mirror, her fine legs perched on the highest of heels, her body leaning slightly towards the glass.

'Good luck, Alison,' I said genuinely. 'You deserve it.'

She stopped and laid her brush on a nearby table, sitting down and turning to me with an oddly sarcastic expression on her face.

'You're right, I do deserve it. After all, I've had such bad luck with men.'

My stomach flinched.

'Matthew seems a good man,' I said lamely, watching as her eyes sized me up.

'"A good man",' she mimicked. '"A good man.'
What the hell's the use of a good man? I wanted
a real man, someone with glamour and style,
someone like Mark Ward. Remember him
— good old Mark?'

I leant against the door of the Powder Room,
my palms flat against the wood.

'Alison.'

'Whatever happened to him, I wonder?' she
continued, ignoring me. 'Did you ever get to
meet him?'

'No . . . I never did.'

'Never, not once? You do surprise me.'

'No, never.'

'You would have liked him, Jill. He was tall
and good looking . . . but then, I've told you all
of this before, haven't I? During our little
conversations at home, when I was so *grateful*
for your help.'

She bit off the last word, like a child snapping
off a piece of rock, and I watched her, knowing
that she was going to say more. Silently, I prayed
that someone would walk in.

'Yes, he was quite a man. Shame that he was
married, after all, you'd done such a good job
trying to work everything out for us. Trying to
help.' She stood up and walked over to where I
was standing by the door. 'Shame he was no
good, when you thought he was the reliable kind.
Hey, Jill?'

She was very close to me; her face perfectly
beautiful, the long line of her eyes unblinking.
Suddenly she frightened me, seeing all her good
humour evaporate and in its place, a peculiarly

brittle hardness. I no longer knew her.

'I didn't know,' I began, and my voice cracked.

'No, I don't suppose that you did. After all, why would you deliberately set out to ruin me, to wreck my chances? Why would you hate me so much that you wanted to hurt me? Why? That was the real question — why? It kept going round and round in my head.' She jerked a finger in front of my face. 'Why?'

Clumsily I moved away from her, and walked over to a small, curtained window in the far corner. She watched me, her hands on her hips.

'Then I thought back over all our years together — all the times you had been jealous of my boyfriends, or my looks, or my success. All the little jibes . . . remember those, Jill?'

'Alison, you've had too much to drink — '

She hurled the lipstick she was holding towards me, though I ducked and it hit the wall above my head.

'Don't you stand there and judge me!' she shouted as the door opened.

The woman who stood there took in the scene immediately and before Alison had a chance to say anything else, she backed out and let the door slam behind her.

'You bitch!' Alison hissed at me. 'You conniving, cunning, spying, underhand bitch! You're rotten with jealousy — do you know that? Eaten with it. Consumed by it. You're sick . . . and all because you're not beautiful, and instead of coming to terms with that, you tried to make me pay for your lack. It wasn't fair.

'Alison, it's not what you think — '

322

She cut me off immediately, her arms folded, her fingers drumming on the sleeves of her wedding suit.

'But what I couldn't figure out was why? Why? Then after all these years it came to me.' She looked squarely at my face, her eyes hard as flint. 'He wouldn't have anything to do with you, would he? You were both in the same business, you and Mark, so you must have met previously — and he'd ignored you. Wasn't that it, answer me!'

I responded dully. 'Yes, I met him before. We went out for lunch once . . . it was a disaster, and yes, he didn't want me. Does that satisfy you?'

It didn't, I could tell that by her eyes.

'So here we have one jealous female, and our dashing hero — enter the sister who had met him before, and bingo! The scene is set for the aforementioned plain sister to encourage her unsuspecting pretty sister to fall in love — knowing that the dashing hero would drop her like a hot brick when the novelty had worn off. I'm not going too fast for you, am I?'

I didn't reply.

'Foolishly, the sister falls madly in love and gets pregnant, thinking that he is the reliable kind and will marry her.' She laughed shortly. 'You must have got some mileage out of that one — quite a giggle, I'd say.'

'I didn't feel that way, I was — '

'What were you? Sorry? Guilty? Ashamed? What exactly did you feel?'

I wasn't going to answer her. I kept thinking that if this was all she knew, we could come out

323

of this without ruining the whole structure of our lives. I kept hoping.

'But that wasn't enough,' she continued, 'was it? Oh, Jill, why did you meet up with him afterwards and get involved, how could you sleep with him when I was having his child? How could you do that to your own sister?'

She knew. She knew everything.

'I hated myself.'

'Some good that did! Did it stop you from creeping off to see him at every opportunity? Did it stop you from climbing into bed with him? How did you feel, leaving me in that house and going off to see him? Lying to Nancy? How *did* that feel, I'm curious.'

'I wanted him.'

'So did I! So did I! He was the one man I *did* want, and you knew that, and then to take him away from me and keep him for yourself.' She looked away, close to tears. 'I want to know one thing — when did he dump you?'

I flushed with indignation, and turned away. I could have told her that he left his wife for me, that he had wanted me far more than he wanted her. I could have destroyed that beautiful woman in front of me, by saying — *yes, I know I'm plain but the man you wanted chose me instead of you, that's how you failed* — I could have, but I didn't.

'He couldn't have loved you!' she said, tears in her voice. 'He couldn't have! You've no style, you're ugly and fat, and have nothing that a man like him could want . . . Mark couldn't have loved you, it's impossible.'

324

'You're right, it's impossible,' I said dully.

'Don't agree with me! Don't do that, thinking I'll forgive you because you've been found out. He couldn't have loved you, he just wanted — '

She stopped short.

'Someone to sleep with?' I finished bitterly. 'Why don't you say it, Alison? There's an old saying from Richelieu I think, something about 'all cats being grey at night'. Well, maybe he did use me, and maybe it didn't matter what I looked like — but he wanted me for a time, and that was enough. I may never get the chance to love anyone again.'

'He didn't love you,' she repeated stubbornly, tears running down her face.

'How do you know?' I asked her,

'I know.'

My fingers played with the floral curtain whilst I waited for her to continue. A minute passed, and then another, before I spoke, unable to remain silent any longer.

'You said that this only came to you the other day,' I said slowly. 'Well how did you know that I was seeing Mark whilst you were carrying Rachel?'

She looked over to me and smiled, her mouth tilting upwards, her small teeth showing slightly.

' 'I'm sorry, so sorry, Alison',' she mimicked so that I recognised the words I had used the night when I looked in on her, and thought she was asleep.

'And that was enough to tell you all this?' I asked, dumbfounded.

'No, I suspected something, but I wasn't sure.

Then that night I heard you come in and I was just about to speak when you said that . . . I knew then. Then I was certain.'

She was calmer after the outburst, and sat down on the chair facing the mirror, so that I could see her face reflected in the glass.

'I'll tell you something,' she said softly, 'you can have that child.' She jerked her thumb towards the door. 'I don't want anything to do with her, she reminds me too much of Mark, and of you.'

'Rachel is still your child, and she needs you.'

Carefully, she dabbed at her mouth with a tissue.

'She was never my child. I wouldn't have given birth to her, if it hadn't been for you and Nancy. I never wanted to be a woman with a child and no husband — it would look as though I had failed.'

'Alison, she's a beautiful child, and she's yours. Not mine, not Nancy's — you can't take it out on the child.'

'I can do as I please,' she said, straightening up in her chair. 'I have a rich husband, and a new, glamorous life, meeting interesting people and travelling. I intend to spend as little time as possible in this country.'

'I'm sorry — that's all I can say to you. What I did was unforgivable, but I had no one . . . and I probably never will again. You came back from the States and said that you'd fallen in love with Mark, and only months before I'd met him and wanted him, and . . . it seemed too unfair, too cruel for it to be the same man.' I didn't know if she was listening, but I continued. 'Yes, I was jealous, but believe me when I say that I only wanted to hurt you to get my own back, just so you would feel some of the agony I'd felt, being the one constantly passed over.' I knelt down by the side of her chair. 'Alison, listen to me, I never meant it to get out of hand, or for you to get pregnant and suffer so much — I never meant that. I never got a minute's pleasure from your distress . . . I nearly went mad with guilt.'

She looked down at me. 'But you still had an affair with him. How did that fit into your guilt pangs?'

'I've told you. He was the only man who had ever looked twice at me. I needed him.'

'But I wouldn't have done it to you.'

'Alison, you would never have needed to,' I said quietly. And that's the difference. You could have anyone, anyone you chose, and I had only the one chance and I took it. Wrong as it was, vindictive as it was — much as it betrayed you and Nancy — I still did it, because at the time it was too strong to resist. I'm not making excuses, I'm just trying to explain that I wasn't gloating over you . . . I was just so hopelessly grateful to him.'

Her face took on the look she had worn so many times before, the look of childhood, the expression of something bordering on arrogance.

'Tell me, when did he leave you?' she asked quietly.

If I told her that he had left me she would be able to keep the upper hand; she would be able to preserve her ego. If I told her the truth, I knew that her face would crumble, and that a steady, grinding doubt would lodge in her and follow her down the years. Mark had wanted me, I thought to myself, he had left his wife for me — maybe it was enough that only I knew the facts.

'The day you had Rachel,' I began, picking my words carefully, my voice by then emotionless. 'He said that he no longer wanted to see me.' I hid my face from her by lowering my head. 'He said that it had been fun, having two sisters, but that I had been a complete fool and a bore . . . he told me to go, and said that he never wanted to see me again.'

After a while I heard her breathing evenly, and when I looked up, she had repaired her make-up, and was smiling at me. She helped me to my feet gently, and kissed both of my cheeks.

'Poor Jill,' she said softly, and walked out.

24

We lived, the three of us, myself, Rachel and Nancy, in the same house that I had occupied as a child, Rachel taking over Alison's old room when she was ten years old, her hair cut short, and her figure boylike and agile as she climbed the apple tree under my window. She altered as she grew, naturally, her oval face enhanced by a pair of splendid eyes, shaped like her mother's, although her skin burnt in the sun if she stayed out too long. Mentally, she was quick to learn and skilful with her hands, achieving and holding her place as one of the brightest girls at her school. Rachel was not the beauty her mother was, but she was very attractive and sometimes when I looked at her, I was dizzy with pride.

She could be lazy though, if we didn't nag her to work, and at every opportunity she sneaked off to climb trees, or play in the park.

'You've got to do your homework, Rachel,' I said, watching her wheel her bike into the garage, her trousers torn round the ankles. 'It's for the best, you know, even if it's a bore now.'

'I've done it.'

'No, you haven't, I've found a half finished essay under one of the cushions in the lounge.'

She looked grudgingly at me. 'If I finish it, can I go out again?'

I paused for effect.

'Maybe. I'll read it before I decide.'

I learnt to be tough with her, as she was left more and more under my control. Nancy stepped back and continued with her own interests, and Alison remained in California, giving birth to a son eighteen months after she married. They called him Robert, after Matthew's father. Now and again, she sent us a picture of the child, who looked remarkably like his father when he was only months old, with the same self-satisfied, worldly air.

Despite her continued disinterest in her mother, Rachel was fascinated by the new baby.

'Do you think she'll bring him over when she comes?' Rachel asked me.

'Who's 'she'?' I replied, knowing full well.

'My mother. Well, do you think my mother will bring him?'

'I can't say . . . why?'

I was sitting by the window in the lounge, Nancy doing her crossword by the fire, and Rachel hovering round me.

'It would be nice to have a baby in the house,' she replied thoughtfully, adding, 'Do you think you'll get married, Jill?'

Nancy snorted with laughter across the room.

'I'm not sure. You think I should provide you with someone to play with — is that it?' I asked her, amused.

She blushed easily, something she had not inherited from either her mother or her father.

'No . . . it doesn't matter.' She walked over to the bookshelves. 'I just thought that you might like to get married, that's all.'

330

'And who would want a plain old stick like me?'

'Sarah's aunt is much worse than you and she's married.'

I could see Nancy's newspaper shaking as she laughed, and for a moment I was too taken aback to answer. By the time I had recovered, Rachel was continuing smoothly, 'I'm sure someone will come along, you're much nicer than most people, so you're bound to find someone.'

It was of much less consequence to me than it was to Rachel. I was happy in the walled house, and settled at work. Edward went into semi-retirement when my niece was eight and from then on I had the run of the place, taking over his duties with a confidence which surprised me. His health suffered and he became bedridden, working intermittently, although he always asked me to bring Rachel to see him once a week, because she made him laugh.

'Do you mind?' I asked her, wondering what she thought of visiting some very old man, in a dusty, faded bedroom at the top of a London town house.

'No. He's odd, like an old fossil, and anyway he's got loads of good stories.' She bent down to pull up her socks. 'Besides, no one at school knows anyone half as scary.'

She had a tremendous gift for making the best out of any situation, and seemed to lack Alison's self-absorption and rather sickly charm. Her attitude was direct and genuine, and the slight awe in which she had held Nancy when she was younger changed, so that a closeness built up between them and they talked for hours, sometimes sitting by the wall in the garden, or laughing in the kitchen when Nancy baked.

So I went from a contented home life to a career which was not exactly brilliant, but very sound. I still responded like a child when someone rang me and asked me to look at a find, or visit a dig in the wilds somewhere. Weather seldom prevents me from driving out to see what some previous generation has left so considerately for us to find centuries later, and there is still the same thrill when I turn a piece of bone over in my fingers, or wait patiently smoking a cigarette and leaning against the car, for something to be uncovered.

Typically, Rachel found my work absorbing, and dragged along her reluctant schoolfriends to listen to my lectures, held quite often in draughty village halls.

'They're not interested, dear, and you shouldn't expect them to be.'

'Nonsense,' she replied, sounding not a little like Nancy. 'You're marvellous.'

It seemed that adolescence troubled her as little as childhood had done, although in her thirteenth year she began suddenly to want to find out more about her father.

'Jill, tell me what my father was like.'

I thought for a long moment.

'He was gentle and kind and good,' I lied. 'He was handsome and clever and he loved your mother very much. He would have loved you too, a great deal.'

'Then why doesn't he get in touch?'

'Because we didn't tell him about you,' I answered, turning back to some papers I had been fiddling with.

'Why didn't you tell him?'

'Because he was married.'

The truth appeared to satisfy her, or rather, my version of the truth, and for a time she didn't ask me anything else. To Rachel, her father was good and handsome, and only fate prevented him from recognising her as his daughter.

So the walled house continued as a house of women; no men intruded into it, and nothing remained of a male presence, other than the photograph of my grandfather on the piano. I thought of Mark, because he was still so much a part of me, and because his child held on to me, and loved me, and through her, he was still present — and what was more important, the very best part of him remained with me. Not the unhappiness, the uncertainty, not the humiliation and deceit, only the soundness of a love I had thought to get from a man, and found in a man's child.

Then when Rachel turned fourteen, she altered, throwing off the tomboy and turning, it seemed almost overnight, into a singularly composed, and well-balanced girl. School became a means by which she could prove herself, and even at that age she decided to become a doctor, and worked towards that goal.

'Are you sure?' I asked her, trying not to let pride bubble up in me. 'It's a long time to spend studying, and a very hard way to earn a living.'

333

She was sitting on the arm of Nancy's chair, her hand resting on my grandmother's.

'Honestly, I've never been more certain of anything in my life. I can do it.'

'That's not what's bothering me,' I continued. 'I know you are perfectly capable, it's just that a decision like that is very important.'

She thought for a moment, and I looked at her. Late spring sunshine fell on her head, and made freckles on the shoulder length dark hair. Her skin was pale, the tremendous beauty of her eyes hidden as she glanced down. Next to Nancy, she appeared very slight, although she was not thin, only finely built, the inheritance of her mother's grace much apparent. Not for the first time did I wonder how Alison could live, seeing her daughter only once, or twice a year. She looked older than she was, and mature. I understood then that she would leave us, one day.

'No, I'm sure,' Rachel said, lifting her head to look at me. 'It's right.'

So we encouraged her from that moment on, Nancy spending hours testing her for examinations, which took her through O Levels, and on to A Levels, whilst she continued to alter and astonish us both.

At seventeen, she visited her mother on her own for the first time, being sure that she could cope with Alison alone. Previously, I or Nancy had gone with her. We waited for news, and when she rang long distance, we sighed with relief.

'Hi! It's me, Rachel — how are you both?'

'We're well,' I shouted down the phone, as Nancy bent her ear to it to hear. 'How was the flight? Did Matthew meet you?'

'Yes, he was there when I got off, and Mother.'

I could see Alison in my mind, her glamorous figure at the barrier waiting for her daughter. Playing the loving mother.

'Is it warm out there?'

'*What?*'

'Is it warm?' I bellowed.

'Yes, it's lovely. Mother sends a kiss to you both.'

Nancy and I exchanged a look.

'I'm off now — I'll see you soon, don't worry,' she said, and put down the phone.

When she returned she seemed altered, and after a little probing it came out that she had met some boy and that he had been interested in her. A slow feeling of dread welled up in me as I wondered if she would be like me, totally incapable of dealing with her emotions.

'Do you like him?' I asked her, as she finished her unpacking.

'A little bit.'

'But not much.'

'No, not much.'

I should have felt relieved.

'What did your mother think about all this?'

'She said that I was old enough to make up my own mind,' Rachel replied calmly.

'Your own mind about what?'

'About whether or not to sleep with him, I suppose.'

A wedge settled round my throat and stuck

there; how could Alison be so uncaring, so cavalier? Hadn't she suffered enough with her affairs, not to give her daughter such a free hand when she was only seventeen years old? I looked up at Rachel who had paused and was watching me.

'I didn't sleep with him, Jill. Why should I? What would have been the point?' she said softly, sitting down next to me on the bed. 'I don't want to end up like Mother, do I? With a child she never wanted, and now resents because it gives away her age? No, that's not for me.' She squeezed my hand, the comforter for once. 'I'm going to be a doctor, and have a career, and one day, if I'm lucky, a man. If not, I'll be very happy to live as you do.'

'Believe me,' I said, turning to her, 'you'll marry one day, and it'll be the right man.' She looked so like Mark — the same expression in her eyes, the same attractiveness without the conceit. 'Trust me, I know.'

She shrugged. 'Well, frankly I don't care . . . Can you help me with this suitcase?' she asked, changing the subject and lightening the atmosphere.

She did keep in close contact with Alison though after that trip and it worried me, until I realised that the main reason was Robert, my sister's son, who had become very close to Rachel. He wrote letters to her, addressed by Matthew at the office, with his child's appalling handwriting telling her that he missed her and that they could go on the beach again when she came back. She laughed when she read them,

336

passing the notes over to me, or Nancy, who always complained about the spelling.

'I spent years with that girl, and she never could spell, and now she's passing all her bad habits on to her son. God help us all.'

But it did me good to see the loving side of Rachel, not merely the affection she had always shown to me, but a caring, considerate nature which extended towards Alison's child and my grandmother, who was growing older.

Not long after the American trip, Rachel began to worry about Nancy.

'Don't you think she's getting a bit rickety?' she asked me one morning, after I had taken up a breakfast tray for my grandmother.

'No. Why?'

Rachel lowered her voice, although Nancy couldn't have heard us from her bedroom. 'I thought she looked as though she's lost some weight. I could be wrong.'

Considering that Rachel seldom said anything without careful thought, it seemed unlikely that she was mistaken.

'I'll have a look at her later . . . Okay?'

She nodded.

'Are you going to school?' I prompted her, and she nodded, kissed me and left.

Alarmed by what Rachel had said I watched Nancy carefully, but she seemed little altered, her temper as hot as ever that day as she ate enough for four, the toaster clicking on and off like a pair of castanets. Whenever I hear a toaster now, I think of her. We went out that afternoon because I got back from work early, and we walked around the shops, looking at what we were thinking of buying for Christmas. I did notice a slight alteration in her step, a slight hesitation, but I refused to see it, and when Rachel came home from school, I greeted her cheerfully.

'She's fine, just a bit tired, that's all.'

But with her usual bluntness, Rachel persisted, 'Is she going to die?'

'For God's sake!' I shouted, unnerved. 'Why do you say such stupid things?'

Her face flushed.

'You can be so . . . ridiculous at times,' I continued angrily.

'I'm not stupid — '

I flared up at her again. 'Don't shout at me, Rachel — you might be able to get away with that with your mother, but not with me.'

'You're jealous of her!' she cried without thinking, and then, seeing the look on my face, stopped short.

'I'm sorry — '

'Oh, why be sorry, Rachel, after you said the words? Sorry, sorry? What does that mean . . . If you thought it, maybe it was better that it came out.'

I was white with anger as I looked at her, even though her obvious misery should have made me realise that she regretted what she had said. It seemed as though she, of all people, was resurrecting old ghosts.

'I was angry — I would have said anything,' she said, trying to appease me.

'But you didn't say anything, did you? You said

that I was jealous of your mother — that is a very specific statement, Rachel, and either you've been thinking it for a long time, or Alison has put the thought into your head.'

'She didn't . . . I said it to hurt you.'

'You succeeded, my girl,' I said bitterly, and left the room.

I think I might have brooded on the quarrel for hours had there not been a knock on my bedroom door only minutes later.

'Yes?'

'It's Rachel, can I come in?'

'If you want to,' I said childishly, and she walked in and stood by the window, the light behind her. I fidgeted idly with something on my dressing table.

'Jill, I'm sorry if I hurt you, it was wrong of me, and I regret what I said, it was just that you seem to resent my mother so much, and you throw her into my face so often.'

I hadn't realised.

'I don't mean to,' I said slowly.

'Why do you hate her so much?'

'I don't hate her, but over the years we've hurt each other so much, and I've been so envious of her, and then she was jealous of me — because you loved me more than you loved her . . . ' I trailed off, no longer wanting to talk about the two of us.

'Don't you think I feel it?' she said savagely, making me glance over to her. 'Don't you think that I know how much you dislike each other? How much do you think it hurts me — that my mother gave me away? She gave me away

— because she didn't want me.' Rachel stopped talking and glanced down, her voice wavering. 'I love you, I've always loved you, and I can't help it if I said something to hurt you, but sometimes,' she put back her head and looked up to the ceiling, 'sometimes I still feel like an associate member of this club, and not really a part of it.'

I did her the courtesy of not interrupting — the wounds were old ones, and needed to be healed.

'You and Alison; you and Nancy; Nancy, you and Alison — all three of you, all bound up in yourselves, so that no one ever really made an impression — even my father disappeared after I was conceived. No one other person has ever been included in your set-up, and even though my mother is on the other side of the earth, the mention of her name sends you in paroxysms of anger. And she's just as bad. I'm with her and I mention you, she explodes and says that I love you better, and that she never had a chance to prove herself as a mother, although how she works that out I'll never know.' She turned away and looked out of the window. 'I've been happy, I've had a happy childhood, but I think that we should all now try and live as peacefully as we can, because otherwise, we'll destroy each other.'

She was right, but I couldn't answer her. For a few minutes she watched the garden and then she turned to face me, her arms folded, her slim figure dark against the light.

'I know why you acted that way just now, it

340

was because I asked if Nancy was doing to die — that's the reason, isn't it?'

I nodded.

'I know how you love her, and I'm sorry if I frightened you by mentioning her death — do you forgive me?'

I held out my arms and she rushed into them, suddenly the child again.

'Nancy will die, Rachel, but not yet.'

'How do you know?'

'I'm not sure but something will tell me.'

I don't understand how I knew, but I developed a sense which I believed would tell me when my grandmother was going to leave us, and as long as I did not feel that deep sense of loss, I continued as normal, and waited.

That Christmas. Alison visited, and remembering what Rachel had said, I made an extra effort not to quarrel with her. She was as lovely as ever, although the bleakness of her personality made her strident at times and there was seldom any warmth in her. Occasionally, though, a brandy could resurrect her maternal feelings.

'She's lovely, isn't she?' Alison said as I cleared the dishes off the table.

'You mean Rachel?'

She nodded, watching her through the kitchen door. 'Do you think she's like me?'

'No, Alison, I think she's like her mother *and* her father,' I said, and waited for the reaction.

To my surprise, my sister smiled, and glanced back to her daughter.

'You know, you're right,' she agreed without rancour.

From then onwards, an uneasy truce developed between us. Perhaps because we had finally acknowledged Mark, the old gremlins fell off one by one, and although we didn't have any overnight revelation, the atmosphere beween us became almost comfortable. Rachel noticed the difference, and had the tact not to mention it directly, although she fussed over both of us as her way of saying thank you.

But after Christmas, and Alison's return to America, a long, dark winter set in on us and made the house cold and the nights long and comfortless. Nancy caught a bad cold and retired to bed with hot water bottles and a tumbler of whisky which was refilled at regular intervals. Her hearing was the first sign of her advancing age; it began to fade quite quickly, making her impatient.

'What did you say?'

'*Are you hungry?*' I shouted back.

'Of course I'm hungry! What sort of a stupid question is that?'

She made both Rachel and I laugh when she pulled faces, and if she answered the phone she roared down it to the unsuspecting party at the other end as all deaf people do. At night she sometimes fell asleep with her hearing aid in, and I took it out and put it beside her bed, laying it near to her clock and whichever book she was reading. I watched her carefully.

But mornings saw her bright and full of enthusiasm, even if it did take her a long time to dress and arrange her hair as she liked it. I never dared to offer to help, and only Rachel could convince her to rest if she didn't feel like it.

'Just for half an hour,' she said, leaning towards Nancy's ear so that she could hear her.

'You're not a doctor yet,' Nancy answered querulously, secretly delighting in the fuss. 'I shall have ten minutes and no more.'

Ten minutes crept round to an hour, and she still slept, her head lolled over to one side, her mouth slackened. When she woke, she grabbed the evening paper eagerly and read out the news to us.

'Right! Now I'll tell you who's died.'

'That's morbid,' Rachel said, screwing her face up.

'Rubbish, it's the only way I can get my own back on some people, knowing I've outlived them!'

But it seemed over the next few weeks that it was merely her bravado which kept her going, the hugeness of her personality which dragged her through each day. She lapsed back into her childhood, and told me repeatedly about her wedding, confiding more about her husband than she ever had.

'We should have tried harder, you know, Jill. We should really. I was to blame for being so . . . hard on him.'

'I don't believe you. He needed to be pushed, otherwise he wouldn't have done anything with his life.'

She turned her head to catch my words.

'And what good did it do him, hey? All that pushing, all that trying, maybe I should just have

343

left him to potter in his garden and smoke his pipe.'

'He wasn't unhappy.'

She thought for a moment, and grinned, a huge crescent of a smile peeling across her face.

'No, he wasn't unhappy, and when we were young he could be very happy indeed.'

'Do you miss him?' I asked her, wanting to keep the conversation flowing about him.

'No, not at all, until lately. Lately I've been thinking about him a lot more.' She pulled herself up in her seat, and nodded her head upstairs. 'She turned out all right, didn't she? That girl of Alison's.'

I smiled. 'Oh, I think she turned out a little more than all right, I think we did rather well with her.'

Smiling contentedly, my grandmother leant her head back against her chair. On her lap was the inevitable newspaper, the crossword page folded over, and the first few clues entered. Beside us, the clock ticked hypnotically and, against the window, a small shower tapped its fingers on the glass pane. For a moment I felt a sense of belonging, of complete contentment, but when I turned round to Nancy to speak again, she was asleep.

Her face, which was totally relaxed then, was older, even I couldn't pretend otherwise. The youth had gone, and in its place was the expression of what my grandmother had become. There was a firmness around the mouth, and even though her eyes were closed, some feeling of humour remained. I watched her

344

avidly, saw the plump hands, and the full flesh of her body filling the chair where she slept, and as I looked, a dull sense of panic ate into me. For the first time ever, I saw that she was going to die. That she was turning already towards her parting, and that there was nothing, absolutely nothing, I could do to prevent her loss.

In her own way she had decided that this was the right time. Her instincts told her that Rachel was mature, and that she was capable and no longer needed her as before, and as for me — wasn't I settled in my own life, and happy? She also knew that I was not going to be alone, that although I had not married, I had someone who was devoted to me, and that child would remain close to me throughout my life. To my grandmother, who had dreaded that I might have been left alone, the knowledge was comforting and absolved her of any further responsibility towards me.

I understood how she thought, but I dreaded her going.

Later I told Rachel what I believed.

'I think Nancy's ill,' I said simply, seeing how her back stiffened and her face flushed.

'Are you sure?'

I nodded.

'You mean,' she said uncertainly, 'that she's going to die?'

'Yes, I'm afraid I do,' I replied softly, holding her to me. In spite of all I felt for my grandmother I was calm, my voice did not break, neither did I feel any anger at her going. She had done enough for me.

'Can I do anything?' Rachel asked me, drawing away and dabbing at her eyes.

'Just don't let on you know, that's all. Carry on as normal.' I glanced up to the first floor, where I could hear Nancy moving around. 'I don't want her to suspect anything — I only told you so you'd be prepared.'

She seemed suddenly young again, all her newly acquired polish cracking under the strain.

'You could be wrong though, couldn't you?'

She was still a child, after all.

25

Nancy died three days later, having fallen asleep with her hand in mine. She faded quickly, her heart giving out abruptly and shockingly, whilst I sat by her. That morning she had been very bright, but then they do say that often happens, just before someone dies, a last burst of energy and then — nothing. I sat there stupidly, knowing that she would have wanted to be efficient and practical, but for almost an hour I couldn't move, and only the sound of Rachel coming home startled me into action.

Reluctantly I walked to the head of the stairs and looked down, seeing her dark head and hearing the bang of her books as she tossed them onto the hall table. She turned and saw me, her face taking on a smile of welcome.

'What an awful day,' she began, and then stopped short, her eyes reading mine. 'How's Nancy?'

'Rachel — '

There was no need to say more, she merely nodded, ran past me and made for her grandmother's bedroom. When I got there she was standing beside Nancy's bed, her hands smoothing the sheet.

'She didn't suffer,' I said slowly, and then sat down without another word.

Rachel leant over the bed and very gently kissed Nancy's forehead. She then straightened up, walked over to me and knelt down. Her eyes were huge with tears.

'How long ago did she . . . ?'

'About an hour, I think.'

My voice sounded peculiar and unreal, and in the room I could smell the faint perfume of freesia from the bunch I had bought her only days before.

'Shouldn't we ring someone?' Rachel suggested practically.

'Yes, yes, that would be the right thing to do,' I began and then drifted away, too stunned to think clearly.

'The doctor?' Rachel prompted me, and I nodded, although what she said next I didn't catch, and never even asked her to repeat it.

He arrived soon afterwards, by which time I had bathed my face in cold water, and tidied the bedroom although it hardly needed it. Rachel showed him upstairs and stood beside me as he wrote out the death certificate, and offered me a sedative.

'No thank you, I don't want anything,' I said firmly, relieved that my voice had returned to normal, and that I no longer felt light-headed.

'It might help,' he insisted, leaving a few tablets in a bottle, in case I changed my mind. He then told us which undertakers to contact, saying that they were sympathetic people, and that he used them often. I thought Nancy would have laughed at the implication.

The doctor was right; they were helpful and kind, and spoke in whispers, and until they removed Nancy I was perfectly in control. But as she was taken to their vehicle outside my throat closed momentarily, and a dull, hammering dizziness began in my ears. Rachel held on to my arm and then turned me away from the front door, and steered me towards the lounge.

It struck me then, as I sat down, that there had never been a photograph of Nancy on the piano. There were all the ones of us, Alison, myself, Rachel, my grandfather and my mother and father, but not one of her. I made a note that as soon as I was able, I was going to get the large print of her developed, and place it, right at the front, in a silver frame.

So the two of us staggered through the rest of the day, and although I did not ask her, I wondered if Rachel listened for the sound of Nancy upstairs, or for the noise of the doors banging as she came in from the garden. We both hung on, dry-eyed, until I found the newspaper on the kitchen table, the one from the previous night, turned to the crossword page, where half the spaces were filled. I was crying when Rachel walked in and we clung to each other and sobbed for minutes at a time, until a calmness came back to the two of us.

'I have to ring your mother, you know,' I said, as I cleaned my glasses on the kitchen tea towel.

'Do you want me to tell her?'

'No, love, thanks just the same, I must be the one to let her know.'

When I did finally get through, it appeared that Alison was holding a party, judging by the amount of background noise, and when I asked her if she could take the call somewhere private, she bristled.

'What for? You're such a dry old stick, Jill.'

'I have something important to tell you, Alison, and I think you'll understand when you hear.'

Her curiosity finally overrode her annoyance, and after a few seconds she picked up another extension in the house.

'Well, this had better be good, I've got nearly fifty people downstairs.'

'Alison — Nancy's dead. She died this afternoon.'

There was silence on the line, then the sound of sobbing, followed by the noise of a phone being dropped, and finally Matthew's voice. 'I'm sorry about that, Jill, but Alison's so upset — she said that Nancy's dead. Is there anything I can do?'

'No, nothing, thanks, Matthew. I merely rang to tell you what had happened and arrange the funeral for when you can come over.'

He took charge easily, and within minutes we had the arrangements settled. He seemed eager to help, and genuinely sorry. A good man, in fact.

The next days followed awkwardly, although Rachel was given time off school, and was a tremendous help. She fielded the many phone calls that came through from people offering their condolences, and passed on only the few friends to whom she knew I wanted to speak. Her attitude was one of calm, steady reliability, and only her constant, unspoken support got me through the days following Nancy's death — days which otherwise would have destroyed me.

The night before the funeral, Alison arrived with Matthew, the rain lashing down on them as they got out of the car, their suitcases dripping in the hall. Matthew greeted me with a kiss to the cheek, and then patted Rachel on the shoulder in a fatherly, sympathetic fashion. They had left Robert behind in California.

'I don't think funerals are good for children,' Alison explained, kissing Rachel and turning to me, 'do you? You know, you've lost weight, Jill, and it suits you,' she added smiling.

I was unreasonably annoyed.

'Do you want to see Nancy?' I asked, watching her face for the reaction. She looked horrified.

'Is she here?' she asked, lowering her voice.

'No, she's in a Chapel of Rest,' I said, 'but you could go and visit her if you want, before the funeral tomorrow.'

Her smile was strained.

'I don't think so, I'd rather remember her as she was alive.'

Rachel moved over to her mother, taking her coat. 'She looks lovely, you'd be surprised. Actually, Nancy looks as well as she ever did.'

'Have you been?' Alison asked, impressed.

'Twice,' Rachel responded and walked off, taking the coat and a suitcase with her. I smiled inwardly.

'Do you want something to eat, Alison?'

'No, I couldn't, it was such a bad flight . . . ' She nodded towards her husband. 'Matthew

351

might be hungry though.'

I made him dinner, and afterwards he retired to bed, leaving Alison, Rachel and I in the lounge. The atmosphere was artificially light, and seemed to threaten either an argument or a display of grief. I poured my sister a drink, and threw some more logs onto the fire, seeing how they blazed up and illuminated Alison's face as she sat there, her long legs crossed, her hair shiny and perfectly arranged. Beside her, only a couple of feet away, was Rachel, sitting in her chair, her hands laid idly on the sides of the arm rests. They were similar, and yet totally dissimilar. Whereas Alison was breathtakingly, unusually lovely, her daughter's face was stronger, more expressive, the deep blue of her eyes clear, and the look even. Of the two of them, Rachel was oddly the most impressive, because her personality swamped the thin charm of her mother, and encouraged interest, more by character, than by initial beauty.

'What time did you say the service was?' Alison asked me, twirling her drink around in the glass.

'Eleven thirty.'

She thought for a moment.

'Did you put a notice in the paper?'

'Yes, Alison,' I replied.

'And rung the people who don't read it?'

'Yes.'

'Everyone?'

'Everyone I could think of.'

She frowned, and took off her earrings, laying them on the table next to her. They caught the

352

firelight and flickered.

'Did she say anything?' she said quietly, and out of the corner of my eye I could see Rachel stiffen and turn her head towards her mother.

'No, she died without saying anything.'

'Are you sure, Jill?'

'Of course I am, I was there.'

'I just wondered.'

'Why?'

She shrugged.

'It was just that . . . I wondered if she missed me,' she said, downing her drink and looking back to the fire, embarrassed.

After all this time she was still jealous of us. Still felt excluded, although she had excluded herself, and still hurt that we had continued happily without her, when she wasn't the centre of our world. She resented our closeness, that bond which Nancy and I had enjoyed, even though she never had the patience, or desire, to sacrifice her own ambitions to achieve it. I looked at her, and felt sorry because I knew that now she was the least happy of the two of us, that although she had been ruthless and ambitious, she had finally discovered that nothing mattered to her other than her family, and what it had represented. She had dismissed Nancy, and abandoned Rachel, and I felt sorry, because she was suffering for it.

'When will you be going back to America?' Rachel asked, breaking into the silence.

'Oh, tomorrow night . . . there seems little point hanging around in such unhappy circumstances.'

She was trying to put on a brave face, and it hurt me more than her usual brashness.

'You could stay on a while if you like.'

She seemed interested, and looked from me to Rachel.

'Yes, I could, couldn't I?' she said slowly. 'But what about Matthew? He has to go back for business.'

Rachel seemed to pick up my train of thought, and continued easily: 'He could go on his own, he's not a baby. And Robert's all right where he is.'

There was a sharp jab of pain in my chest as I watched Alison hovering, wanting desperately to be needed by us, and yet frightened to stay. She was wondering if we meant it, if we wanted her, and I recognised the feeling well.

'Alison, stay with us, just for a few days, it would do you good . . . and besides, we'd like you here.'

I thought she was going to cry, that her immaculate face might turn into a parody, but instead she swung round happily in her seat to face me.

'I'll stay, you're right, I can go back on my own.'

'That's good,' I said quietly, smiling across to my niece. 'That's the right thing to do.'

The day of the funeral was overcast, the sun hidden behind clouds, the house cold. I locked the door behind us, and got into my own car with Rachel, Alison and Matthew sitting in the back. From my sister's face it appeared that she had been crying, although her mood was calm.

354

We drove in silence to the church, and as I walked in I was astonished to find that it was full. People I had not seen since my childhood crowded the pews, and all the men and women who had come in and out of my grandmother's life were there to pay their last respects. I nodded to several as I passed and then took my seat next to Rachel, Alison on my other side. The faint scent of her perfume came over to me as she moved.

The coffin had been placed in front of us, facing the altar, and it seemed far too small for Nancy, far too confined. I couldn't take my eyes off it, and kept staring all the way through the hymns, although I could hear Rachel singing now and then. There was a slight draught in the church, and the ribbon which was tied to the flowers fluttered gently, whilst two birds flew past outside and made a pattern against the stained glass window.

The reception afterwards was confused, although that maybe was only the way I remember it. Rachel was very controlled, and greeted people easily, recalling names that I had long since forgotten. It was held at the walled house, the lounge being rearranged so that the people could be accommodated easily, the drinks being served in the kitchen, where Nancy had spent so much of her time baking, or eating.

By the time everyone had arrived, the noise was deafening, each person apparently remembering something that my grandmother had said, or done, and all of them trying to outdo the other. It became suddenly overwhelming, and I turned to look for Alison or Rachel, only to find that my sister was sitting in a corner talking to Matthew, and that my niece was walking round with some sandwiches. Perilously close to tears, I ran upstairs to Nancy's room, closing the door behind me.

'Why the hell did you have to go and die?' I said out loud, picking up her hairbrush and pressing it into my chest. 'Why? Everything was going so well, we were all so happy — why did you go and do it?'

Frustration made me bitter, and I threw the brush on the bed.

'You were always so reliable, you were always there . . . why did you die? I loved you so much . . . so much.'

I hadn't heard the door open behind me.

'Jill?'

I swung round, embarrassed — it was Rachel.

'Are you all right?'

'No, I'm not! Nancy's dead, and I can't get her back.'

'She was old,' Rachel said practically.

'I know. I know she was old, but I still didn't want her to die,' I said childishly, turning from her to the window. 'When I was a child she was everything to me. Everything. I loved her, and she was always such good fun; and when we got older, your mother and I, she was there when we needed her.' I stopped, my eyes filling.

'I'm sorry.'

'I know, I know you are . . . but she was so special. I can't think of life without her. She was so loved.'

Rachel walked over to my side, and put her arms around me, although I was still facing the window. Leaning her head on my shoulder she breathed deeply for a moment before she spoke.

'I know what it is to love someone very deeply — just think for a moment of how I will feel when you go.'

A minute later, we both went downstairs.

26

Everything changes, of course it does, and we changed over the years. Alison did not stay after the funeral as she had planned, and cornered me in the hallway to make her excuses.

'You see, Jill, Matthew needs me, and I feel I should be there for Robert.' She stopped talking momentarily and looked round. 'Are you going to sell the house?'

'I hadn't thought,' I replied honestly. 'I don't want to — '

She interrupted. 'Listen, you take what you want — whatever Nancy said in the will. I've got more than enough, and it seems the least I can do.'

We hovered for an instant. I could have kissed her, she could have kissed me, but we merely smiled awkwardly.

'I have everything I need,' she said quietly. 'Can you do something else for me though?'

'Go on.'

'Look after my daughter,' she said, and then stopped abruptly. 'God, that sounds as though I'm criticising, and I'm not, I just wanted to say thanks, and . . . well, look after her for me.'

I nodded. 'Don't I always?'

And then she had left, Matthew dispensing invitations to visit them in California, which I knew Rachel would accept, even if I didn't. I watched Alison's tall figure bending down to get into the back of the car, and the long line of her elegant legs in their black stockings. Her face was close to the window as she waved, and for an instant there was a look which was almost regret, before the car made its way down the path and passed through the gates. Momentarily, I missed her, then walked back into the house and Rachel.

My niece soared like a kestrel over the next year, passing her exams well, and gaining a place at university, achieving something that I hadn't managed. She didn't visit her mother that year because of her studies, but the following spring she went out and spent several weeks with Alison, and her beloved half brother, Robert, who apparently thought the world of her. I could see why.

When she got back, little letters floated through the post, the handwriting improving as he grew older.

Dear Rachel,
Just a note to say it was lovely to see you and that we want you to come again soon. I told them at school about you and they want to meet you next time. Will you send that stuff we talked about, and collect the stamps from Jill? Thanks.
Nothing else to say for now —
Robert

It seemed as though the children were achieving what Alison and I had found impossible — a comfortable closeness — and

359

through them we became gradually more friendly, her telephone calls to the walled house occurring at least once a week.

'Hi! How are you?'

'Well. And how's Matthew and Robert?'

'Blooming. I was offered a modelling job the other day, in New York, at my advanced age.' She paused on the line. 'Do you think I should have a go at it?'

'Why not?'

'Because I'm getting on, and besides, my looks aren't what they used to be. I don't want to make a fool of myself.'

'Why stop now?' I said, and was relieved to hear her laughing down the line.

'You are such a bitch! Seriously, what do you think?'

I answered without hesitation.

'Have a go! You've nothing to lose, and besides I need some more cuttings for the scrapbook.'

She did the job a month later, and it went well, if not brilliantly. She was still powerfully attractive, but the thrill she had experienced before when she modelled, had faded, and she found it easy to walk away from the business, concentrating instead on entertaining Matthew's business colleagues.

I went from strength to strength at work, and as Edward gave up more of his commitments, I took over from him, taking on outside engagements to lecture, although I lacked his tremendous aplomb in front of an audience. People rang me direct with queries, or contacted Mrs Wren, who had become my secretary, asking for my time and opinions.

'Miss Henly, we were wondering if you would like to come and talk at the school', or 'Mrs Wren, can you ask Miss Henly if she can look at this pottery we discovered?'

I build up the work assiduously, because I know that the time will come when it will be very important to me, when Rachel has left. I don't brood about it, but the thought is in the back of my mind, always.

Needless to say, I have not married, which is not the same as saying I never will — it just seems unlikely, and it doesn't bother me much anyway. I have the house, and I have Rachel, and that seems more than adequate. I never heard directly from Mark, although when I was talking to Edward only the other day, he mentioned an article in a magazine he had been reading.

'Do you remember that man called Ward, Mark Ward — he was an American?'

I was surprised that my heart still lurched when I heard his name.

'He's in South America now, doing something for the Government. Quite a high-flyer,' he added, pushing the paper away from him. 'I always said that he'd do well. You can tell.'

South America, North America, or on one of the polar ice caps — it didn't matter to me because he was no longer any part of my life, he was still locked back in those few boiling, unsteady months of the summer that Alison carried Rachel; he was still tied to the memory of small, intimate restaurants, and furtive meetings in cars. Now Mark exists in Rachel, the best of him lives daily in her, and the worst stays somewhere in another country, well apart from us. I am glad of it.

Anna's dream of returning to Malta kept her going for years, as she worked for Edward and hoarded all her wages in those two small rooms at the top of the stairs. We continued with the ritual of the afternoon tea, until one morning she knocked on my office door.

'Well hello, Anna — what is it?' I asked as I saw the look on her face.

'No good,' she said softly, a piece of paper in her hand.

I got up from my desk and walked over to her, taking the letter from her and trying to read it.

'Anna, I can't read this, it's in Spanish. Tell me what it says.'

'He's dead,' she replied, throwing the paper into my waste paper basket. 'My husband is dead.'

'I — '

She interrupted me.

'Yes, I know, no matter.'

Without another word, she walked out. I expected her to cry, or to hear the sound of doors banging, but after a few minutes, the hoover began its dull humming as she worked her way up and down the stairs. A week later, she sent all her savings to her children, although she stayed on at Chestnut Walk, dusting and polishing from room to room, as she had always done. When Edward was finally bedridden she worked in her bedroom slippers all the time, as a form of defiance, taking them off only when she